Praise for

Laurel Osterkamp's Books:

Starring in the Movie of My Life

Award Winning Finalist 2011 International Book Awards (Women's Fiction and Young Adult Literature)

Award Winning Finalist 2011 Indie Excellence Awards (Chick Lit)

"A riveting romance and drama. Highly recommended." —*Midwest Book Review*

"Two stories collide in this novel that deals with acceptance, love and revenge. This story will stick with you long after it's come to an end." (4-Star RT Rating) — *RT Book Reviews*

"*Starring in the Movie of My Life* is fast-paced, engaging, and a recommended read." —*All Books International*

"This is a great love story, very deep and complicated and messy, but very real." —*ChicklitPlus.com*

"I'm not one for giving out 5 stars all willy-nilly. I am deadly serious about my 5 star rating and have only given out two so far this year. Pretend you can see my serious face. Okay? Well, I am giving my third 5 star rating for this incredible and surprising novel by a new favorite author, Laurel Osterkamp." —*StephTheBookworm. blogspot.com*

"Laurel Osterkamp is an author to watch." —*GirlyScribbles. wordpress.com*

"*Starring in the Movie of My Life* is about second chances at any age. It's also about discovering how to fulfill your needs without expecting an outside source, especially a relationship, to magically fix everything. I really enjoyed reading this novel." —*Bitchlitblog. wordpress.com*

"The story is emotional and intense… I can certainly see why *Starring in the Movie of My Life* is a 2011 International Book Award (Women's Fiction and Young Adult Literature) and 2011 Indie Excellence Award Finalist. I can't wait to see what's next from Laurel Osterkamp!" —*ReelSwellBlog.com*

"*Starring in the Movie of My Life* was immensely involving. I truly enjoyed Laurel's writing and I am looking forward to her next book." —*PiaBernardino.com*

"This book definitely took me by surprise and really held my attention the whole way through. If you are looking for a great read then this is it!" —*ChickLitCentralTheBlog.blogspot.com*

"Get your copy today & weigh in on a rising star, before she jets off into the Milky Way." —*ElsieLovesFiction.blogspot.com*

"This is one of those rare reads I come across where I'm so enthralled from the first page that I can't stop reading and nothing else gets done until the book is finished." —*TheBookFetishBlog.com*

Following My Toes:

Winner! *2008 Indie Excellence Award for Chick Lit.*

"A wonderful story of learning to forgive yourself and others, trusting your instincts and not giving up… a great read." —*Muse Book Reviews*

"Ms. Osterkamp has penned a tale that is pure delight and will touch the reader on many emotional levels." —Love Romances June 2006

"*Following My Toes* connects the reader to the feeling of chatting with a close friend." —*TCM Reviews*

"Osterkamp's background as a comedy writer is readily apparent with the nice balance between the humor and the serious." —*Book-Pleasures.com*

"Faith's realization of her faults and that she is more than everyone thinks she is, makes a very good story." —*Coffee Time Romance*

November Surprise

"Well developed and spotlessly executed... Bravo to Laurel Osterkamp for yet another chick-lit title that charms the reader, and leaves us rooting for Lucy and Monty as if they were friends of our own." -Keri English for *IndieReader.com*

"Very well done! I enjoy books that mix politics and love, they give more depth and texture to stories, so I would highly recommend this book for anyone who seeks a good, brainy romance." --*Fountainheart* "Z," Amazon reader

"Having read everything Laurel Osterkamp has published, *November Surprise* continues to reflect Ms. Osterkamp's excellence as an engaging, intelligent, creative author. Stylistically interesting with each chapter written beneath a short depiction of what had recently occurred in the political arena, the main character of November Surprise is a young woman whose depth, nature, and relationship style evolved like a fine wine throughout her life (and therefore throughout the book). --*Love to read chick lit and beyond*, Amazon reader.

"I absolutely loved this book! It was a great read from start to finish! I really liked the main character Lucy. She is smart and interesting and I was rooting for her throughout the whole book. The author's writing style is excellent. I can't wait to read more books by this author. I definitely recommend reading this book!" *--kateshines,* Amazon reader

Campaign Promises

"Short and sweet, Osterkamp creates a world of politics and high school memories that meld together to form a novella that works." – Keri English, *Indiereader.com*

"*Campaign Promises* is a intelligent peek into one woman's journey into adulthood as her naivety and idealism are nurtured into mature self-awareness. At 75 eBook pages, *Campaign Promises* is the perfect companion for short trips, lunch hours, or an early afternoon with a cup of tea that leaves you feeling accomplished and satisfied. " — Christine, *Bitchlit.com*

the holdout

Also by Laurel Osterkamp

Following My Toes

Looking for Ward

Campaign Promises

November Surprise

Blue State

the holdout

a novel

by

Laurel Osterkamp

PMI Books

Boulder, Colorado

This book is a work of fiction. Names, characters, places and incidents are products of the author's imagination or are used fictitiously. Any resemblance to actual events or locales or persons, living or dead, is entirely coincidental.

ISBN: 978-1-933826-40-0

Front cover photo © VibrantImage/Bigstock.com

Author photo © Richard Fleischman

Published by
PMI Books
an imprint of
Preventive Measures, Inc.
254 Spruce St.
Boulder, CO 80302

Printed in the United States of America

For information regarding special discounts
for bulk purchases, visit our website at:

pmibooks.com 

the holdout

Prologue

November 2012

My only mistake was falling in love. Other than that I played a nearly perfect game. But it doesn't matter. Do you remember Janet Jackson's halftime performance during the Super Bowl back in 2004? It was stunning but nobody will ever recall the actual dance because at the end of it, she showed her nipple on national television. Well, Janet and I have something in common. I didn't think things through, I exposed myself to the nation, and now that is what I'll be remembered for.

Except it hasn't happened yet.

I filmed the current season of *The Holdout* months ago, but it's still airing. There are three episodes yet to be broadcast, and my most humiliating moments are still to come. Right now I only occasionally get spotted on the street, but I was edited out of a lot of the earlier footage. I'm not naïve enough to believe that will be the case later on. What happened was devastating but it will undoubtedly make delicious TV.

So I'm wondering if anyone will recognize me today, and if so, will that increase or decrease my chances of being dismissed? I park my car and walk from the lot to the federal court building, clutching my jury summons in my hand. If I'm chosen, it will be the second jury I've been on in a year.

Inside, I give my bag to the security guards and walk through the metal detectors. They give me my bag back on the other side, and I take the elevator to the fourth floor, which is where my summons said to go. When the elevator doors open I immediately see a desk and behind it stands a perky brunette wearing an adorable suit jacket with bell sleeves and a Peter Pan collar. She totally pulls it off.

I pull on the edges of my oversized sweater and smooth out my skirt. My outfit seemed reasonable when I left this morning but I've never worked downtown and I've never owned a pair of heels. What do I know?

"Hi," she says, with a floating voice. "Can I help you?"

I hold up my summons. "I'm here to report for jury duty."

She takes the summons and looks it over. "Robin Bricker. Great. Please sign in." She gestures toward a clipboard with a sign-in sheet. Mine will be the fourth signature.

"Here's your card." She gives me a new piece of paper, and it has a stamp with today's date on it. "Hold on to this. If you're selected for a jury, you'll present it every morning to be stamped and that will be documentation for your boss."

"Oh," I stammer. "I'm sort of between jobs right now, so there's no need." I tilt my head to the side, trying to stretch away the tension. Who cares if I don't have a regular, nine to five gig? I'm not obligated to explain how I support myself.

She nods and oozes sincerity, and even though she's wearing heels I tower over her. She's the sort of girl I wanted to be when I was in high school. "Well, then you'll get paid for your time here!" Her perfect brown bob curls just so, right under her ears. Maybe if I blow-dried my hair every morning I could get my hair to do that too. "You're a little early, but go ahead and have a seat in the lounge. There's coffee, juice, and muffins, and in about half an hour, we'll get started!"

I thank her and walk into the lounge, a large room with oversized windows and strategically placed tables and chairs. Although I've had breakfast, I grab a chocolate muffin because I'm still hungry, and besides, it's my policy never to turn down anything chocolate. I lost a lot of weight while filming *The Holdout*, but even if I gain it all back I'll still be thin. For the first eighteen years of my life I hated that I was always the tallest, scrawniest girl in my class. No cute curves for me. But once I went to college I appreciated that I could eat cafeteria food and still fit into my size six jeans, while my friends all struggled with the freshman fifteen.

I sit down in one of the many cushy chairs, take out my book, and settle in to read while enjoying my muffin. Who said jury duty has to be awful? But then the television that's mounted to the ceiling switches from the morning show to commercial, and an ad for *The Holdout* comes on. My castmates are walking along the beach, some wearing teeny tiny bikinis, others shirtless in swimming trunks. Joe Pine's voice can be heard over it all, loud and clear.

"This week, on *The Holdout*. The stakes are high, loyalties are tested, and hearts are broken." Then it switches to a close up of Grant. He's sitting and smirking; even the way he blinks seems self-satisfied while the waves lap the shore behind him.

"*The Holdout* is a game," he says, "and I'm not here just to play. I'm here to win. I'll do whatever it takes."

Then – oh my God – it switches to a shot of Grant and me, locked in an embrace. But even worse, it switches again, and now Grant and Klemi are making out. Finally it switches back to Grant, sitting alone on the beach, laughing to the camera and clapping his hands. Joe Pine's voice comes on again. "Will lover boy Grant endure? Will he persist? Will he be the holdout?"

The commercial ends and I shrink down in my seat. I look around the room and see that others are all busy on their phones or reading the paper or nodding off as if they're practicing sitting in the jury box. Nobody seems to recognize me, which is my goal. I've cut my hair since the show and I dyed it a darker blonde. I'd have gone more extreme, but contractually I'm only allowed to make minor changes to my appearance. So I'm wearing thick rimmed glasses with fake lenses, and I dress in ways that will hopefully help me blend into the wallpaper.

All my life I've wanted to be famous. Now that my day has arrived, I'm clinging to my old, faceless existence like J.D Salinger gone into exile after writing *Catcher in the Rye*. Except instead of publishing a groundbreaking classic novel, I got duped by a pretty boy and his girlfriend and cheated out of a million dollars. What's worse though, is soon the world will see it all play out on national television.

Chapter 1

December 2011

Imagine you were born with only one arm. If you had never known what it was like to have that second arm, would you miss it or would you just never think about it at all? I suppose you'd have to think about it sometimes. Gym class. Grocery shopping. Finding sneakers with Velcro. But other times, would the idea of a second arm seem unnatural or even unnecessary?

That's what it's like for me. I have two arms but I don't have a mother. She died in a car accident when I was two, so my memories of her are predominately from stories or old photographs. And most of the time I don't think about her. My older brothers and my dad took terrific care of me even though I was the only girl, born years after my parents thought they were done with babies. We all got by, however, and now I'm a fairly well-adjusted, thirty-one-year-old woman (with a focus on the *fairly*.)

But there are times when I feel a part of me is missing. There was never a smooth voice or soft arms to soothe me when I fell. I missed her then. I missed her when my dad left a copy of *Growing Up: It's a Girl Thing* on my pillow one night, which was his attempt to guide me through puberty. I wanted her then. And every year, I wish she was around for Christmas.

I take a bite of turkey and mashed potatoes, glued together with buttery gravy, and wash it down with a sip of merlot. The food here is always tasty because my Aunt Natalie does most of the cooking, and she reads *Martha Stewart Living* the way middle-aged guys read porn. Dad invites himself, me, my older brothers Ted and Ian, and their families to her house every year for Christmas dinner, even though his brother (Aunt Natalie's husband) has been dead for over ten years.

Across the table my dad is describing, in detail, his latest injury. Aunt Natalie takes neat bites of turkey and little sips of wine while he talks. "I didn't even see the dog coming," he says. "Ran right into my bike. Fell head first onto the sidewalk. Good thing I was wearing my helmet. But I busted my knee. Had to wear a brace for over a month."

She nods patiently. "Was the dog okay?"

On the other side of the table, Lucy and her parents coo over the newest addition to the family, baby Noah. Lucy's married to my cousin Monty and she has no siblings. Since her parents live in town, they come to Christmas dinner too. But they always seem sort of shell-shocked, as if they were airlifted into this loud, messy meal without their consent.

Beside me sits my oldest brother, Ted, and his cologne is even more powerful than the wafting aroma of the green beans in mushroom sauce. He's taking efficient bites of the salad his wife brought, and he's baiting our cousin Monty.

"So Monty, how's the job going? Have you moved up yet?"

Monty's dark head turns away from his daughter and his dimpled chin shifts in tension as he answers Ted. "It's great. I'm actually happy in the position I'm in. What I was hired for is higher than what most people ever get at the Bill and Melinda Gates Foundation."

Ted straightens the collar of this polo sweater, swallows a bite of turkey and smiles. "What's your title, again?"

Monty's face remains stoic. "Senior Program Officer and Counsel for the Malaria Initiative."

Ted nods. Under the ceiling chandelier, the frosted tips in his light brown hair are more noticeable than usual. Nobody would ever guess that my brother Ian is the gay one. "Wow, that's great. If it was me, I'd be frustrated that so much of my job isn't about law, but if you're happy with that, more power to you. Personally, I spent far too much money on my MBA to be happy with anything less than a high level gig in business administration."

"Well," says Monty, "I had more scholarships than you did, so my tuition wasn't as expensive as yours."

"Harvard is simply more expensive than NYU." Ted laughs, but actually it's a challenge with a squint, and Monty raises his chest as if to accept.

Lucy, who had been focused on their baby son, pops her head up as if propelled by instinct. She puts one hand on Monty's arm while using her other hand to tuck an escaped corkscrew curl into her bun at the back of her head. "How's the restaurant, Jack? Have you recovered from the recession yet?"

Monty's younger brother Jack smiles with his entire face and his hazel eyes shine as he answers. Drawing my cousin Jack into conversation about his restaurant is a temporary solution; Jack isn't super competitive but the subject morphs into talk of money, time management, and family. Soon my two brothers and my two cousins, all of whom are in their late thirties to early forties, are one-upping each other like they're in a high school locker room. They do this every year and nobody ever bothers to ask me about my life. It's hard to get upset though, because I usually don't have much to brag about.

I majored in theater in college, and I've spent most of my post-college years floating from one job that's beneath me to another, and my taste in men is even worse than my taste in employment. But this year I can actually compete in the game.

It's hard to hear myself think over the cacophony of voices and the clink of silverware, but when there's a lull in the conversation I take my chance. "I have news," I say.

All heads turn towards me. My aunt Natalie brings her hands together and smiles. She probably hopes that I'll announce a new relationship; Natalie worries a lot about my romantic life. "What's your news, Robin?"

Everyone is listening. My skin prickles underneath the cashmere sweater my father gave me this morning for Christmas. "I've been selected to be on *The Holdout*!" I smile in triumph, ready to accept everyone's sincere congratulations and expressions of pride. Instead, I'm met with blank stares.

Jack's wife, Petra, breaks the silence. "You mean the TV show?"

"Yeah!" I say, and again I wait for the response I'd anticipated. Aunt Natalie, bless her heart, at least tries.

"I watch it. They all wear bathing suits all the time. God knows you have the body for it, darling. But I certainly wouldn't want to be on that show. It looks pretty difficult."

Jack speaks up. "Is that the one where they're all on an island, and they have to find their own food and water, and every week someone gets voted off until the last person gets a million dollars?"

"Yes." I say, trying not to let desperation sneak into my voice. "I could win a million dollars. And it's an epic show. Tons of people watch it, and this year they'll be watching me."

"What about your job?" asks my dad. "Are they going to let you take several weeks off to film a TV show?"

I suppress a sigh. "I'm sure they won't, Dad. But who cares? I can get another stupid office job that I hate anytime. Being on *The Holdout* is a once in a lifetime opportunity."

Monty starts to speak, but Lucy drowns him out. "That's great! Congratulations, Robin."

"Thank you," I say. Finally one person is happy for me.

But Ted has to ruin it. "Don't you have to be good at sports and survival skills to do well on that show?"

"I am good at sports and survival skills."

Monty, Ted, Jack, and Ian all laugh.

"I am!" I insist. "I'm a strong swimmer, and my survival skills are fine. Just because of that one camping trip back when I was eight…"

My brother Ian cuts me off. "Do you remember?" He speaks to Dad, Ted, Monty and Jack. "She cried the whole time. That seagull pooped on her head and she couldn't take a shower, and that was it. Her meltdown lasted the entire trip."

I tap the end of my fork against the table. "A seagull pooped on my head, and I couldn't wash it out. That was disgusting. Besides, I was eight, and the only girl on that stupid trip…"

Ted directs his comment to Dad. "I still don't know why you insisted on bringing her."

"I did offer to take her," says Aunt Natalie.

Dad speaks through a bite of turkey and potatoes. "I didn't want her to feel left out. But I admit it didn't go terribly well."

"It would have been fine," I say. "I blame the seagull."

"It wasn't just the seagull," Monty says. "I remember you wouldn't go hiking because you kept getting blisters. We had to take turns carrying you back to camp."

"That's true," says Jack. "And then at night you were afraid of the dark."

"No," says Monty to Jack, "that was you."

Ian laughs and shakes his head at me. "Is it too late to tell them no? Have you signed anything yet? Because if you have, I'm sure Monty could look at the contract and get you out of it."

"I don't want out of it!" I'm yelling now. "Do you know how hard it is to get on this show? Thousands of people audition every season, and they only pick sixteen. I had to make audition tapes, fill out pages and pages of applications, and go through interviews and background checks, all to prove that I'm watchable and not easily intimidated. And guess what? I convinced them. So I'm going on *The Holdout*, and I will kick butt, and I plan to come home with a million dollars. Next year at this time you all will be kissing my ass."

"Robin!" Aunt Natalie purses her lips. "Language, please."

"Well," says Ted. "Let's just hope there aren't any seagulls."

§

Later in the kitchen, Jack, Monty, Ian, Ted and I clean up. Tradition dictates that this is our job. Normally I don't mind; I like having something active to do after such a heavy meal. But this year our dishwashing chore has turned into an extended opportunity for my brothers and cousins to mock me.

"You'll all be kissing my ass!" Ted mimics me and the others laugh. I pretend to chuckle along as I scoop the leftover potatoes into a Tupperware container. "What if you're voted off first? How are you going to deal with the humiliation?"

"I'm not going to be voted off first. I'm going to win."

Ian hoots. His rosy cheeks and spiky brown hair make him look more like a teenager than a guy in his late thirties. And even though we're the same height, it doesn't stop him from talking down to me. "Look at you, Robbie! Such confidence. I suppose you need to go into it with that attitude."

"It's not like I haven't thought about this, you know." I hand Ian the container and he makes room for it in the refrigerator. Then I start wrapping tin foil over bowls of vegetables. "I've been practicing."

Jack is loading the dishwasher. He and I inherited the family's tall blonde gene, and he's bent over at an angle where the light is bouncing off his head, like a halo. "How do you practice for it?" he asks. "You won't know until you're there what the challenges are going to be."

"Well, I've been swimming and running a lot, working up my speed and endurance, and I time myself solving puzzles, and I go for as long as I can without drinking any water. Things like that."

Ted scoffs. The sleeves of his expensive sweater are pushed up as he wipes down the greasy turkey platter, and he looks afraid to stand too close to it. "Isn't it a social game? I thought the whole point was not getting voted off by the rest of your tribe."

"It's both," I say. "You have to be tough and you also have to be likeable."

Lucy walks into the kitchen. "Hey," she says to Monty, who has rolled up the sleeves of his flannel shirt while he rinses wine glasses in the sink. "My parents and I are taking the kids back. Abby's having a meltdown."

He turns toward her and asks expectantly. "Do you want me to come?"

Jack stands up straight. "I can drive you home," he says to Monty.

"You don't want to shirk your cleaning duties." She goes and kisses Monty on the cheek. "I'll see you back."

Before she can step away, Monty gently grabs her arm, pulls her close, and leans down and whispers something in her ear. She laughs. "No," she says to him and she shakes her head. "I don't think so."

He laughs back. "Oh yes. I absolutely think so."

She places both hands on his chest, pushes him away, and Monty is grinning more widely than I've seen him do all evening. Their casual, intimate moment happens so quickly and suddenly that it doesn't occur to me to look away until after it's already over.

Monty goes back to washing glasses. Lucy steps over and hugs Jack, promising to call him tomorrow, hugs both my brothers, who she obviously doesn't plan on calling, and then she hugs me. "Good luck Robin," she says. I'm a full head taller than she is, but I feel so immature in her presence. "I'm going to want to hear all about it."

"It should be interesting," I say.

"Hey!" Lucy's eyes light up. "After it's done, you should come to Seattle and lecture my students about your experience. I could make it a special topic."

Ted scrunches up his face. "Don't you teach history? What does reality TV have to do with history?"

"She teaches social justice," says Monty. "And I can totally see the connection. Societal dynamics and so on…" He stops talking when a child's wailing can be heard from the other room.

"Well anyway, it's an idea." Lucy gives me an extra hug and pulls away. "I should go."

As Lucy walks out, Jack's wife Petra comes in. "Jack!" Her voice is shrill. "Can I get some help here? Mikey just spilled apple juice all over your Mom's new book and she's freaking out."

Jack wipes his wet hands against his pant legs. "What am I supposed to do about it?"

Petra's face hardens and her request comes out like a demand. "Can you please just come here?"

Jack slumps a little and follows his wife. Ian and Ted snicker after he leaves, and Ted makes that whip/meow sound, communicating exactly what he thinks about the dynamics of his cousin's marriage.

Ian finishes putting away the leftovers. "Well Robbie, I'll be rooting for you. If you win, next year you can take us all out for dinner, then there won't be any dishes to clean up afterwards."

"I wouldn't get my hopes up about her winning," says Ted.

Monty turns off the sink and throws the dishtowel at Ted. "Why do you have to be such a dick?"

Ted steps out of the line of fire, not wanting the stained, damp towel to make contact with his dressy casual pants and sweater, an outfit which must have cost hundreds of dollars. "I'm just being realistic. It's a hard game to win."

"There are only sixteen contestants," says Monty. "She has more than a six percent chance, which is a higher chance than you've ever had of winning a million dollars."

Ted responds. "Some people have a higher chance than others though, based on their skills or their social game. So you can't look it at that way."

Ian picks up the towel from the floor and puts it on the counter. "I suppose you think you could win."

"I'd have a decent shot." Ted squares his shoulders. "I'm athletic and I went to Harvard business school, after all. I think I know how to sell myself."

"Dream on," says Monty. "You'd be voted off first. They always vote the arrogant ones off first."

"Well I wouldn't know." Ted walks over to Monty, invading his space. "I don't watch the show. I don't have time for things like television."

"Eddie and I have watched it," says Ian. "And you both would suck. They always vote out the old, bossy players right away. Plus, you need to be skilled at building things, and neither of you are."

Ian owns his own contracting company, and his claim to fame is that he's handy *and* business savvy, which nobody else in the family can maintain. "I'd totally win the million before either of you."

The three of them continue to argue, and I leave the kitchen without notice.

Chapter 2

May 2012

My going-away party is an informal affair. I was actually surprised when Ian and Jack insisted on throwing one, after how dismissive they were at Christmas. Neither Monty nor Ted live in town, but all my family members who live close by are at this shindig, along with my handful of friends who swear they're going to watch every episode of *The Holdout*, even if I get voted out first.

The low-lit room is drafty and overly air-conditioned, and I hug my thin sweater tightly around myself. I take a swig of beer and wonder how many beers it will take to feel warm and at ease.

"You packed sunscreen, right?" Ian pops a chicken tender into his mouth. Chicken tenders are a signature item at Jack's restaurant. I've never tasted any, anywhere that are better. We're all back in the party room of his restaurant, and plates of chicken tenders, bruschetta, and crab cakes are set out, along with pitchers of Fat Tire and of soda.

"I don't have to pack sunscreen," I tell him. "They provide all the contestants unlimited amounts. Condoms too. We get all the sunscreen and condoms we want, no questions asked."

Ian's face contorts and his eyes skip spastically with distaste. "You won't have need for condoms, Robbie."

Ian's husband Eddie laughs and pats him on the back. "She's not a teenager anymore, hon. Robin's an adult and there's no telling what she might 'have need for.'"

Ian winces. "But out there, in all that sand, where you won't have had clean underwear or a shower in weeks? Ick."

Eddie places his hand on the top of Ian's short brown hair. "I seem to remember a time when sand and poor hygiene wasn't standing in your way."

"That was a long time ago and I was very drunk." Ian's cheeks turn pink and he looks toward me. "They're not giving you an unlimited amount of tequila, are they? Please tell me they're not."

I exchange a knowing glance with Eddie. "I think tequila is only ever distributed after reward challenges."

"Good," Ian says. Eddie hugs Ian to his side, and they exchange an affectionate, brief kiss.

I look up, and my friend Isobel catches my eye and waves. I excuse myself and walk over to her. "How long have you been here? I didn't see you come in."

"Only a couple of minutes." Isobel hugs me even though I just saw her a few hours ago. We've been friends since college, when she was a senior in the theater department and she cast me, a lowly freshman, in her student director showcase piece. We kept in touch over the years; she even helped me find an apartment in the building where she lives.

"So," she says as she pulls away. "Somebody from our theater department is actually going to achieve stardom!"

"Who?" I ask.

"Duh…" Isobel responds, crossing her eyes.

"Oh!" I cry, comprehending. "You mean me. I don't think reality television counts though. All our classmates will probably make fun of me behind my back."

"Only because they're jealous," Isobel rubs her hands over her bare arms. "It's freezing in here."

"I should have warned you to wear a sweater. This place is always too cold in the summer and too warm in the winter." I look around the room. "I don't see Jack. I'll go find him and ask him to adjust the thermostat." I tap her lightly on the shoulder. "I'll be right back."

I go through the doors and past the kitchen. I used to wait tables here while I was in college. I know my way around, and some staff are even still the same. So it's without a tinge of trepidation that I walk headlong into Jack's office, where the light is on, but dimmed. Luckily I have on soft-soled shoes and I don't make much noise, because what

I end up seeing is not anything I want to answer to.

Jack is making out with a brunette wearing a waitress uniform. Her hair is long, and it's pulled back with a large red barrette. She's kissing him like she could swallow his head whole, and he's kissing her like he wouldn't mind if she did.

I stand there for a moment, stunned and voyeuristic, already wishing I could delete the image that's burning into my mind. But then I hear laughter from the distance, and it breaks me out of my paralysis. I turn silently on my heel and hurry back, hopefully unnoticed by anyone.

The first person I see when I return to the party room is Jack's wife Petra.

"Robin!" She grins, grabs my hand and gives it a squeeze. "There you are. How are you? All ready to go compete and win?"

I feel myself flush. My cheeks, legs, arms, and everywhere else I have skin must be turning bright pink. Petra has always seemed sort of ice-princess-ish to me, with her porcelain doll looks and her hot/cold mood swings, but nobody deserves to have her husband making out with a waitress mere feet away from where she's standing.

"Ummm…" I stammer. "I …" I place a hand to my forehead, which feels damp. "What was the question?"

Petra pulls her eyebrows together. "Are you okay?"

"Mmm hmm." I nod my head. "Anxiety. Nerves. You know."

She squeezes my hand again and gives me an empathetic look. "You poor thing. Let's get you some water." Petra looks around the room, and sees what I see. All the pitchers are filled with soda or beer, none with water.

She lets go of my hand and her jaw sets. "Wouldn't you know it?" Blame floods her voice, as if this is only one of many injustices that she's had to endure since this morning. "Jack might have thought to put out some water. I'll go find some." She starts towards to door.

"No!" I'm loud enough to attract attention and surprise from nearly everyone in the room. Conversation ceases and all eyes are on me. This means I'm the only one who notices that Jack has finally made an appearance at this party for which he's the host.

Our eyes lock, and in an instant I know he knows that I know. Perhaps he saw me scurrying away, or maybe it's because we're both younger siblings, and our genetic similarities extend beyond being tall and blonde. But we silently communicate in that moment; he begs me not to say anything and I tell him that I won't.

I look back at Petra. "Sorry," I squeak. "It's just not necessary to go to the trouble.

These moments come and go. I'm fine."

Jack approaches us. "Hey, Robin." He puts his hands on Petra's shoulders, but she steps away from his touch.

"Thanks for the party," I tell him.

"Of course," he says. "I had to do something now, *before* you're famous. In a few months you'll probably be too rich and popular for any of us."

I laugh because he says this in sweetness, like a kid who just wants to be liked. He may be a decade older than me, but he's always been that guy who tries to make everyone happy. Maybe too happy.

Then my dad clears his throat from several feet away. "Can I have everyone's attention?" His words resonate across the room. "I want to say a few things while everyone is still here and still sober."

There's a collective chuckle and Dad smiles at the encouragement. He raises the glass of beer in his hand. "To my brave daughter, Robin. May you be safe, and may you be successful in this latest adventure of yours. We're all in awe of your courage, strength, and willingness to make a fool of yourself on national television…"

"Hear, hear!" shouts Ian.

"…just kidding about that last part," says Dad. "Robin, win or lose, you'll always be one in a million to us, and we wish you all the luck in the world."

Everyone claps and I blush again, this time in pleasure.

Jack stands next to me, close enough that he can speak without raising his voice. "My money's on you. Go show them what a bad-ass you actually are."

I step back and our eyes meet again. I'm about to thank him for the encouragement, but his gaze shifts and I follow it. A waitress with long brown hair clasped in a red barrette is clearing some empty trays, and she briefly looks up at Jack. The smile they share goes unnoticed by Petra, but to me it speaks volumes.

And it tells me to be glad that I'm leaving the country tomorrow.

Chapter 3

May thru June 2012

Ican't let myself be tired. My trip took thirteen hours, longer if you count airport time and connecting flights. But it was uneventful; the only thing that kept me awake was my heart, vibrating in my chest like a tightly wound alarm clock. Oh, and the rocking turbulence also tugged at my insides. So my limbs are heavy and I'm moving slowly, as if I've aged twenty years since yesterday.

There were several other cast members on my flight, but we were escorted by a *Holdout* representative and instructed not to talk to each other. When we landed in Kalibo International Airport our luggage was scooped up and we were ushered into a van without delay. I wish travelling was always so efficient.

Now I'm sitting in a docked boat with my castmates and all we're allowed to do is eye each other up and down. I'm trying to look both useful and non-threatening while I drink my bottled water and eat the chewy beef jerky that the crew provided for us. It's the last chance for food and the first chance for strategy, and turning down either would be like sacrificing sleep just to gain weight.

A shiny black limo pulls up. Out of it emerges Joe Pine, the host of *The Holdout*. He's wearing a blue safari shirt and khaki pants, and a red baseball cap covers his dark, movie-star type hair. My head swims and I grab the armrest of my seat to steady myself; maybe it's leftover vertigo from the flight or new vertigo from the boat sway-ing, or perhaps I'm just star-struck. Joe confers with the cameramen, and their voices pool with ambient sounds from the dock. It strikes me that he looks smaller in real life, like a punter who is suddenly diminished when he stands next to a linebacker.

Moments later we take off. Soon we're clipping along, cutting through waves and rocking back and forth, while the wind is rushing past and blowing my hair into my eyes. I pretend like I ride on speedboats with camera crews every day, but already I doubt myself. They told me to wear green, so I have on a green t-shirt, cotton leggings, and a grayish green zip-up hoodie sweatshirt. My swimsuit is of course underneath my clothes, but looking around I see most of the young women are wearing skimpier outfits than mine, showing a lot of leg and even more cleavage.

I've watched every episode of *The Holdout* in its eight seasons, and it doesn't seem like winners ever get ahead simply by using sex appeal. And no matter what I use, I have to be smart in how I use it.

Joe Pine gets a signal from a bearded guy standing in the back. Is that the director? Before I can figure it out, Joe grins at the camera and it's the sort of smile you could snag your sweater on. No wonder he's on television; even the air around him confirms that he's smooth at being smooth. Then he speaks.

"These sixteen castaways have not yet spoken to each other. They do not know each other at all. But over the next thirty-nine days they will be forced to work together, live together, and survive together, as they determine who will become the ultimate holdout."

Joe looks away from the camera, shifting his gaze to the sixteen of us sitting here on the boat as we get wet from the rough, lapping waves. "Castaways, it is time to separate into tribes. If you are wearing red, you are in the Tapang tribe. If you're wearing green you are a member of the Lakas tribe."

I look around for the other seven people wearing green. Among them are a beautiful Hispanic girl wearing a tight miniskirt and a cardigan over a bikini top; a seventyish looking man sporting a buzz cut and a stern expression; a solid looking woman with frizzy, blondish hair; a guy in his forties who's wearing a straw fedora; and a lean yet muscular hottie with a mop of short, dark curls and eyes like freshly-brewed espresso.

The cute dark-haired guy meets my gaze and gives me a shy smile, the sort that seems to say, "Can you believe this?" I smile back, as if to say, "Hell, no." It is the first conversation I have with anyone here, if you can count it as one. No matter. I'll be talking to him soon.

Joe signals to the two rafts that are hitched to either side of the boat.

"Castaways, you and the rest of your tribe will have three minutes to board your raft and procure any of the provisions we have for you on this boat." He gestures towards the back, where tarps, baskets of food, tools, and other survival gear are sitting out. "You are not allowed to move or talk until I say, and at that time, your three minutes will have begun. After the three minutes are over, anything that isn't on your raft will be left behind."

The guy with dark curls meets my eyes again, and silently and subtly he gestures towards the snorkeling gear with his head. I see it, and I give him a tiny nod in response. The snorkeling gear was what I was going to go for anyway.

"Castaways ready, and go!" Joe Pine shouts, and we're all up like a shot. This could be the most decisive moment of the game. The supplies I score will help feed and protect myself and my tribe, and it's also a chance to be the cool, capable person that always gets picked first for teams. I'm not the only one who thinks so. We're all like anxious children who have been let out for recess, instantly hunting for the fiercest set of monkey bars or the highest slide. The pushiest kids are going to win, and in the frantic, crazy noise, we all want to be at the top of the food chain.

Which is why I push away a skinny, nerdy-looking guy dressed in red. He's got to be on the other tribe, so he's my enemy. He lands on his butt, and under normal circumstances I would apologize, extend my hand, and help him up. But crap. I play to win.

I lunge towards the snorkeling gear and the tarp that he was about to take, and I hop over him and towards the edge of the boat, realizing that stress feels like wet plastic. I jump into the ocean, and my treasures want to slide out of my grasp when they become slick with water.

I swim towards our raft like I'm a River dancer, ridiculously gesticulating in the ocean without my arms. When I get to the raft I hurl everything onto it, making sure the gear and the tarp are in the center where they won't easily slip off. Then I do the crawl stroke back to the boat and hoist myself up. I start grabbing whatever is in my range, whether it's a lantern or a cooking pot. I throw them overboard towards my fellow Lakas tribemates who are still in the water. This is more difficult than you would think, because salt water is stinging my eyes and it's hard to see, but I can still identify the other members of my tribe. I just hope the stuff I jettison over doesn't hit any of them in the head.

The thirtyish woman and the old military guy know what to do without being told; they catch whatever I launch at them, put it on our raft, and then come back for more. But the younger people seem kind of lost, like they don't know whether they should be swimming or climbing. Meanwhile, my new dark-haired friend has taken hold of our raft, and is making sure nothing gets stolen or falls off into the sea.

"Over here!" and "Hurry, come on!" He yells to anyone dressed in green, somehow becoming the leader of our tribe.

Way too soon, Joe warns us that our time is almost up, so I dive back in and climb aboard our raft. The dark-haired guy offers me his hand and helps me up.

"Good job on the snorkeling gear. I had a feeling you'd come through." He smiles at me again, and his eyes crinkle in this way that makes me want to trust him. "I'm Grant," he says.

Our hands are still clasped, so I squeeze and shake. "Robin," I say. "Nice to meet you, Grant."

§

"We have to be careful about who we align ourselves with." The next day Grant is walking ahead of me. He lifts a low-lying branch and holds it up as I pass underneath. The result is that for a moment we are standing very close to each other. He doesn't even smell bad. We've been out here for more than thirty-six hours, and after sweating through the building of our fort, the clearing of camp, the first immunity challenge and the pursuit of fire, you'd think he'd be a little ripe. But no. Unless I stink so bad I can no longer smell anyone else's stench, he's fine.

"Who do you suggest?" I ask.

He pulls his eyebrows together in concentration. "I think we should establish a tight alliance of four with people who need us more than we need them. I say we go with Bailey and Beth."

Conrad Bailey is in his seventies and he used to be a Merchant Marine. Beth is in her late thirties and she works in a middle school cafeteria. They're both hard workers but they did little to secure our win in the first immunity challenge. Part one was physical, with lots of running and climbing, and Grant and the younger tribe members were the best at that.

The second part of the challenge was about putting together a puzzle. All my hours spent practicing at home, timing myself doing the Rubik's cube and word scrambles paid off, and I was able to step up and lead my tribe to our first victory.

"Are you sure?" I ask Grant. "There are other strong players."

"We don't want someone who is too strong," Grant explains. We continue to walk and search for our clean water source. We'd found it yesterday, but I've already lost my bearings. I wasn't prepared for how thirsty I'd be. I feel like I swallowed a carpet sample.

Grant continues. "We don't want to be up against anyone who is too likeable in the finals. And if we align with someone who could win a lot of individual immunity challenges at the end, we could also really get screwed."

A sudden rustling startles me, and I panic, thinking a tribemate has followed us. But it's just the camera guy. I've already gotten so used to being followed by him that I barely notice his presence.

I hitch up my leggings, which are grubby and damp and falling off me. I can't have lost a lot of weight yet, unless it's water weight. I'm only wearing the pants to keep my legs from getting scraped and bitten, but I'm starting to wish I had left them back at camp.

"So you think Bailey and Beth are the best to go to the finals with?"

"They're likeable, but not too likeable. We can depend on them. They both have good work ethics. But in the end, we could beat them."

I stop, and once he realizes I'm no longer walking, Grant stops too. The camera guy has got to be thrilled; we're giving him the perfect angle from which to film us.

"*We* can't beat them, Grant. Only one person can win."

He laughs, and his teddy-bear eyes crinkle around the edges. "Well, yes," he says. "Of course. But we can take each other to the final two and then let the jury decide."

I rub my fingers together and knot them up into little balls while I look off in the distance, away from the camera and away from Grant. Should I trust this guy?

He's the sort of guy you meet in a coffee shop while you're standing in line for a skim latte. He's standing behind you, his hair still damp from his morning shower, and the scent of his shampoo mixes perfectly with the coffee smell that lingers in the air. He accidentally bumps into you when you get your drink, causing you to spill and stain your new cream-colored coat and he feels so bad that he offers to pay your dry cleaning. He also insists upon taking you out for dinner at the newest, swankiest restaurant where only big names can get a reservation on such short notice. While there, over wine and under mood lights, he confesses all his insecurities. You quickly fall in love.

No, wait. That sort of thing only exists in romance novels. I have absolutely no reason to trust this guy.

"Do you think I'm really weak?"

Grant's eyes widen in surprise, and he does a double take. "What? No. Of course not."

"Then why do you want to be sitting next to me in the final two?"

"I don't!" he says. "I…I just mean," he stammers and runs a hand through his thick hair. I can't help but appreciate the sight of his bicep and well-developed chest when his arm is at such an angle. "I have to find someone to trust out here, right? You seem like the best choice. You're obviously smart and you'll be good at the challenges. If the jury picks you over me, so be it. But I plan to align myself with someone strong."

I squint at him. Is he for real?

Right now my power of reasoning is about as strong as it was during those late night cast parties from my college years. God knows I made some bad decisions when I was sleep-deprived and strung out from adrenaline, chips, and cheap beer. But going home with the hot but unavailable stage manager is nothing compared to the monumental missteps I could make out here, when a million dollars is on the line and millions of potential eyes are on me.

Now I'm thirsty, hungry, and I feel like I slept on a bed of rocks, probably because last night I did. I don't want to be this season's empty-headed blonde, naïve and near-sighted. I can only imagine what the viewing audience will think of Grant, but if he's half as appealing on screen, packaged into good-looking sound bites, as he is in unedited real life, then he'll be this season's fan favorite.

Without making a conscious decision, I'm extending my hand to Grant.

"Fine," I say. "But if you lie to me, you're going to pay."

He shakes my hand, and his grasp is warm and dry. It is the first thing I've touched all day that hasn't been damp.

"I know." He smiles at me again, and he lets go of my grip, slowly, like he wishes he could hang on. His gaze drops down and follows my hand, falling to my side. Then he looks up at me, and I feel myself breathing, each inhale and exhale, a little more vividly than I had a moment ago. "I won't screw you over, Robin." He's whispering now, and he steps in, just a little bit closer. "We're in this together, okay?"

I nod and try to calm my racing pulse. Then off in the distance, I see it. The water source.

"Oh, thank God!" I say. And I rush to go take a drink.

"Who let the fire go out?" Joel, a lawyer in his forties, yells this to nobody and everybody. "I leave to go fishing and when I come back, the fire is out!" His face reddens and I see a vein popping out of his neck.

Joel fixes his gaze on Klemi (short for Klementina), who is basking in the sun, wearing nothing but a tiny string bikini that shows every curve and possible inch of her skin to its best advantage.

"Were you on fire duty?" He demands.

She barely raises an eye. "Last time I checked it was going strong." Her Puerto Rican accent makes everything she says sound like a line from a Rita Moreno movie.

"Yeah, well, it's not 'going strong' now." Joel uses air quotes to emphasize his point. His voice is like Alan Alda's, so everything he says sounds like a line from *Mash*. "It's out. What are we going to do?"

"Well…" Klemi puts her index finger to her chin, and tilts in her head in a way that's obviously meant to be mocking. "We could restart it?"

Joel kicks at the half-burnt firewood, swears under his breath, and storms off. Klemi laughs, rolls her eyes, and returns to sunbathing. I continue to scrub the pot we used for breakfast and say nothing.

But inside me a knot unravels.

Our tribe suffered its first defeat today at the immunity challenge and now one of us has to go. Klemi's neglect at letting the fire go out simply fans the flame for her expulsion.

I'm not going to cry about it. Klemi is only happy when she's putting someone else down. You would think she and I would be friends, since we're tribemates, female, and close to the same age. But Klemi claims that all the "female bullshit" is too much for her and she can only get along with guys. I look over and see that she's basking in the sun, a self-serving smile plastered to her face, and I imagine what her expression will be when she gets voted out tonight.

So yeah. I could have saved the fire from going out but I chose not to so Klemi would get blamed. Now the dead flames and smoldering wood smell like victory. I put my bowl down and walk to the beach, where Beth is gathering driftwood.

"Can I join you?" I ask.

She nods, and her hair, now more bleached and damaged from the sun than it was when she arrived, blows in the wind. Beth more than anyone has lost noticeable weight in the ten days we've been here. Eating a diet of rice and the occasional fish will do that to you.

I pick up some sticks and inch closer to Beth. "We need to talk," I say.

"Has Bailey or Grant said anything?" Beth asks.

"Not yet. There hasn't been a good time." I look around, and when I'm sure the only extra pair of ears belongs to the cameraman, I say, "I think we should vote out Klemi. She's weak in the challenges, and until we get to the merge we need all the muscle we can get."

"I'm fine with that," says Beth. "That girl is lazy as shit. Good riddance, I say."

I intentionally give Beth my best unintentional smile. The hardest part of being out here is all the self-monitoring I have to do, like I've become my own parole sergeant. I have to stay safe and safety comes from always playing to the middle. Work hard, but not so hard that the slackers around camp resent you. Be good in the challenges, but not so good that you'll be perceived as a threat. Be nice, but not so nice that you're popular enough to win, because that's the quickest way to get voted out. And if the stress from being pulled in a million different directions makes your head explode, pretend to be fine.

My degree in theater gave me practice at pretending, though acting on a college stage is a million miles from this island I'm on. There aren't any costumes or curtain calls out here, and if someone tells me to break a leg, it's during a challenge and it means they hope to see bone sticking out from my skin. But I'm still playing a role, and when I see the cameras I remember to be sort of likable, uncontroversial, and never brash.

I grab another piece of wood, the last I can possibly hold, and head back to camp. "I'll tell Grant and Bailey that it's Klemi tonight," I say to Beth. "I'm sure Joel will be on board too."

But on our way to Island Assembly, Grant walks up to me, his unlit torch wavering slightly in his grasp. "It's got to be Joel," he whispers.

"I thought we agreed on Klemi," I whisper back.

"I know. But Joel is more of a threat."

I look up at him, maintaining my pace as we walk. "Should we be worried about that before the merge? We need Joel for the challenges."

Grant looks both ways. We're at the back of the line, and quickly, before anyone can see, he places his free hand on my shoulder. "I know. You're right, I know. But Bailey wants Joel out, and the merge is coming soon. Don't worry. The four of us are tight, and we'll have plenty of time to vote out Klemi."

"Why does Bailey want Joel out?"

Grant's eyes twinkle in amusement. "He doesn't like him. You should have heard the expletives he used. Bailey thinks Joel is gay because of the straw fedora he wears."

I clench my torch tightly, dig my toes into the sand as I walk, and make my whisper fierce. "Joel's been married for fifteen years! But what if he was gay? That's not a reason to vote him out!"

"I know that, but this is Bailey we're talking about. He's a military guy from a different generation." Grant steps on a small rock and falters for a moment, but he quickly self-corrects. "We're not going to change his mind, and I don't want to be political. I'm trying to keep our alliance together so one of us can win."

I don't respond. I set my face into a scowl and stare straight ahead. Grant taps my shoulder. "Robbie, you know I'm right."

I whip my head toward Grant. "Don't call me Robbie."

Grant raises his fingers from my shoulder as if I'm a hot stove he accidentally touched, and I'm cursing myself in the same moment that I'm letting it happen. I try so hard to betray nothing, yet this time I couldn't help but let my anger out. Only Ian calls me Robbie. Ian, who is a great big brother when he isn't talking down to me. Ian, who is sweet and strong, and who never mentions how hard it must have been to come out during the early 90s in suburban Iowa. What will he think when he watches this at home, on his couch, with Eddie and their adopted son, Charlie, by his side?

I sigh. "I know this isn't your fault," I tell Grant. "But voting someone out because Bailey's a homophobe makes me really uncomfortable."

Grant reaches for my hand, gives it a tight little squeeze, and then quickly lets go. "Calm down, Robin. This isn't a Pride parade, and I'm not Lindsey Graham." Grant speaks just loud enough that only I can hear him. He keeps his tone light and friendly. "I get how you feel. I do. But Bailey's right about one thing. If Joel made it to the end, he'd be very persuasive to the jury. He's a lawyer for God's sake. Do you want to be sitting up there with him? I sure as hell don't. So if we have a chance to get rid of him now, I think we ought to. Besides, we need to keep our alliance cohesive at this stage in the game. When it's our turn to vote out Bailey, I promise to draw rainbows and purple triangles all over the ballot. Okay?"

I smile at the thought, but don't say anything.

I need to think. Joel reminds me of my cousin Monty: same age, same profession, same sort of temper that flames yet extinguishes quickly, and same ability to charm and make you laugh. Other than Grant, I enjoy talking to Joel more than anyone else at camp. He reminds me a little of home, and I feel slightly safer when he's around.

I'd vote for him to win the million dollars. There isn't anyone here who would get my vote over Joel, which means Grant is right. Joel needs to be voted off tonight.

What sort of game is this, where you make friends only to betray them?

§

A little over a week later the tribal merge happens. Luckily, our Lakas tribe goes into it with five people while the Tapang tribe only has four. Grant, Bailey, Beth and I maintain our alliance, and even though somebody from Tapang wins the first individual immunity, we manage to vote off another one of their original members.

The day after our first Island Assembly as a merged tribe I'm lying on the beach, taking a rare break. I try never to be alone, because that's when other people start conspiring against you. But if I don't have a little downtime I'm sure to lose my sanity. I knew this would be difficult, but what I didn't understand was how much I'd miss the opportunity to sit by myself, comfortable on my couch, with no company other than the television and my two lifelong friends, Ben and Jerry.

The sand warms my back and the sun's rays beat down on my face. Then there's a shadow. I open my eyes to see the cause, and find Grant standing over me.

He smiles. "Hey." He says. "Whatcha doing?"

"Solving world problems."

"Oh good," he replies. "Somebody needs to."

"Well, I'm on it." I pat the sand next to me, signaling him to sit. As much as I want time alone, I can't seem rude or standoffish. It's just not an option.

Grant sits. "I think the next challenge is going to be a swimming one."

"How do you know?"

He shrugs his shoulders. "I don't know for sure. But we haven't had one in a while. And I thought I heard Joe Pine mention something to one of the camera guys at Island Assembly last night."

"Hmm."

"Anyway, I hope so. You or I would have a good chance of winning."

"You think?"

Grant brushes some sand off my shoulder. His touch is warm, warmer than the sand and sun together. "We're the best swimmers out here."

Earlier, Grant told me that he works as the high school swim coach in the town where he lives. I bet all the girls have a crush on him.

"You're an amazing swimmer," I say. "But I can get really water logged."

He chuckles and leans in close. "It's safe, Robin. Nobody else is around."

Nobody except the camera guy, of course. The omnipresent camera guy. I look at Grant with a widened, innocent gape. "I don't know what you mean."

He rolls his eyes and looks towards the sky. "You can admit that you're a good swimmer. I already knew you were, anyway. But even if I didn't, I still wouldn't hold it against you." He speaks in an exaggerated whisper. "And I promise not to tell." Now he raises his eyebrows and grins at me, like a little kid telling a dirty joke. I can't help but return his smile.

"Fine," I say. "I'm a good swimmer."

Grant digs his toes into the sand and inches ever so much closer to me. "There," he says. "That wasn't so hard, was it?"

I shake my head and sniff in response, and Grant looks at me in fascination, as if he's never seen anyone sniff and shake their head simultaneously. He seems so genuine that I'm almost convinced that I actually did something to merit his reaction.

"So, what else are you good at?" Grant asks.

I chuckle and sit up before he can lean over me and match his suggestive tone with a suggestive posture. "Oh no," I tell him. "Your turn. I already confessed something. Now you."

"I don't have anything to confess," he says. "I'm actually a very boring person."

I pass my tongue over my teeth, and hope my breath isn't too bad. He's sitting awfully close. "Please. If that were true, you wouldn't be here."

"Oh yeah?" He laughs. "Does that mean you have some juicy reason behind why you're on this show?"

"Not at all." I run my fingers through my hair, trying to shed some of the sand that's stuck to my scalp. Grant has changed the subject again by putting the focus back on me. I shouldn't fall for it, but I admit it's fun to have his attention. "My reason is really boring. I didn't know what else to do. I have no career or family that I'm obligated to. I like the show, I like competing, I want the money, and I thought I might be good at it. That's all there is to it."

"Hmm." Grant eyes me up and down, as if he could decipher the truth by inspecting the sand on my arms and the dirt on my bathing suit. "I don't believe you," he says. "There has to be more to it." He closes his eyes for a moment, and pretends to be deep in concentration, wrinkling his brow and biting his lip. He reopens his eyes and looks at me with unreserved confidence. "I think you're here because you have something to prove."

A self-conscious chuckle escapes without my permission. "Like what?"

He presses his thumb against my shoulder. "I don't know. That you can handle adversity?"

I pick up sand and let it fall through the spaces between my fingers. "And I have to demonstrate this on national television. Wow. I must have a lot to prove to a lot of people." I keep my head down and watch the sand flow instead of staring at Grant to detect possible changes in his facial expression. If I see his face, he'll see mine, and I can't broadcast any truth or fear too blatantly.

His hand lingers in the air before it lands on the back of my neck. My head snaps up and our eyes meet, shifting the mood between us like a cloud covering the sun.

"Robin, I'm sorry. I didn't mean to insult you."

I offer him a cautious smile. His hand is still lightly resting against my skin. Despite the heat, I have shivers.

Grant moves away so he's no longer touching me and looks off toward the ocean. "I'd tell you the reason why I'm here, but my reason isn't like yours. It will make you think I'm weak."

Now I'm dying to know. I place my hand on his bare, sandy back, but I allow myself to do so only for an instant.

"That's okay, Grant. You don't have to tell me anything. But whatever you say is between us."

He scratches his head, and then his hands come together. As he massages his knuckles the tension in his grasp is clear. "I don't actually need the money," he mumbles. "My parents died when I was young and they were loaded. So I just do whatever I want now. I drift." He rolls his head and I hear a little pop. "This seemed like a good way to fill the time."

Inadequate words of sympathy loiter in my head, but I don't release them. "How did they die?" I ask softly.

He takes a deep breath and turns his face towards mine. "They died in Iraq. But not in combat or anything. They were working with Halliburton and they got killed by a roadside bomb." His eyes tear up a little, but he blinks it away. "I was a senior in high school and I was staying with my grandparents in Connecticut, but as soon as I turned eighteen I left, and I've been on my own ever since."

"Are you an only child?"

Grant shakes his head no. "I have a little sister. She was twelve when I took off, and I've only seen her a handful of times since then." He rolls his shoulders back and stretches out his neck, as if releasing physical tension could diminish the pain of what he's trying to say. "Last I heard, she ran away to Mexico to live with her druggie boyfriend. My grandparents have no idea where she is… " His voice trails off and he switches course. "I haven't talked to my grandparents in months. They blame me for Molly's disappearance. They say I failed her. If I had been around more, been more of a role model, maybe she would have been okay. But she's been in and out of rehab and she's a total mess." His chest rises and falls, and he dares to meet my eyes. "That is, if she's even still alive. We don't know. Of course, we hired a private detective when she first disappeared but he hasn't found anything. My grandparents are convinced Molly is dead and they're angry with me for that."

I shudder. "They can't put that on you. You were just a kid yourself when your parents died." I almost mention my own mother's death and how my brothers and I dealt with it, but I stop myself. This conversation is about Grant.

"I could have done better for her." He squeezes his eyes shut before his lids rise back up. "Being a kid is no excuse. I should have been there for Molly, and now I can't tell her I'm sorry. So I guess I'm here because I don't know where else to be."

His normally dark eyes are especially black as they pool with ache, and I long to make it better. Before I can figure out how, he laughs and shakes off his mood, like rainwater from a tarp. "Want to hear the really twisted part? Part of me thinks I'm doing this so I can reach out to Molly. Like she'll see me on television, and decide to come home. How sad is that?"

"Maybe it will work."

He smiles in appreciation. "Don't tell anyone, okay?"

I marvel at his ability to smile. What else is he hiding? What other painful secrets lie behind his cheerful façade? "It's our secret," I say.

Grant was right. The next challenge involved swimming and I won individual immunity. Grant came in second.

"Did you throw the challenge?" I asked him afterwards.

He scrunched his face in confusion. "Why on earth would I do that?"

"To seem less threatening and to put me in the spotlight."

He sighed. "Don't be so paranoid, Robin. I got a cramp and it slowed me down. Relax and enjoy your victory."

So I did. Besides, Grant won the next challenge, and the one after that was won by Bailey, who must actually be a robot in disguise. My theory is he had some top-secret surgical implants during his time in the military. How else do you explain a guy in his seventies having perfect balance and unrelenting endurance?

Whatever. I don't care, because the short version of the story is that as long as people in our alliance continue to win, we can pick off the remaining members of the Tapang tribe. True, I'm as anxious to vote off Klemi as I was to start tweezing my eyebrows in the eighth grade (we're talking blonde unibrow), but luckily my need for immediate gratification has diminished since my middle school years. So I'm biding my time.

There are six of us left: Me, Grant, Beth, Bailey, Klemi, and Henry, the last member of the Tapang tribe. Henry is a physics student at Princeton, and he meets every stereotype you would expect from an Ivy League genius. He's slight, nearsighted, bad at the physical challenges, and even worse at social skills. But he can talk circles around us, and half the time I wonder if he just operates on his own, separate whiz kid plane. Grant says we'll vote him out next, but I'm thinking Klemi should go first. She has a better chance of winning a final individual immunity than Henry does.

But before the next immunity challenge there is a reward challenge. I'm wondering what it will be as we line up behind a roped off obstacle course.

"Welcome, Castaways!" Joe Pine is wearing his usual blue safari shirt, his dark hair is styled just enough to look attractively windswept, and his well-chiseled cheeks are freshly shaved. Meanwhile, the rest of us look like exhausted, homeless beach dwellers. Only because we are.

"You all have been out here for 31 days. Anyone can tell you: that's a long time to go without seeing or speaking to your family.

Well, today we have a special surprise for you."

Now I know what's about to happen. Every season when it gets down to six people, they bring in the players' "loved ones" to team up in some sort of reward challenge. It's the perfect way to manipulate our already unstable emotions and get us to cry. Silently I vow not to dissolve into a pool of tears like past players have, because it seems so silly. I go weeks without seeing my family all the time, and that's a GOOD thing. However, the other players are already reacting. I guess I'm not the only one who knows what's coming, because Beth gasps and brings her hands to her face, Klemi widens her eyes in anticipation, Bailey inhales deeply, and Henry shifts his weight from foot to foot. I can't see Grant's reaction, but I'm curious. Is he hoping one of his grandparents is waiting to see him? Or maybe he's thinking that against all odds, Molly is about to come out and shock him with her reappearance.

Joe continues. "I can tell all of you are anxious to see your surprise. Well, I won't keep you in suspense. Beth, your husband Mike is here."

Mike, a paunchy, balding guy in his forties comes running out, and Beth squeals and jumps into his arms as if he was Ryan Gosling in a wet t-shirt. They lock in a passionate embrace. I look away to give them some privacy, and see instead the large camera zooming in to capture their intimacy.

Joe continues to call out family members. "Klemi," he says, "your sister Irena is waiting for you." Irena comes running out, and she's a cleaner, less emaciated version of Klemi. Of course they're both gorgeous, and they grasp each other in a tight, full-body hug that is sure to thrill all the male, heterosexual viewers with a pulse.

Next comes Henry's mom, who is very put-together in a pair of khaki shorts and a fitted black t-shirt. She looks like she never has a hair out of place, but that doesn't stop her from squeezing Henry like he's still her baby. Henry rests his head on her shoulder and his body wilts, as if all the stress has been sucked out of him. After that Bailey's daughter appears. She's tall, broad, and has the same tough exterior as her dad, but when Bailey sees her his face actually betrays itself and shows some vulnerability. Everyone is emotional and ecstatic, touching each other's faces and speaking softly in familiar terms, and I'm nearly in tears myself, watching the reunions.

Joe directs his attention to Grant. "Grant, I'm afraid I have bad news for you. We contacted your best friend, Cody, and he wanted to come, but his work schedule wouldn't permit it. He said to wish you a lot of luck."

Grant's face remains stoic, but I can see the hurt behind his unyielding expression. I want to reach out to him and tell him he's not alone, but Joe addresses me first.

"Robin," he says. "You must be wondering who is here for you."

I exhale in relief. I was worried for a moment that my news would be the same as Grant's. But no. Is Ian here? Or, possibly, my dad? Surely not Ted?

"Robin," Joe says, "Say hello to your cousin Jack."

Jack comes running out, and his hug is quick and strong. He looks like every picture I didn't know I had stored of him in my mind. His smile is for me, and there are no ulterior motives or hidden agendas. He is the first person in a month that is unquestionably on my side; he is the only one here who knows who I really am. Damn it. The tears start to form, but I laugh them away. I look at him in confusion. He answers my silent question out loud. "Ian and Eddie's adoption finally came through," he says. "They had to go to China. Otherwise he would have come. Ted had to work and your dad sprained his ankle."

I hug him again. "Thanks for being here."

"Are you kidding? It's a free trip to the Philippines and a chance to be on national television. I should be thanking you."

Joe explains the reward challenge. We are to navigate our way through the rope course while carrying buckets of water. The ropes are set up so we have to climb over and under them, making it virtually impossible not to spill. Once we get to the end of the course we dump our remaining water into our designated tank and go back for more. When our tank is completely full a flag will automatically rise and the first team to raise their flag wins.

"Want to know what you're playing for?" Joe asks.

We all nod our heads in excitement. "You and your loved one

will be whisked away to a private yacht, where you will enjoy a lunch of hamburgers, beer, and brownies for dessert. Afterwards you will receive a once in a lifetime chance to swim with dolphins. Losers will say goodbye to their loved ones immediately. Worth playing for?"

Beth is already crying. She must know she doesn't stand a chance. Henry shouts "Yes!" and crouches before he's even standing at the start line. Bailey and Klemi play it cool, but Bailey's eyes are darting around and Klemi's hands are clenched into fists. Of course they all really want this.

I turn to Jack. "I am so hungry that I would eat *you* if you were cooked right, and served with a little garlic butter. We have to win. I need a burger."

"No problem," he says. "I was all-conference in ropes courses in high school and I even played intramural ropes courses in college."

"Really?"

Jack is deadpan. "No. That was a joke. But I still think we can win."

I blink a few times and shake my head out. A sense of non-reality settles over me. It's a shock to my system to have Jack here. Combine that shock with the fatigue, thirst, hunger, and emotional exhaustion I'm experiencing, and I've lost my ability to separate logic from emotion.

"Then let's win," I say. "If we don't, not only will I go hungry another day, we'll never hear the end of it at Christmas."

"Castaways, take your place at the starting line." Joe Pine orders us, and we fall into place. "Ready, set, go!"

Jack and I quickly drop into an easy rhythm, where he carries the water behind me while I maneuver my way through the ropes. Every time I climb over or under, he reaches his long arms out, and my long arms receive the jug of water. Then once he's through, he takes the water back.

I become focused on my goal of winning and nothing else. I shut out my competition, and I don't even notice how the others are progressing through the course. I don't hear Joe's running commentary. At one point I hear him say, "Grant is still in this, even though he's competing on his own," but that's all I hear. And all I see are the ropes, the water, and Jack.

I don't know if it's our third or fourth trip, but when I pour the jug of water into our tank, our flag pops up.

"And Robin wins reward!" Joe shouts.

I squeal and jump up and down. Jack whoops, and we give each other a triumphant high five. The other contestants stoop in defeat.

After we're ordered to line up again so the cameras can catch us at a good angle, Joe speaks to us. "Okay, Robin, you and your cousin will be treated to a cruise on a private yacht, complete with lunch and a chance to swim with dolphins. Sound good?"

"Oh, yeah!" I say. Then I look around, and see how sad and dejected everyone else is. They will have to say goodbye to their loved ones momentarily.

Joe addresses me. "There's just one thing. A reward isn't complete if you can't share it. For that reason, you get to pick one castaway and their loved one to join you this afternoon."

This is not good news. If I have to pick someone, then everyone else will be mad for not getting chosen. I feel like hitting myself. Moments ago I was focused only on the idea of success, a cheeseburger, and time with my cousin Jack. Now that I'm the winner, victory is not so sweet.

They're all throwing their desperation at me, and the injustice of the situation darkens my mood. Beth is obviously much more attached to her husband than I am to Jack, and she probably needs this visit the way a skydiver needs a parachute. She already looks like she's curling up to break her fall.

But that doesn't mean I don't need it. And it doesn't mean that Bailey, Klemi, and Henry don't need it either.

Okay. There's no way I'm picking Klemi. And I'm not picking Bailey either. Henry is a possibility, because I could use his vote if I make it to the final three and he's on the jury. Then I see Grant, standing by himself. He lost because he was playing alone. And I never have seen anyone look so alone in all my life.

This could literally be a million dollar decision. I know that on past episodes, while the winning contestants are experiencing their rewards, the other contestants back at camp plot against them. All I could think of before was the chance to eat a real lunch, but now I have to remain clear. Who is the person with the most influence? That is the person I have to choose.

"Joe," I say. "This is an impossible decision. I know how much everyone wants a chance to spend time with their loved one, but for that reason, I can't pick one team over another. And since Grant was playing by himself, against impossible odds, I am picking him to come with us today."

Grant's face changes in that instant. He goes from being the sad, lonely child to the one who was just awarded the biggest ice cream cone in the history of the world. He runs over to join Jack and me, and I wonder if I'm doing the right thing. Then our eyes meet, and he mouths a silent "thank you." My breathing turns to liquid, warm delight, spreading from the top of my skull all the way down to each pinkie toe.

I shake myself a little. "Snap out of it, Robin," I whisper to myself.

"Robin?" Joe says. "Did you say something?"

I look up at Joe, aware of all the cameras pointed in my direction. Falling for someone is risky enough under normal circumstances, doing it with millions of people watching and a million dollars at stake is beyond insane. I inhale sharply and square my shoulders. "I'm ready to go," I reply.

§

Later, on the yacht, Jack and I lounge in the sun while Grant swims. My belly is full of beef, beer, and chocolate. I'm surrounded by a sparkling ocean and deep blue sky. A warm ocean breeze teases my skin and hair. There's even a real chair with a soft cushion to sit on. Forget about swimming with dolphins. Right now I could go for the once in a lifetime opportunity to take a nap.

"So, tell me how it's going." Jack says. "You're in the top six. That's pretty impressive. Do you think you'll win?"

I sigh. "I try not to let my mind go there. Then I tell myself I have to. But I'm at the point now where I probably can't win unless I start backstabbing people. Do I want to be that person? Is it worth a million dollars to be a jerk on national television?"

Jack grins and looks out into the horizon. "Very few people get through life without some backstabbing here and there."

"Yeah, but usually it's done with a little more privacy."

Jack squints and bites his lip. There's a wrinkle across his brow that I can sort of see, but he won't meet my eye. "This is what you signed up for Robin. I say get the job done."

"Really? That surprises me. You always seemed like the nice one."

"I am nice. But there comes a time when you say 'screw it' and start going after what you want."

The image of Jack in a lip-lock with that waitress crashes into my mind. "Are you speaking from experience here, Jack?"

Now our eyes meet, but only for a moment. Then he looks at all the cameras and he looks back at me, like he's issuing a silent warning to keep my mouth shut. As if I would out him in front of a camera crew.

Jack scoots closer to me, and places a fraternal hand on my shoulder. He speaks softly. "You need to ask yourself what you want. Why are you here? Is it to win a million dollars or is there something else that you're after?"

I contemplate this and try to form an answer. Of course I want the money, but it's more complicated than that. I open my mouth to explain, but at that moment Grant appears, climbing the ladder up and over the side of the boat.

"The water is amazing!" he says. "And I came this close to touching a dolphin before it swam away." He holds out his hands to indicate the space of about a foot. "I'm not exaggerating. Seriously, Robin. You have to go in."

He holds out his dripping arm. I place my dry hand in his wet one, and he pulls me up from my comfy chair. But his smile is as warm and infectious as a hot rash and if I'm itchy now, so be it.

I turn towards Jack. "You coming?"

"Go ahead. I need to change into my suit, but I'll be there in a minute."

I grab a snorkel and a scuba mask. Then Grant tugs me toward the edge of the boat. We both climb up, but I dive in a split second before he does. Once we're in the water he swims towards me and takes my hand again.

"Let me show you, Robin. Trust me, it really is amazing."

So I swim with him and I trust him, even though right here, right now, trusting anyone is the last thing I should do.

Chapter 4

November 2012

Back home in Iowa I am still under water. Only I've lost my snorkel, and instead of chasing after dolphins I'm swimming away from sharks. Every week a new episode of *The Holdout* airs, and every week I dread feeling exposed, icky and vulnerable, like it's time for my yearly gynecologist exam. I sit on my couch, knees drawn to chin, arms hugging ankles, and I stay like that, a tall little ball of tension, until scenes for next week fade to commercial. And before I have time to ruminate on all the crap that went on behind my dense, closed eyes (and it turns out a buttload of crap went on) my family and friends inevitably call, wanting to know how I could have been so blind.

But family and friends are the least of it. I disabled my Twitter account because I was getting, like, a thousand messages a day from people who watch the show. Some were from fans, but a lot more were from critics, and I was stunned by how harsh people could be in 140 characters. But even on the days when I can forget that Twitter exists, I'm still left with a dilemma: do I go on the message boards, or not? If I was strong and smart, like the Robin I thought I was being on the show, I would stay away. But now I realize that ignorance is not bliss. The more I know, the better, even if the truth stings like salt and vinegar in a paper cut. So I read the comments, and I am privy to America's opinion about how dim-witted I am.

"Lol! Robin is so stupid! I stopped being fooled by guys like Grant in middle school."

Remarks like that are of the kinder variety.

"Robin thinks she's hot shit, but she's as dumb as a brick. I guess her last name fits her. I can't wait for her to get voted off so I don't have to see her ugly face pouting every time some 'injustice' is done to her. What a loser."

So when I get my jury summons, I'm relieved. Maybe I can be an anonymous face, a number sitting on a bench, an audience member for someone else's drama. Maybe I can have something other than my own stupid life to worry about, to think about, to obsess over. Maybe I'll have somewhere to be for a week or two, where I am both unimportant and instrumental: A cog in a wheel that turns in the machine of justice. And maybe this time, justice will make sense. Justice will be what is *supposed* to happen.

§

By 9:00 a.m. the conference room has filled with what must be thirty to forty people. There's a pretty even distribution of males to females, and there's a variety of ages present, but mostly I see white faces. On *The Holdout* they made sure to represent different ethnicities, but this is real-life jury duty in Des Moines, Iowa, and old demographics die hard.

The perky brunette who checked me in earlier this morning walks to the front of the room, turns on a microphone, and addresses us all.

"Hello and good morning! My name is Madison, and I'm the jury clerk for federal court here in Des Moines." People around me put away their cell phones or reading material and direct their attention toward her. "Thank you all for performing your civic duty by showing up today. This is an age-old process, and the justice system needs you. It may seem like a pain, but jury duty is actually one of the most sacred foundations of our democracy!"

The guy to the left of me snorts in exasperation. How charming. Luckily our speaker doesn't notice. I would hate for Madison to pick up on the cynicism; she seems so committed to what she's saying.

"I hope all of you had a chance to help yourself to breakfast treats. If you are selected for a jury, please feel free to use this room during your downtime. You are welcome to use the microwave, televisions, and Wi-Fi. There will be refreshments put out twice daily as well. We want jury duty to be pleasurable, so if there's anything we can do to improve your experience, please let us know."

Wow. Treats twice a day, and free Wi-Fi! To get that on *The Holdout* I would have had to jump over hurdles, or dive for bottles, or put together some impossible puzzle after lifting twice my body weight while balancing on a board half the size of my feet, and I would have had to do it better than everyone else, and even still, the treats would have come at the cost of the jealousy of all the other contestants. Here, I can just go up to the table and grab whatever I want, and unless I take it all, nobody is going to care. I never knew jury duty could be so plush.

Maybe it's just a federal court thing. I bet county court juries don't have it so good.

Madison's smile gleams as she continues to speak. "Right now Judge Sanchez and the lawyers for both sides are upstairs, preparing for trial. In a few minutes you all will be led upstairs for what we call "voir dire.'" She pauses after she says this unfamiliar term, as if she's just disclosed a juicy secret. "But first we watch our orientation film, *Jury Duty and Me*."

She dims the lights and lowers the screen, and moments later the film starts. A woman stands outside the court building in a wide shouldered, bright blue suit and a Katie Couric haircut, circa 1994. She speaks to the audience in a grave yet confident tone. Katie Couric would be proud.

"We've all heard about jury duty. But what exactly is your responsibility, as a juror, and as a citizen? And how can you get the most out of jury duty?"

The scene switches to a doctor's office. A nurse is taking a child's temperature, but she looks up from what she's doing and speaks to the camera. "I never thought I'd be selected. Once I was, I had questions. Are there rules I'm supposed to follow? And what about work? A lot of people rely on me."

The woman in the blue suit comes back, nodding her head with downright solemnity. I haven't seen such focus from anyone since Ms. McCarthy, my middle school gym teacher, explained tampons to a room full of thirteen-year-old girls during Sex-Ed class. "Many people feel anxious about jury duty," says the fake Katie Couric, "and they're nervous about the time they'll be spending away from their work and families. But if you follow these simple guidelines, being on a jury just might turn out to be a fun, rewarding experience."

The guy next to me snorts again as the peppy elevator music swells and the title screen appears. Then a farmer, standing with some cows against a fence, faces out and talks.

"I really liked that I got a say. Nobody ever listened to me about important stuff before. And on juries, everybody has an equal voice."

The film continues, and it keeps switching back and forth between blue-suited "Katie", and "citizens" describing their jury experience. In the midst of it all, some useful information is imparted:

Voir dire is when the jury members are interviewed by the judge and lawyers. We'll be doing that next.

If you're on a jury, and you eat lunch or go on a break with someone else from the jury, you're not allowed to talk about the case unless everyone else on the jury is around to hear you.

You're not permitted to do outside research on the case. This has to include Google searches, but the blue-suited lady doesn't mention the internet since this prehistoric film was obviously made before the web had invaded our lives.

Talking about the case is a no-no, because somebody might say something that will sway your opinion. Only the lawyers are allowed to do that.

§

When the lights come back up, Madison announces that it's time to go upstairs to the twelfth floor for voir dire. My stomach flips a little. I wonder what the lawyers and the judge will ask us. Whatever it is, I hope I have a good answer. I hate feeling stupid. Hopefully this won't be like a citizen test or something. I scan my brain for leftover information from my high school civics class. Who came up with the jury system anyway? Was it Thomas Jefferson? That information should have been included in the film we just watched.

I'm walking towards the elevator when a curvy lady in her late fifties catches up with me. "Do you think they'll notice if we make a run for it? We could just say we got lost on the way up." She laughs, and I laugh back.

"Yeah," I say. "Great idea. But I don't want to get busted." I walk past her as I push down my true desires. Hiding what's inside of me should come naturally at this point. Nobody can know I'm a weirdo who actually *wants* to get picked.

I make it to the elevator, packed tightly with other potential jurors, and ride up to the twelfth floor. On the way up other people make comments.

A skinny guy wearing a suit and glasses says, "So I counted. There are 43 of us. Assuming they pick twelve, that means we each have roughly a 28% chance of being selected."

A woman wearing a bright pink blouse groans. "That high? Oh God help me."

Everyone laughs and I pretend to laugh along. But on the inside I'm making calculations. Surely some people will be excused, right? They'll act crazy or say they have some conflict of interest, which could raise my chances to around 35%, if not higher. That's not too bad. My chances for getting picked to be on *The Holdout* were much smaller, and for better or for worse I was, after all, picked.

We reach the twelfth floor and shuffle out of the elevator and into the courtroom. We're escorted towards some plush seats in the back. The judge, clerks, and lawyers for both sides are milling around. Once the last elevator load of jurors arrives and everyone sits down, we're all given a number. Then they start randomly calling our numbers out. I feel like I'm a bingo hall.

When the clerk calmly and clearly announces "fifteen," I resist the urge to shout and wave my card in victory. Instead I walk towards the jury box as if I'm actually sane, and I have a seat. So far, so good.

There are sixteen of us who had our numbers called. The judge looks down at us from her perch. She's got to be approaching sixty, but with her grey-streaked, thick dark hair coiled into a bun atop her head, the robe she's wearing looks like a smart fashion choice.

"Good morning," she says, in a commanding voice. "I'm Judge Sanchez. Thank you for being here today. To get started I need you to all say your names, age, marital status, and your job." Then her clerk hands a portable microphone to the first guy sitting in the booth. He does as the judge instructed, then hands the microphone to the next person.

This is worse than a citizenship test would be. Do I mention *The Holdout*? That sort of counts as a job, and it's a large reason for why I'm not currently employed. But if I admit to it, than I might not get picked. Would a quasi-celebrity be distracting as a juror? I don't want to risk it.

I decide to tell the truth, but not the whole truth. When it's my turn I say, "My name is Robin Bricker. I'm thirty-one years old, unemployed, and single."

Ouch. Not fun to say that out loud.

The judge nods her head. If she thinks I'm pathetic, she doesn't show it. "Robin," she asks, "Would serving on a jury at this time present you with any sort of hardship?"

"No."

She nods again. "Do you believe you could be a fair and impartial member of the jury?"

"Yes!" I say, perhaps a little too vigorously.

Judge Sanchez seems to swallow a laugh, and moves on to the person next to me. After several people are excused due to potential hardship or conflict of interest, people whose numbers weren't originally called now must come and sit in the jury box.

Finally, the lawyers ask us questions. Have any of us heard of this guy, Mark Smythe? One person has and I wonder who Mark Smythe is. Do any of us work in retail? If so, have we ever had a bad experience with returning damaged goods? One lady raises her hand. What do we know about yachts?

For this one I'm compelled to speak.

"I was on one recently," I say.

The lawyer turns to me. "Oh. Where?"

"It was in the Philippines." I inhale deeply, hoping he won't ask for further details.

He just chuckles. "Lucky you."

Soon the interviews are over. I don't know if it's my darker hair and nerdy glasses, or that nobody here watches the show, but there has been no spark of recognition from anyone. Maybe since nobody is expecting to see me here, nobody has.

The lawyers on both sides write down names, and pass a sheet of paper back and forth. After a couple of minutes or so, one of them hands the piece of paper to the clerk, who hands it to the judge, who hands it back to the clerk after looking it over and nodding.

Judge Sanchez speaks. "Tommy, our clerk, is going to read off the names of those who have been selected. If your name is not read, you are free to go."

I can hear my pulse inside my head. This is like my college theater days, when I would wait for a cast list to go up and pray that my name was on it. Tommy reads off the first name; it's not mine. The thin, suited guy from the elevator moves down to the first seat. The second name belongs to a young woman with bright red hair, and she takes her place next to juror number one.

Then, miraculously, my name is third to be read. "Robin Bricker," he says, clear as day. Woo hoo! Feeling like I won something, I move down to the third seat. I guess that makes me juror number three.

After the other nine people have their names called, and the rest of the people leave, we're immediately sworn in. We all have to raise our right hands simultaneously and repeat after Tommy, as he leads us through our oath. I swear to be fair and impartial, to the best of my abilities.

My raised hand is shaking, out of excitement and nerves.

I'm a member of the jury.

Chapter 5

The trial begins immediately and it all goes by in a blur. I take notes on the little notepads they supply for us because it helps me stay focused. The case is about yachts. One guy says he got poorly-made yachts and he wants his money back, plus restitution, and the other guy says the yachts he made weren't cared for, and he wants the rest of the money he's owed, plus restitution.

During breaks I subtly study the faces of the other jurors, and I try to attach identities to them. This time I'm going to pay attention to everyone. This time I won't let myself be blinded. I realize I'm on a jury now and not a reality show, but group dynamics are group dynamics, and when it comes down to it I want pull. I want to have my say.

So I make idle chitchat with everyone, ask their opinions in ways that don't break the rules, and memorize details for later. I'm already thinking long term and this time I'm not going to let a random group of people get the better of me.

The day goes like this: opening statements, lunch in the cafeteria where I sit with the other jurors, the first witness, afternoon break, more testimony, and then evening recess at 5:00 p.m. By that time I'm ready to go home. I check my cell phone on my way out because I wasn't allowed to have it in the courtroom, and I see that Jack left me a message. We don't talk super often, especially since he left Petra to move in with his girlfriend earlier this fall. But I expected him to call today, because tonight the episode of *The Holdout* that he's in will be aired. I dial his number.

"Hi," I say. "How are you?"

Jack says nothing about the show. Instead he pauses before answering, and his silence is like that sinking moment when you realize you've gotten an unwanted surprise party. "I need a favor," he replies. "Jessie and I sort of had a falling out, and I need a place to stay."

I raise my eyebrows and feel my jaw drop. "Oh. You want to stay with me?" I'm sure he can hear my shock.

"All my friends are on Petra's side," he says. "And Ian doesn't have room with their new baby, and so, yeah…"

"So you're desperate," I respond. He would have to be to want to sleep on my couch.

"Do you mind?" he says. "It will only be a couple of nights."

"I don't mind," I say. "It will be fun to have some company." And I mean it; after all, even reality TV stars get lonely. The elevator I've been waiting for dings and the doors open. "I have to go, Jack. But I should be home in around twenty minutes. Come by any time after that."

§

It takes me longer than I thought it would to find my car in the underground garage, and then to navigate my way home during rush-hour traffic in downtown Des Moines. I walk into my apartment and barely have time to pick up the stray pairs of underwear off my bathroom floor before the doorbell rings. When I open it I find a very haggard-looking version of my cousin Jack. Pale blondish gray stubble covers his chin and cheeks. His hair is darker than usual, like it's stained with dirt and grease, and it's sticking out in short clumps. There are gloomy circles under his eyes, and his eyes themselves are pinkish and squinty, probably the result of a headache.

"You look like you either want to crawl into a hole, or like you've just crawled out of one. I can't decide which."

He shrugs his shoulders like they each weigh fifteen pounds. "Same difference, right?" Clutching his overnight bag, he shuffles inside, drops his bag by the coat rack, removes his scuffed-up loafers and hangs his parka vest among my many "vintage" thrift-store jackets. Then he moves slowly, laboriously towards my couch. Once there he sags until he's sitting, leans his head back, closes his eyes, and rubs his temples.

"My life has imploded," he says. He's speaking to the ceiling, eyes still closed, as if he's talking to God. Am I supposed to respond, or should I wait for some divine intervention?

I take a seat across from him, on my green floral print armchair. I wait for a moment before I say anything. He's like he's a cat I've just brought home from the pound, and I don't want to spook and cause him to hide under the bed. But after it becomes clear that God isn't going to contribute to this conversation, I decide it's time that I do.

"Do you want to talk about it?"

He opens his eyes and tilts his chin down, so he can look at me. "I'm a terrible person and I've managed to alienate everyone who has ever been important to me."

"You haven't alienated me," I tell him.

He closes his eyes again, laughs a little, and shakes his head.

"Oh," I say. "You mean really important, don't you? Top-tier important, like your son, wife, and girlfriend?"

Now he sits up, places his elbows on his knees, and puts his head in his hands. "It sounds even worse when you say it like that."

I look down at my hands. "Well, yeah, I suppose it does." With a sigh I get up. "Come on; wining and moping isn't going to do you any good." I walk around my coffee table (which is actually a bunch of orange crates nailed together, sanded down, and stained blue) and I stand over him with my arms crossed. "Jack, you're welcome to stay here as long as you need. But you have to pull yourself together. Why don't you start by taking a shower, and I'll order us some dinner, and then we can eat and you'll tell me what's going on."

Jack lifts his head from his hands and looks at me like I'm a stranger. "How old are you now, Robin?"

"Thirty-one. Why?"

He shakes his head. "I can't believe that. In my mind, you stopped aging at twenty-three. I always think of you as being twenty-three."

"Does that mean you're still only thirty-three?"

"I only wish." He stands. "Thanks for letting me stay. I'll try to snap out of this funk."

I give him a smile and a pat on the shoulder. "I'll find you a clean towel." I walk over to my linen drawer and grab one. "Lucky for you I've matured a little in the last eight years, because back when I was twenty-three not only would I not have an extra clean towel, I wouldn't have had an extra towel, period. And the one towel that I did have wouldn't have been washed in the last two months." I laugh a little and hand him the towel, and he takes it.

"I suppose learning that stuff didn't come easy, given the circumstances."

I cock my head in question. "What do you mean? What circumstances?" I ask this, stupidly, when I know what the answer will be, and I also know I don't want to hear it.

"You know," Jack responds. "Growing up surrounded only by males. I'm sure there's all sorts of stuff you missed out on."

I inhale sharply through my nose. "Like learning to do laundry? Because only women can do laundry, right?" My voice stiffens. "Ted and Ian lost their mother too, and they're both capable of having clean linens. They have been for years. It just so happens that my father did a fine job at all that stuff."

"Calm down, Robin." He moves past me and into the bathroom. "Boy. I really have a talent for saying the wrong thing lately." He closes the door behind him and it's the end to that conversation.

It's probably for the best.

I find my takeout menus in the cubby by the phone, and I peruse them all, trying to figure out if I'm in the mood for Mexican, Asian, or Italian. But I can't focus. What is wrong with me?

I should welcome the excuse to play the "dead mom" card every time some flaw in my personality is betrayed. Instead I always insist that my many downfalls and foibles have nothing to do with growing up without her. And the worst part is I don't know why I do this.

After a few moments the water stops running. "Robin!" I hear Jack call. "Can you do me a favor, and place my bag by the bathroom door?"

I get up and grab his bag, which is heavier than it looks, and put it outside the bathroom. "Done," I tell him.

I walk away and hear the bathroom door open then close again. I sit on my gray, sagging couch and read the latest issue of *In Touch Weekly*, hoping there will be no mention of *The Holdout* or of me. I've gotten to the last page and I'm breathing a sigh of relief when a freshly clean, livelier cousin Jack emerges from the bathroom.

"I ordered a pizza," I say. "I hope that's okay."

"Sounds great." Jack smiles and sits across from me in the chair, our positions now reversed from how they were before. "Hey, I'm sorry about what I said. I know you don't like talking about your mom."

"Don't mention it," I say, not to forgive but to intimidate. If I squint at him hard enough and make my voice sound cold enough, maybe he won't bring up my mother, or my lack of one, again.

Jack scratches behind his ear. "What day is it?"

"Tuesday," I murmur and look away.

"Isn't today the day?" Jack's eyes widen in anticipation. "I almost forgot." He looks past me, at the blinking clock on my cable box. "Isn't your show on in like, two minutes?"

"Huh. Wow. I guess *I* forgot."

Jack smirks at me. "You're such a bad liar. Take it from one bad liar to another: don't lie if you don't know how."

"I know how to lie," I say, my defenses going up for the umpteenth time in the forty minutes or so since he's been here. "I lied all the time on *The Holdout*."

"Apparently not enough." Jack laughs and starts looking around. "Where's your remote?"

I get up and power on the television old-school style, sans remote. "I have no idea. I lost it around a month ago. I've looked everywhere, and it's just gone. I think it's the universe's way of telling me that I shouldn't watch TV until this stupid show is over."

"Too late." Jack sits back on the couch and pats the spot next to him. I sit down, and we settle in. I have to admit, watching the show actually feels more appealing than hearing about Jack's messed up personal life. Jack must agree, because he is smiling and he looks way happier than he did when he first walked through my door.

I understand. There's no better way to forget about how damaged your own life is than by watching someone else's stupid, even more damaged life on television.

No wonder reality television is so popular.

The episode starts with a testimonial by Grant. He sat on the beach; the sun was bright and the ocean filled the frame behind him. Grant's curly hair had grown into a white-man-fro and he had three-day beard growth. But his eyes twinkled with joy and the elements had done little to diminish his natural beauty. Even knowing what I now know, I still feel myself responding to him. He must have learned long ago that he's appealing enough to get away with whatever he wants. Because, so far, he has. He faced the camera and spoke without regret.

"I've been playing this game for almost a month. Before I left all I heard was how hard it is to be on *The Holdout*, but it's not hard. It's easy. All you have to do is appeal to their emotions. If I make them think I'm attached to them, they'll become attached to me. I give them a reason to be sentimental so they'll stop using strategy. And every few days I wave goodbye when somebody else gets voted out." He held his hand up, and waved with a smile. The corners of his eyes crinkled with charm. He's a piranha disguised as a lovable puppy dog.

Jack and I watch and the loud shimmer of the television hypnotizes and renders us mute. By the time the reward challenge is shown, the pizza is here and we stuff our faces as we relive our victory.

"Wow," says Jack. "We rocked that ropes course. Maybe I missed my calling."

"Mmmm," is all I say as I lick the pizza sauce from the corners of my mouth. I can't tear my eyes from the screen. In a moment Joe Pine is going to ask me to pick someone to come with us on the reward challenge. *"Pick Beth,"* I say to myself. *"Don't be an idiot, Robin. Pick Beth pick Beth pick Beth pick Beth."*

But no. On screen I started talking, and I said exactly what I remember saying several months ago. "...since Grant was playing by himself, against impossible odds, I am picking him to come with us today."

Uhgg! I see that Beth's face fell as she had to tear herself away from her husband. Even as she cried she shot me the death stare. I see that Grant barely contained his gloating. I see that Klemi met eyes with Grant for a mere second or two, but it's long enough to suggest the intimacy between them that I had missed before.

They say hindsight is twenty/twenty. No. Not when hindsight is aired every week on broadcast TV. Then it's beyond twenty/twenty. Hindsight is Superman, x-ray vision with psychic powers built in.

"You know," says Jack, "I still don't get why you chose Grant to come with you. He didn't even have a loved one."

"Not a visiting one, anyway."

"Huh?"

I wave my hand dismissively at him, telling him to back off. "I'm not allowed to reveal any secrets until after they've been aired and they're no longer secrets. Just watch the show."

Jack looks back towards the TV and watches the commercial for *Drama*, the nighttime soap that comes on after *The Holdout*. Somebody is about to betray someone who's been in a terrible accident after having an affair with a government official who might be a traitor but is definitely hiding a covert identity. "Your show's not back on yet," Jack says. "What secrets?"

I get up to avoid further interrogation, and move to the kitchen to refill my glass with water. We already emptied a leftover half-bottle of wine while we watched the first part, and I'm cursing myself for not buying straight-up, hard liquor in anticipation of tonight's episode. I know what's coming and I should have known I'd need it.

I sit on the couch as the show comes back on, and I bring my knees to my chin. "Are you okay?" Jack asks me.

I nod my head as much as I can, as my chin is resting on my knees.

Jack and I see ourselves on the boat. We listen to ourselves having a heart-to-heart about what I really wanted. We see me smile as Grant took my hand and led me into the ocean and I swam away with him.

Then they cut to the other contestants back at camp. Henry was taking a nap. Beth was tending the fire and doing dishes, muttering to herself. Then she had a testimonial to the camera.

"I never liked Robin," Beth said. "She's a spoiled princess type, and she thinks she's entitled to whatever she wants just because she's tall, skinny, and blonde." I'm so tense that as I hear this, I bite my lip and contract every muscle that was formerly relaxed. Her words are as grating as laughter from a party I wasn't invited to. "I was only in an alliance with her for strategy." Beth grimaced at the camera. "That girl thinks way too much of herself."

Is that how I came off, as stuck-up? I was just trying to lay low. Beth continued. "And now, when she could have chosen me, she chooses that pretty boy Grant? Please. Everyone is kissing his ass but me. I know his game and I'm going to make sure other people do too."

Jack raises his eyebrows at that. "Did she ever tell you anything?" he asks.

"No. She stopped speaking to me, and then she got voted out." As soon as I say it, I clap my hand over my mouth. "Oh my God!" I say. "I didn't just tell you that."

Jack smiles and reaches for his phone. "I'm going to Tweet and let the world know that Beth gets voted out of *The Holdout* tonight," he says.

I grab his phone. "No! The show will sue me if they find out I've disclosed any information."

Jack doesn't try to get his phone back. "Relax, Robin. You're secret is safe for the next sixteen minutes. Besides, I'm not even on Twitter."

I shove him in the arm and we return to watching.

Bailey and Klemi conspired as they went for water.

"We obviously need to talk to Grant," Klemi said. She was wearing her mint green bikini and nothing else. She tossed her long, sun-kissed locks as she spoke in an utterly serious tone. "But I think we should vote off Robin next."

Bailey shrugged and looked away, clearly unimpressed. "Whatever Grant wants is fine with me."

I glimpse over at Jack, and he doesn't flinch. If he's been watching the show like he says he has, then it's no surprise that Grant had formed one alliance with Beth and me, and another one with Klemi. Bailey was the only one privileged enough to be in both of Grant's alliances.

I chew the sides of my mouth and consider getting up for Chap-Stick, but decide against it. Nothing is going to ease the sting of what's coming next, not even medicated wax. The scene cuts again to me saying goodbye to Jack, and then to Grant and me arriving back at camp. I got the cold shoulder from everyone. Beth wouldn't even look at me.

"Should I try and catch some fish?" I asked. "The Silver Perch were out in droves the other day."

"Did you guys hear something?" Beth said. "It's like a weird, annoying echo is ringing in my ears." Klemi and Bailey snickered and Henry stayed quiet. Grant shrugged it off the way he shrugged off everything.

But not me. Getting shunned always hits me where I live, like cheap toilet paper or rough, pilling bed-sheets. Of course out there I would have loved to have had either, but I couldn't stop myself from bristling from the harsh treatment. Later at nighttime I wandered off by myself to lick my wounds.

But then Grant was behind me. "Hey," he said. "Can I sit with you?"

Tell him no tell him no tell him no, I say to myself now. "Sure," I said.

He sat next to me. It was dark, so it was hard to see, but his smile was bright enough to read and I remember this moment well. I know that for a moment I was smiling too.

"I had a really good time today, Robin. I appreciate you bringing me, and I'm so sorry that you're paying for it now." He said this softly, so soft that it's a wonder the microphone could pick it up. But I have no memory of a camera or a microphone. Just him.

"It's okay," I said. I was fighting back tears, wondering if I'd just cost myself the game. I took a deep breath of the exotic evening seaside air.

He stroked my knee with his finger, tracing my leg all the way up to my thigh. "So you and your cousin must be really close, huh? Closer than you are to the rest of your family?"

I tried to keep my voice free of any self-pity or sadness. "My dad is accident prone. My one brother just adopted a baby, and my other brother…" I started to tell him how Ted can be a real ass, but I remembered the cameras and microphones just in time. "…he's a high-powered business man with a tight schedule. And my mom, well, she's dead."

I almost didn't get that out without tears. I barely remember my mother, and the memories I do have are more manufactured than real. So why was this so hard?

"Anyway," I told him. "I shouldn't complain. I'm not complaining. I love my family; and my cousin Jack, it was amazing to see him and it was amazing of him to come."

At home my cheeks grow warm. Jack just smiles and pats me on the knee. On television I keep talking.

"But, even still, I know what loneliness feels like. And I didn't want you to have to feel that today."

Grant's eyes glistened and he looked right through me, as if he could interpret my thoughts. "I won't let anything happen to you because of this. I promise. I promise on my little sister's life."

He brought his thumb to my face and wiped away the stray tear that had fallen. I sniffed and smiled.

"You put yourself on the line for me and nobody ever puts themselves on the line for me," Grant said. He blinked and I knew I saw bare, naked emotion in his face. Was he faking that too? His eyes opened again and they were gazing into my own. "Robin, I feel…" his voice faded away.

"What?" I asked, desperate for him to finish the thought.

"I feel close to you," he said.

Then he leaned in and kissed me. Deeply. So deep that I can still feel his lips on mine all these months later.

"What?! No! No!!!!" Jack throws a couch pillow at my television. I had momentarily forgotten he was there and I'm startled back to reality.

Jack turns to me, waving his hands in the air. "How could you kiss that asswipe?" he sputtered. "He's so obviously playing you!"

I clench my jaw and my words come out in a ball of tension. "Obvious to you! Okay? Obvious to you."

"He was protecting Klemi!" Jack looks like he wants to smack me in the head to further drive home his point. But he settles for a verbal blow instead. "I mean, if he wasn't having sex with her, it's not because he didn't want to!"

I sigh. I guess that part isn't a secret after all. "Yes, but I didn't know that at the time. It's not so easy when you're there, and you're not privy to EVERYTHING that is going on, all right? So leave me alone." I stare at him with stones in my eyes before I deliver the final punch. "Who are *you* to judge, anyway?"

Jack's face falls and I regret my last three seconds, in addition to my last six months. Silently we turn back toward the television.

Cut to the next day. They show the immunity challenge. Henry won because it was a test of knowledge. It's almost like the producers wanted him to win and they came up with a challenge they thought he'd be good at. Huh. Then we're back at camp. Beth "accidentally" tripped me as I went to tend the fire. I could have fallen into the pit if gravity had decided to pull me the opposite way.

Afterwards I pulled Henry aside. "I'm thinking we should blind-side Beth," I said.

Henry scrunched up his face in surprise. "Didn't you promise each other that you'd go to the end together?"

I wipe my mouth with the back of my hand and nod. "Yes, but she's unpredictable. If you do one thing to cross her then she's done with you. I'd rather be in the final four with you."

Henry's eyes widened behind his square-rimmed glasses. "What about Grant?"

"I'll talk to him," I said.

Later Beth sat under the shelter, next to Bailey, who was taking an afternoon rest. "We've got to vote out Grant," she said. "Not that I wouldn't love to get rid of Robin first, but she's more annoying than she is a threat. Grant could win though. And he's lying to everyone. He's dangerous, I tell you. We need to do it now while he doesn't have individual immunity."

Bailey nodded his reclined head. "I'll see what I can do."

The first chance he got, Bailey found Grant and told him what

Beth said. "I'll take care of it," Grant told him. He was as calm as concrete. Then Grant found me.

"She's useless in the alliance now," Grant said. "And she's turned against you. She wants you out. Better to vote her out now before she can convince the others to write your name down. "

I nodded my head. "You're preaching to the converted. I'm totally voting her out, and I think we should include Henry in our alliance instead."

Grant looked to make sure nobody was watching. "Really? Should I be jealous?" Then he stroked my cheek. We shared a hushed smile.

"We'll be in the final two together." Grant was all but whispering sweet nothings in my ear. "If I'm not going to win, I want it to be you."

"I feel the same way," I said. I closed my eyes and fantasized about one of us winning and then both of us going away somewhere, together. We'd have nothing but time and a million dollars to spend. I hugged him, and for the first time in a while I felt rooted to the ground.

Cut to Grant shaking hands with Henry. "I'll carry you as far as I can as long as you vote with me," he said.

Henry nodded his head. "Okay."

Cut to Grant and Bailey sitting waist deep in the ocean water, while the sun set behind them.

"Just tell me what the plan is," Bailey said.

Grant punched him fondly in the shoulder. "It's the two of us until the end. That's the plan."

Bailey nodded his head. "Okay."

Cut to Grant with his arms around Klemi. They were hidden in a thicket of trees as dusk settled into shadows.

"Beth is trying to vote me out, and she has to pay for that."

Klemi sighed into his shoulder. "But you promised this time it would be Robin's turn to go."

Grant smiled at her with tenderness. "Robin will go next time," he said. "Not just because she could win, but because her stuck-up routine has gotten pretty irritating."

"I know," said Klemi. "That's what I've been saying all along."

Grant laughed. Then he kissed her. "You and me until the end," he said. "I promise."

She giggled and nodded her head. "Okay."

And months later, watching the exchange, my heart dies a little, like a battery that needs to be recharged.

They show Grant one last time, by himself, speaking to the camera. "See?" He said. "This game is easy."

Chapter 6

The next morning Jack is still asleep on the couch as I prepare to leave for the day. But the smell of coffee and the sound of my shuffling about must wake him, because he straggles into the kitchen just as I'm filling my travel mug.

He notices my hair, pulled back in a severe bun, my fake, thick, dark-rimmed glasses, my purple sweater with shoulder pads, and my knee-length black wool skirt.

"Why do you look like a secretary from a cheesy 1980s television show?"

I secure the cap on my coffee mug. "I'm not really allowed to disguise myself, but I'm dressing in a way that doesn't look like me. I don't want anyone to recognize me from *The Holdout.*"

He rubs at his eyes. "Why not? After last night I bet you have the sympathy of every woman in America. At least the ones who have been lied to." He raises his eyebrows and scratches his head. "So that means all of them."

"Uh huh." That's all I can say, it's all I want to say, and it's all I'm ever going to say about last night's episode. I've already endured numerous phone calls and chat rooms, and each friend, family member, or online community member marveled at my incompetence. It's like Valentine's Day and I'm Charlie Brown, and everyone would feel bad for me if I wasn't such a blockhead.

After last night's episode I could barely sleep. The only thing that comforted me was the thought that this morning I actually have somewhere to be. I am drinking coffee before 10:00 a.m., I'm dressed in something other than sweatpants, and I will be too busy to go on my computer and read about myself. I prepare to go. Jack follows me as I walk to my coat tree. I select a gray felt jacket I refurbished with a wide collar and red buttons. "Will you be at the restaurant tonight, or will you be around when I get back?"

"Back? Back from where?"

I button my coat with the hand that isn't holding my coffee mug and grab my purse. "Didn't I tell you? I have jury duty!"

"Seriously? How'd you get so lucky?"

I decide to ignore the sarcasm. "I know! I can't wait. So…Will I see you later?"

Jack yawns. "I'll probably be at the restaurant until 10:00. If you're up, you'll see me after that."

I grab the spare key that is hanging by my door and hand it to him. He sighs and smiles. "Thank you, Robin. I really, really appreciate this."

"No problem. But bring home leftovers tonight."

§

I arrive at the courthouse in plenty of time, although several people got here before me. There's a refreshment cart with coffee, juice, bottled water, fruit, and pastries. I refill my travel mug, grab a banana and a Danish, shuffle around the large conference table and take a seat in the same spot where I sat yesterday.

We get our own individual jury room now, and I sit here undecided about whether I should stare at the gray walls, gray carpet, the white board at the end of the room, or out the large picture windows on one side. We're on the fourteenth floor, so there is a postcard view of downtown Des Moines. They don't make too many postcards of downtown Des Moines – go figure – so I suppose I should take this opportunity to focus on that.

Sitting beside me, Juror Nine sighs and mutters more to himself than to anyone else. "Here we are. Day two. Yeehah." He's as dejected as someone who just graduated college with a philosophy degree.

Okay. So not everyone is jazzed about jury duty. I wonder: If this was *The Holdout*, and we had to vote each other off, which one of us would get voted off first? Who would be the lone survivor, privileged with getting to decide the verdict of the case?

But of course that's not how it will work, and instead of being stuck on an island we're stuck in a room. Nine has a cold and his stuffy, nasal breathing fills the silence. Jurors number two, six, and twelve are here as well. Yesterday we said our names at lunch, but at that point the excitement of being chosen was still charging through me and I've since forgotten them.

But I remember other stuff.

I turn to my right, where Nine is sitting, reclined, with his legs stretched out. His salt-and-pepper hair is a shade lighter than his mustache, which accentuates his big face on his even bigger neck. "How was your drive this morning?" I ask.

He sniffs thickly and wipes his nose with a tissue. "Good. When I left it was so early there wasn't any traffic." Nine lives outside of Ames, and he's the system op for a grain company. Since this is federal court, people were summoned from all over the state.

Two lets out a deep and throaty laugh, unintentionally displaying the dimple on the left side of her cheek. I think she's close to my age but her dyed red hair and dog-collar necklace make her seem young. "My drive wasn't like that. I was coming from Ankeny."

Six, who is sitting to the left of me, looks up from her phone. Her cologne reminds me of apples and air-freshener. Six's round cheeks and prominent chin make her face memorable, and her blond hair looks natural even though she's got to be in her sixties. "I'm from Ankeny too! I manage a clinic out there. What do you do?"

"I waitress at an Olive Garden," answers Two.

"Really?" I say. "I love their breadsticks."

Twelve, who could be a model with her dark wavy hair and lipstick that always seems freshly applied, takes off her iPod and joins the conversation. "My fiancé and I got engaged at an Olive Garden!"

I do my version of a mini-squeal, which comes out like an injured meow. "Oh, that's so awesome! When did you get engaged?"

Twelve describes the entire evening of the proposal, shows us her ring, and tells us all about the wedding plans. I try to follow along, but inwardly I sigh. I'm so bad at small talk. But I want to fit in this time. I couldn't take it if another group of people thought I was stuck up.

Two, Six and I continue to chitchat, while Nine feigns no interest and plays with his phone. One comes in. He was the only guy dressed in a suit yesterday and he's in another one today as he sits in his chair, skinny legs crossed, and reads the *Financial Times*. When Four enters she does so in a flurry, with quick, erratic movements that contradict her large frame and composed appearance. She takes a restless seat next to Six.

"You wouldn't believe the morning I had! I got up early to make sub plans, and I found my classroom had been completely rearranged! The desks weren't even in rows anymore. Seriously! How am I going to be gone for two weeks if this is what happens when I'm not there?!"

Six gives her a maternal pat on the knee. "Don't worry. Your students will get by."

I chime in. "I'm sure it's stressful though."

She turns to me as if her problems are all my fault. "Stressful? You'd better believe it's stressful! Grades are due next week, and the kids have a test coming up. I'm going to be grading and lesson planning when I'm not in court. It's like I'm working two jobs now."

I nod and express sympathy, but already I'm thinking she'd be voted off first just for being annoying. Yesterday she was always on her cell phone because she's trying to plan her wedding and buy a house, and she made sure everyone knew it so she could inhale their sympathy like a huffer on glue. Oh well. Let her have her freak out. As long as she doesn't recognize me, she can curse her bad luck all she wants and I'll listen to every word.

Eventually the other jurors come in. All the females join in conversation, while the men act like there's somewhere else they'd rather be, or like they're hung-over, or both. Except for Number Ten. He sits and listens to the women talk, nodding his head without saying much.

Ten's a real-estate agent; I remember that from yesterday. This is his third jury duty in two years. One was for state court, and the other was for county. So now he's doing federal. It's rare that each type of court would contact someone in such a short amount of time but he's living proof that it can happen. The system just really likes him, I guess. Now he stares at me with squinted eyes and I pretend not to notice. Maybe he watches *The Holdout*. Maybe he knows who I am. But that doesn't mean I have to give him an opening.

Finally Tommy the clerk, as cute and bright as a candy apple, comes to get us.

"Good morning, everyone! Your presence has been requested."

We put our phones down. I grab my court-sanctioned notebook and my bottle of water. We make our way into the hallway, and get in numerical order.

Tommy the clerk goes inside first.

"All rise for the jury!"

And everybody stands up. I should enjoy this. It will probably be the only time in my entire life that a room full of people will rise just because I'm entering it.

The trial certainly isn't as interesting as the ones I watch on TV, like on *The Good Wife*. There's no Josh Charles-type lawyer, the handsome bad-boy in good-boy clothes, who comes in to plead the innocence of the mentally ill woman accused of murdering her philandering husband because a drug company gave her harmful medication and her swimming pool was emitting poisonous insecticides, which proves negligence by the neighborhood association.

No, this case is about yachts.

Here's what I've learned so far: One of Iowa's multi-millionaires, Mark Smythe, has a son, Silas, who is fascinated with yachts. Several years ago, before the recession, Silas decided he wanted to buy and sell high-end, wooden yachts. He hired a company in Greece to craft the yachts for him. He found a shipyard in Florida to which the yachts could be shipped. From Florida he transported the yachts all around the country to boat shows. He sold several yachts that way, but he was unable to sell all of the original hundred that he had ordered. These yachts went for a million dollars each. Then some of them started to show flaws, specifically cracks in the hull, which is the foundation of the boat. One sank (nobody was on it when that happened.)

Mark Smythe is suing the Greek company, Potenza, for the cost of all the boats, plus lost wages and expenses from marketing them. Potenza is countersuing, saying that the Smythes didn't store the boats correctly, and they're making all this up because the real reason the boats didn't sell was that the recession hit. They say the Smythes owe them for several boats for which they have not been paid.

Yesterday Mark Smythe testified. Today it's Silas's turn.

He's sworn in and he sits down in the witness box. The Smythes' lawyer, a generic white-haired expensive-suit sort of guy, questions him.

Silas's testimony begins with questions from his lawyer about his age, his background, and his personal life. The lawyers ask all the witnesses these questions, as if they were a candidate for Match.com rather than part of a multi-million dollar civil suit. Silas is thirty-two, majored in Peace Studies at Grinnell (the Ivy League of the Midwest), and he's worked for his dad ever since graduation. Oh, and he's single. Now he sits with excellent posture and answers all the questions with rosy, dimpled cheek eagerness.

"Selling yachts from Iowa, that's sort of unusual, is it not?" asks the lawyer.

"Ever since I was a little boy, I've been fascinated with water and maritime activities." Silas's voice reminds me of caramel and pretzels, sweet yet salty, smooth yet sticky. Like every word he says is infused with entitlement, but he's packaging it all in self-deprecation and handsome good humor.

"And you're lucky to have a father who can subsidize your interests, are you not?"

Silas brushes his dark bangs out of his eyes. "I won't pretend to be something I'm not. I realize people resent guys like me, a trust-fund kid who's never had to hold down a real job. Boating is my passion but it isn't just a hobby. I was pursuing a legitimate business venture and I cared deeply about the integrity of those yachts. I'm not here for the money as much as I am for justice."

I look down and write in notebook: *Pretty boy rich kid used dad's money to fund yachts. Pissy because it wasn't as easy as he thought it would be to sell them.*

Then I read what I wrote and cross it out. The judge asked me if I could be fair and impartial, and I said yes. So instead I write: *Wealthy son who likes yachts is upset when he can't sell them because they were damaged.*

The lawyer scratches his forehead, as if he's just now thinking up his next question. "What about the claim that you stored the yachts incorrectly?"

Silas sighs as if he's spent his whole life rehearsing for this moment. "These yachts were selling for a million dollars each. They should be able to withstand the elements. I can't fathom how a little bit of sun, or a few weeks in the water, justifies cracks in the hull. We're not talking about cosmetic damage! The flaws in these boats were both structural and dangerous."

The lawyer nods gravely. To my left, Four scribbles fervently in her notebook. I'm tempted to look over and see what it is that she's writing, but I don't want to mooch off the smart kid's notes.

The testimony goes on. They show us pictures of yachts—how they looked when they were new, and how they looked once they were damaged. The cool part is there is a screen in front of each juror's chair, like we're all flying first class. The lawyers have some electronic port where they can put the pictures up, and display them on all our screens. We see beautiful, golden brown yachts glistening with fresh varnish. We also see cracked, damaged yachts. They're broken and ugly, past redemption, a cautionary tale of great boat potential gone wrong.

After a couple of hours worth of testimony about hull cracks and damning emails on how badly the boats were selling, the judge tells us to go to lunch.

Back in the break room, the jurors grab their phones and bags as they prepare to leave.

"Okay, we're all still here, so I can say this," Four declares. "Silas Smythe is kind of hot!"

Two giggles and Twelve laughs her loud, braying guffaw.

"I agree!" says Six. "He reminds me of a younger, American, Pierce Brosnan."

"Totally!" Two grabs her purse and puts on her jacket "I was thinking the same thing."

"Yeah, he's pretty magnetic." I say this not so much because I think it's true, but because I'm trying to be "one of the girls". However, the only response I get for my comment is a raised eyebrow and smirk from Ten.

"Where are we going for lunch today?" Asks Twelve.

All the female jurors, except for Seven, who brought her lunch, decide to walk a couple of blocks to an Asian restaurant.

"Are you coming?" Six asks me.

"You all go ahead," I say. "With all the treats we've been served, I'm not really hungry."

The ladies shrug and exit toward the elevators, rice, and overpriced pot-stickers. I use the bathroom, pretend to make a phone call, and wait for the break room to clear out so I can raid whatever is left of the treat table. They'll put something new out in the afternoon anyway, so it's not like I'm committing a crime.

But when I reenter, Ten is still sitting there, reading a copy of The *7 Habits of Highly Effective People*.

"A little light reading?" I ask.

"My boss is requiring it," he responds, without looking up.

"Oh." I grab a water, an apple, and another breakfast pastry. Not the best lunch ever, but it will do.

Ten raises one eye from his reading and without judgment, observes my pillage of the treat table. "I thought you said you weren't hungry," he says in a gravelly voice.

I toss a diplomatic smile towards Ten, but he doesn't notice because he's back to looking at his book. "I was just embarrassed," I say. "Money's been tight lately, so if I can score some free food, all the better."

Ten uses both his eyes to look up at me now. His mouth twitches and he subtly tips his head.

I bite my apple and juice drips down my chin. "What?" I demand.

"Do I know you from somewhere?" His tone, his face, and everything about him suggest that he's indifferent to me, which makes it tempting to tell him who I am.

But I don't confess. I give him a close look even though I know we've never met. The collar of his tan oxford shirt is so tidy against his tan skin, like they were color-coordinated to go with each other. His light brown hair is short, like a shorn animal, and his eyes are neither small nor large, just medium-sized brown dots that never rest in a face that is otherwise still. Then he smiles and I remember why yesterday he struck me as semi-interesting. It's the sort of smile you could use for a flashlight, were the power to suddenly go out.

"I don't think so," I reply, making my tenor soft, like yogurt.

"You seem really familiar."

I could say something about *The Holdout*, and I would if I was an idiot and I wanted everyone on the jury to know about me. Instead, I wrap a napkin around my muffin and put it in my purse. With my water bottle in one hand and my partially eaten apple in another, I raise both arms in a sort of goodbye gesture.

"Wow," I say. "Sitting so long in one spot turns my legs into a pair of temperamental toddlers." I kick and twitch my legs a little to reinforce my point. "I think I'll go for a walk."

Ten looks outside the large picture window. "It looks kind of cold and rainy for a walk."

"I'll be fine! Enjoy your lunch."

He smiles and thanks me, even though he obviously isn't eating a lunch, and I make my smooth, stupid exit into the sleeting November afternoon.

§

After lunch the defense finishes their cross-examination of Silas. Then it's time for Robert McDougal, the business manager of Smythe Company, to testify. Although I'm sitting too far away to know, he looks like the kind of guy who wears too much cologne and spends his secret alone time in his own tanning bed. But he's good looking and polished enough that he could be in politics if he wasn't the human version of Guy Smiley, that game-show host Muppet on Sesame Street.

His testimony reveals that he's married to Mark Smythe's daughter, so he's not just the business manager, he's also the son-in-law.

McDougal is asked questions about the pricing and selling of the boats. Both sides ask him how the recession affected business.

"Our decision to return these boats to the manufacturer has nothing to do with the recession," McDougal says through twinkling teeth. He tilts his head, but his hair remains perfectly coifed, and not a single strand breaks away from its wind-swept mold. "We were promised a certain product, and we were excited about the beauty of the yachts. So were our customers. But when a product is defective, you return it. End of story."

A couple of time my eyelids start to droop when I'm forced to look at the same email between McDougal and Mark Smythe that I've seen four times already, or I'm presented with the same ad in *Yachting Magazine,* or I hear another explanation of what a hull crack is. Yet all the while Four scribbles away in her notebook, and the competitive part of me feels compelled to keep up. So I take a lot of notes too. Then, finally, it's 5:00, and we're all done for the day.

§

Later when I'm home my friend Isobel, who lives in my building, stops by.

"Can you hem this for me?" She holds up a Tiffany-blue chiffon dress that's as wispy as a cloud. "The last time I wore it the stitching came loose. Now I have a wedding next weekend, and this is my only dress that's formal enough."

I take the dress from her and look at the hem. "Yeah," I say. "If I have the right color thread, it should be no problem."

I go over to my ironing board, which is set up by my living room window, and turn it on. I let the iron heat to steaming before I start pressing. My favorite smell in the world just might be a steaming iron against cotton; it's like fresh candy that won't ever get stale or gritty.

As the iron hisses and wheezes Isobel stands over my sewing table. She picks up my latest creation, a dyed and distressed long-sleeve t-shirt with an embroidered collar and paisley cuffs. "I love this!" she cries. "Can I buy it from you?"

I smile. "It's already spoken for. I just sold it a few minutes ago on eBay. But I can make you another one that's like it."

Isobel puts the shirt down and leans against my couch. "You really should have a website. It sounds like you're selling these shirts faster than you can make them."

"That's almost true. But that's also sort of the reason I don't feel like I need a website."

Once I got back from filming *The Holdout* I slipped into a bit of a funk. Unemployed, I tried temping for a while, but the stale-coffee, mindless work, and colorless cubicles depressed me even more. Luckily, a friend from my college theater days hired me to do costume construction for his theater company, but the hours are irregular and the pay is pretty bad. So mostly I stay home and live off my show stipend from *The Holdout* while I try to figure out my next step, whether it's grad school or a job search. I do take advantage of the many free online college courses there are available, especially the ones in entrepreneurship and design.

But to supplement my income I often comb thrift stores for interesting cast-offs, rework them ala' *Pretty in Pink*, and post/sell them on eBay. My theater major in college included hours spent in the costume shop and I picked up a thing or two when it came to clothing design.

It's been something to do and it keeps me from wallowing in self-pity. Plus, business hasn't been half-bad.

"Of course you need a website," Isobel says. "Think of how much more you could accomplish if you had one."

"Ummm…" is all I say. I know she's right, but I've learned a thing or two from my online courses. If I'm really going to launch my own business, complete with a website, I need to be ready and I need to do it right. I don't bother to explain this now. Isobel speaks with such authority but it's hard to take her seriously sometimes. It's no wonder. I've sung karaoke with her when she was drunk off Bacardi & Diet Cokes and belting out the lyrics to "I Will Survive."

"Yeah, yeah. I'll think about it once my jury duty is over." The iron has heated up, so it's 'full steam ahead.' I place the dress along the edge of the ironing board and start pressing the hem, careful not to singe the delicate fabric.

"Jury duty. That's right." Isobel raises her well-tweezed eyebrows. "How was your day in court?"

"Well, obviously I can't talk about the details. But it's about yachts."

Isobel crosses her arms and crinkles her forehead. "Yachts? Why is there a case about yachts in Iowa?"

I wave my free hand up in the air. "I can't go into that. But today, the son testified. And you know who he reminded me of?" I pause dramatically. "Grant. He reminded me of Grant."

"How does he remind you of Grant?" She scrunches up her tiny, animated nose. Isobel is always self-conscious about her weight, but she has these amazingly high cheekbones and the sort of nose most of women would pay for. Combine that with her pixie haircut and huge blue eyes, and Isobel would look beautiful in a Bill Cosby sweater and Zumba pants.

I keep my gaze down as I press the thin blue dress beneath the steaming iron. "Same entitled attitude." I struggle for more words. "You know what I mean."

"Actually, I have no idea what you mean," says Isobel. "I have no idea who this 'son' guy is, or why he is into yachts. I also have no idea what happened between you and Grant, because you won't tell me."

"You know I'm not allowed to!" I pick the iron up, scoot the fabric down, and place the iron back down with firm pressure. Steam rises up into my face.

The hardest thing, hands down, about being back from the show is I can't tell anyone what happened. And here I am, a virtual treasure chest full of secrets, juicy details, and angst. Sometimes I feel like I need to duct tape my mouth shut just so I won't leak out classified information. Now I'm in another situation that I can't talk about.

My life is a situation I can't talk about.

"So is the son a womanizer? Is he good looking? Was he making eyes at you?"

I finish pressing the dress and unplug the iron. Then I move over, sit down at my sewing table, and start searching for the right color of blue thread.

"Of course he wasn't making eyes at me," I murmur with a straight pin in between my teeth. "That would be completely inappropriate."

"Well, then what? Give me something."

"I can't." I look up from pinning the hem and embrace my sanctimoniousness. "I'm not allowed. Talking about the case might prejudice me in some way."

"It sounds like you already are prejudiced!"

"Never mind," I say, and the whirring of my sewing machines effectively ends our conversation.

But an hour later we're sitting on my couch and talking about Isobel's life, which usually includes spats with her identical twin sister, her ongoing divorce, and her dating misadventures.

"How did the date go with the guy you met online?" I ask.

She shakes her head and sighs. "The evening had been going great. We went to that new steak place downtown, and he seemed normal and fun, and even sort of good looking. Then, after his second scotch, he started talking like a chipmunk."

I squish my eyebrows together. "Huh?"

Isobel blinks and laughs. "You know, like *Alvin and the Chipmunks?* He spoke in one of those fast, high-pitched voices. And I thought, 'Okay, it's sort of funny. I can work with this.' But then we went back to his place and we were making out, and he was still using his Alvin voice, saying things like 'Ooh, baby, you feel so good,' and I had to run out of there. Thank God we drove separately."

Laughter fizzes out of me and the knots in my shoulders relax. "Oh, Isobel. I'm so sorry."

Then Jack comes in.

After I reintroduce him to Isobel, he sits down and shares the bag of food from his restaurant. As Isobel and I dive into the jalapeno bacon crab-cakes, he leans back and rubs his temples.

"Another rough day?" I ask through chews.

He sighs. "Maybe you can give me the female perspective."

"Sure," I reply. "But I'm surprised you need it. Don't you have Lucy for that?"

"Who's Lucy?" Isobel asks.

I explain. "She's Jack's sister-in-law. But he actually dated her in high school, and they became best friends after they broke up."

Isobel addresses Jack. "So your brother married your ex? That's kind of rude."

Jack examines his fingernails rather than looking at Isobel. "It's fine. I was never in love with her, so it's fine."

When Isobel and I both give him blank, questioning stares, Jack feels the silence and looks up. "What?" he demands. "Everyone always thinks that, but I was happy for them. Really."

I take a swig of beer to wash down my most recent bite of food. "Okay. I don't know who 'everyone' is, but I never assumed that you were in love with Lucy."

"Good. Because I'm not." He runs his fingers through his balding hair like it's a recycled gesture from his youth. "But now, I don't know, Lucy and Monty both just annoy me. They think because they've been married for what – three years or so – and because they're happy, that they can judge me? Neither of them has any idea what it's like for me. They're in their own little self-satisfied couple bubble."

Isobel and I meet eyes, and she cocks her head, asking her soundless, subtle question, *What's up with him?* Jack doesn't notice, but I guess he doesn't have to.

"I know I sound bitter." He releases a woeful, self-loathing kind of exhale. "But my wife stopped loving me. I still don't know why." He shrugs his shoulders. "One day she just lost interest. She stopped talking to me, stopped letting me touch her, and she'd barely even look at me. I tried to talk to her about it, many times, but she always refused. I kept hoping, especially for our son's sake, that she'd come back. This went on for years. Then I met Jessie and her I just clicked. And all the love I'd been missing was offered to me again. So I took it."

Isobel adjusts herself in her chair. "But technically, you and your wife…"

"Petra," Jack interjects. He looks at Isobel with widened eyes, like he had been talking only to me and had forgotten she was there. "Yeah, technically we were still together." He scratches his forehead and speaks to Isobel. "You don't know me at all, and you're probably thinking I'm the asshole who should have left a lot sooner than I did. I just couldn't. I kept thinking about my son, and joint-custody, and I couldn't bring myself to do it."

Isobel presses her lips into a slim, crooked arc. "My soon-to-be ex-husband was having an affair for months before he left me, so I'm probably the wrong person to ask."

Jack hangs his head for a moment. "Sorry," he says.

We let the silence hang in the air before I break it. "How did Petra find out?" I ask.

"I finally told her. I didn't want to hurt her, but I couldn't live like that anymore. And now she's suing me for everything I have, including full custody and the restaurant. So I had to borrow money from Lucy and Monty, which was a mistake." He closes his eyes and rubs at them. His voice softens. "I feel guilty every time I talk to either of them. That's not their fault, but I do." He reopens his eyes and talks a little louder. "And the last time I talked to Lucy, I told her that Jessie and I were getting married and she literally yelled at me, told me I was forbidden to get remarried so soon. That it was a mistake, that I was rushing things."

That sounds like the kind of honest advice a best friend is required to give. But looking at Jack right now is like looking at a guy who's just had the crap beaten out of him because he didn't notice the 'kick me' sign taped to his back.

I stay silent and let him vent.

"I tried not to listen to her. But I let her voice stay inside my head. I wasn't returning her phone calls but I still couldn't turn her voice off.

"Then yesterday, Jessie shows me this bridal magazine, with a $2,500 gown that she'd look perfect in, and she wants it, and she's going on about how she has to have it, and my throat suddenly felt like it was lined with cotton. So I walk away to get a drink of water and Jessie follows me, and I must have been pale and sweaty, because she asked me if I was having a heart attack."

As Jack continues his story, his voice fades as if he has a sore throat and it hurts to speak. But the urgency behind what he says builds. "And when I opened my mouth to respond, what I said was, 'I think we need to wait a little while before we get married.' And instead of smiling and agreeing with me, her face hardened into this weird, plaster-like thing that I didn't recognize. And I tried to explain, but I couldn't think straight and my words just came out like vomit. I don't even remember mentioning Lucy's name, or that she was the one who first planted this idea of putting off the marriage in my mind, but I know I did, because then Jessie accused me of being in love with Lucy. And she threw me out." Jack holds out his arms to either side, a gesture of guilt and loss. "Here I am, forty-one years old, no wife, no friends, no life. So you can see now, how totally screwed up everything is."

Jack punctuates the end of his tale with a loud sniff, and his face and posture settle more deeply into gloom. Isobel and I sit there, like we've just watched a M. Night Shyamalan movie with an ending we don't completely understand.

Isobel tucks her short hair behind her ears as she speaks. "Wow. I thought my life was messed up. You've made me feel a lot better about myself."

Jack emits a long, low sigh. "I guess that's one good thing I've accomplished."

I look over at Jack. He's pressing his fingers against his eyelids.

"Do you love Jessie?" I ask. "Or were you only with her because she loves you?"

His hands fall into his lap and we make eye contact as he meets my scrutiny.

"I don't know," he says without apology.

"Well," I tell him gently, "my 'female' advice is to figure that out first."

He nods, agreeing without saying so, hanging his head like he's about to cry.

I make my voice tender, a consolation prize. "And you get to stay here, in my luxury apartment while you do."

"Thanks. I appreciate it." Jack's forehead wrinkles as his eyes narrow. "But at the same time, if five years ago someone had told me I would screw my life up so badly that I'm forced to sleep on my unemployed, reality TV star, younger cousin's couch…"

He winces as he realizes how bad what he's saying sounds. But I just laugh.

"The world works in mysterious ways." And I pop the last jalapeno-bacon-crab cake into my mouth. Then I get up for another beer.

§

Later that night I'm lying in the dark, alone in my bed, as awake as if I'd indulged in a late afternoon latte. This is when I am most likely to replay my own set of unmet expectations, my own series of disappointments and mistakes, a guilty pleasure movie replayed in an endless loop inside my head. I'm curled up underneath my comforter and I tug on a wad of the acrylic stuffing that escaped from a small rip in the lining. I rub it between my fingers and it reminds me of sand. I close my eyes and I can see myself back on the beach; I feel myself back in his arms.

"You smell like limes," he whispered into my neck.

I pressed my lips against his forehead. "We should probably get back before anyone notices we're gone." I gave him a baby kiss against his hairline. "They'll vote us out the minute they realize we're a couple."

He laughed, and I wanted to swallow that laughter up and keep it in a safe, hidden spot. He planted kisses up and down along the curve of my neck and my bare shoulder. His arms tightened around me, one was grasping my waist and the other was around my thigh. He gently pushed me back so I was lying in the sand. Then he was on top of me.

His t-shirt and the scant fabric of our bathing suits were all that separated us from being skin against skin. Even still, I could feel the heat dispensing from his body, a blanket that could shield us both. His sigh caused his ribcage to raise and lower against my chest and

I wanted to reach under his shirt with both hands. I wanted to press every bit of me into every bit of him, and I wanted to make it all last indefinitely.

But I rolled my head to the side and through squinted eyes I saw a camera lens peaking out of the bushes that we had thought were hiding us.

"Grant," I mumbled, not yet able to find my voice.

He took that as an expression of desire and went in for a deep kiss. His mouth on mine, his lips sucking and caressing, his teeth gently nibbling my bottom lip, his tongue flicking and plunging, in and out and against my tongue, like neither of them has ever been intended for any other purpose. Everything inside of me turned to warm syrup on Sunday morning waffles, and it took some Iron Woman type of strength to push him away and opt for the protein shake instead.

"There are cameras," I told him. I gestured towards the bushes.

He was adorable, his lips rosy from kissing me and his hair sticking up as a result of my fingers delving through his curls. He looked around and spotted the camera, and then gave the operator a smile and a wave. He turned back to me, his expression joyful. "I don't care," he whispered. "Let the world know how I feel about you. That only makes it better."

He started kissing me again and for a moment I relented. But when I closed my eyes I could see my father watching this scene on television. His feet would be propped up on the coffee table and he'd be nursing his most recent injury and a beer. His face would be full of pride and expectation until Grant climbed on top of me, then quickly Dad's eyes would lower into slits, his hands would clench into fists, and the skin beneath his beard would turn red. No. It couldn't happen like this, not with my dad watching.

"Grant," I said again, and this time I pushed him away with a bit more force. "I can't. Not in front of a camera. Not on national television. Sorry."

By then we were both sitting up. He rolled his shoulders and shook his head rapidly, like he was fighting against himself. His mouth was a straight line and he was biting his bottom lip.

But he took a deep breath, and on the exhale everything in him relaxed.

"Don't worry about it," he said. And to show me he meant it, he brushed the back of his hand tenderly against my cheek. "You're right. We should wait." He scooted closer to me so he could whisper something that the camera's microphone couldn't pick up. His breath was hot against my ear as he made his promises. "When the show is over, we'll go away. We'll be alone and we'll finally start living."

And then he leaned back so he could meet my eyes. "Okay?" He raised his eyebrows in question and my heart dived and danced simultaneously.

"Okay," I said, and he went in for another kiss.

"Wait," I said, as I half-heartedly pushed him away. "How can I go away with you? I don't even know your last name, or where you're from, or what you want to do with your life."

He held up a hand and counted off on his fingers. "One, my last name is Hamilton-Leonard."

"That's a mouthful."

He shrugged. "My mom wanted to hyphenate. Two, I'm from Laketown, Connecticut. Three, I plan to save the world, and afterwards I'll spend all my free time with you."

I giggled. Yes, giggled like a fifteen-year-old girl at a Justin Bieber concert. But I was sure that this moment, and all the ones with him that would follow, were what I was meant for.

We got up and straightened ourselves out, laughing as we brushed sand and twigs from our hair. He took my hand and led me through the jungle path, telling me to watch out for that branch and don't trip over that rock. And after weeks of trying to survive on my own, the feeling of being protected was more welcome than the feminist side of me would care to admit.

My eyes were gazing up at him and I was laughing over his impersonation of Joe Pine, *Castaways, take your place at the starting line*, or, *Beth, the tribe has decreed. You're out*, when Grant leaned down for one more kiss. As we pulled away and resumed walking I ran, smack, into Henry carrying a pile of kindling.

Grant and I released our entwined hands, but Henry's gaze stayed on the space where our clasp had been as if it still remained.

"Hey, Henry," I squeaked, and I could feel my cheeks growing flush. I bent to retrieve the sticks I had caused him to drop. He took them from me, wordlessly, and his silence shouted his disapproval.

"Thanks." He took the last stick. Henry's wavy light brown hair was sticking up, and his pink, peeling nose was the same color as his dirty, faded red, button-down dress shirt. Since he originally came from the other tribe he was the only one of us not dressed in green. But Henry didn't need a clothing difference to establish his outsider status; he was probably born with his outsider-membership card tucked inside the pocket of his oversized brain.

"Gathering firewood?" Grant clapped his wide palm against Henry's sunburned shoulder and Henry winced at the contact. "Good man!" Then Grant took my hand again and pulled me away. "Talk to you later!" Grant cried over his shoulder, and we left Henry standing there, like we were walking together towards the dance floor and he was awkward, alone and abandoned - the guy who travels stag on an island full of couples.

How silly was I in that moment? I was the smug cheerleader at the high school party, proud to be dating the quarterback. I could sense Henry's discomfort but I figured he was just jealous of our happiness. If only I could return, knowing what I now know. This time I would listen to the smartest kid in the class.

Chapter 7

Cold molding epoxy is a process of shaping wood. Typically the structure of the boat is turned upside down. The cold-molded wood boats, comparable to the Gougeon brothers' boats, are actually cold-molded wood laminate boats, rather than fiberglass boats, because most of their strength and assembly comes from a wood seal." The expert witness pauses for a moment and he scans the jury box. He must have been trained to make eye contact with us. He smiles and shrugs, as if to concede that he's going to speak in more simple terms now. "The epoxy used in their creation is principally to guard the wood and act as glue. However, regular fiberglass boats rely upon the strength that comes from the fiberglass and not the wood, depending upon whether it is dense fiberglass or bared fiberglass laminate." Next to me, Four is recording every detail of the expert's testimony. I bet she got all A's in college. I bet guys flirted with her just so they could borrow her notes and pass whatever class it was that they slept through most mornings. And I bet she let them; she seems like an attention whore to me.

But who am I to talk? I am after all, a reality television star. That's about as attention whorish as you can get.

I flip back and forth through the notes I've taken and attempt to refocus. Each witness' name is scrawled on top of a page, and I tried to transcribe all the salient points of what each person said underneath. There are around thirty pages total, which averages out to six pages per day, roughly one page per hour.

Four has written more than me. I bet if we were on the island she would have gathered more firewood, caught more fish, and solved more puzzles during the challenges than me too. And I'd have voted her out first chance I got.

I look up at the clock. It's 11:30. Half an hour until lunch.

It's now day six of the trial and my excitement has ebbed. I catch myself thinking bitchy thoughts about my fellow jury members. I have learned more about boats, specifically cold-molded wooden yachts, than I ever thought I would learn in my lifetime. Do you know that the Gougeon brothers wrote the definitive book on boat construction? Well they did, and they've been referenced several times during the trial.

I flip to a new sheet of paper. I write, *Cold molded epoxy boats aren't fiber glass boats.*

Then I draw a picture of me on the edge of a yacht, about to jump into the depths of the dark, dangerous ocean. Grant is in the picture too, but I draw him into the shape of a hungry shark, teeth barred, ready to devour me the moment I'm in the water.

The plaintiff's side finishes the examination of their witness. I'm sure the judge will let us all go to lunch early rather than having the defense start in on their cross-examination. But no.

"Let's take a stretching break," she says.

Stretching breaks are when we stand up at our seats, stretch, and sit back down again. We can talk softly for around thirty seconds but we can't go anywhere. Still, I love stretching breaks. A woman in a robe, holding a gavel and sitting high on a pedestal tells a dozen adults to get up and stretch, and they obey every time. How awesome is that?

I turn at my waist and roll my shoulders. Ten, who sits behind and diagonally from me, catches my eye. He is chuckling.

"What?" I ask.

His eyes move down to my seat where I placed my notebook, open to the page with my drawing. "You're pretty good," he says. "But did you have a bad boating experience? You should have spoken up. You might have gotten out of jury duty."

"But then I would never have learned about cold-molded epoxy boat construction." I smile. Ten is harmless enough.

We sit back down and the defense cross examines the expert witness. The lawyer for the defense is that guy you sort of remember from your freshman year college dorm, and eight years later, when you're walking down the aisle of Home Depot, you're sure it's him but you're not confident enough to say hello. Besides, he used to argue with his teachers just to get a rise out of them, and if you spoke to him now he'd probably do the same thing to you.

Now he cross-examines with his default sardonic smile. "What do you know about Greek cold molding boat construction? Are you aware that there are boat-building authorities other than the Gougeon brothers? Do you realize that the Greeks have their own method of cold-molding epoxy, and it involves having the boats right side UP?

The expert witness answers in concise little bullet points. I gaze at the defense lawyer's hand to see if there's a ring. There isn't one, and he isn't my type anyway, but I can't help but be curious

I sigh and look at the clock again.

Finally lunch comes. I stall and check my phone and go to the bathroom so I won't have to eat lunch with Four. She usually engineers the outing, so not eating with her most likely means eating alone. Honestly, that would be better.

Maybe I am actually stuck up.

When it's safe I take the elevator down. Outside I see Ten sitting in the courtyard. He's reading The *7 Habits of Highly Effective People* again but he looks up and sees me, so I go over to say hi.

"How's the book?"

He scrunches up his face and jabs the page he's on with his index finger. "There's this guy, and he's trying to chop down a tree. But he's tired and he doesn't have a good saw."

"Okay," I reply, as if we just reached the end of a long conversation. I start to walk away but Ten continues so I stay put.

"The point of the story is you need to take care of yourself and be prepared if you want to get things done. But here's my question: why is he cutting down the tree in the first place?"

This is most I've ever heard Ten say all at once.

"Umm, does he need firewood?"

"It doesn't say!" Ten snaps his book shut. "It ought to say! Does he need firewood, or wood to build a house, or is he just an environmental terrorist? I can't understand why Stephen Covey would have someone be so destructive without an explanation." His jaw shifts and hardens in exasperation. "If a real estate agent needs to chop down a tree for any reason, he has hoops to jump through and papers to fill out." Ten shakes his head in disgust, and suddenly switches gears without loosing his intensity. "I'm hungry. Are you eating lunch?"

The sun is shining today, a rarity for November in Iowa, and I'm warm enough with just my cardigan sweater. "I was going to Subway to pick up a sandwich and then go for a walk."

Ten stands up. His eyes don't reach mine. I'd guess he's an inch or two shorter than me. "Do you mind if I tag along?"

I think of Grant. He was always finding me alone, wanting my time, invading my space. But I was a willing party.

The wind gusts suddenly, and it reminds me that winter is rapidly approaching, no matter how deceptive today's weather might be. I button up my cardigan and pull its long sleeves down so my hands are covered.

"Umm…" I stall. I shouldn't say no. "Maybe I'll actually sit there and eat. It's funny how quickly the weather can change."

Ten's eyes crease as his mouth shifts into a crooked smile. "Well, you know what they say. If you don't like the weather in Iowa, just wait five minutes."

One of the oldest, stupidest jokes in the world. Is there anywhere that "they" don't say that about? When I don't laugh or even smile in appreciation, Ten's face drops. "I don't have to come, if you don't want me to. I understand needing time to clear your head. Listening to that trial is enough to drive anyone crazy."

Then he grins at me again and lopsided dimples appear.

"No, no," I answer. "Of course you should come along. I'd love the company."

We walk together companionably down the sidewalk. Cars are chugging along on the street beside us and the wind is still strong. Neither is conducive for talking. But I try anyway.

"So this is your third jury duty in two years? How is that even possible?"

"Because I was called by different branches of the court." We start to cross the street, but he raises his arm without quite touching me, holding me back as a car speeds by. After it's safe, we continue walking. "For example," he says, "you won't get called by federal court for a while after you're done with this jury. But state or county court could summon you any time."

"And you've been called by all three?" I ask.

He nods his head. "The first one was just for a DUI, so it didn't take long." Ten puts his hands in his pockets, his book now tucked underneath his arm. "The second was for state court. That was a bigger deal."

"Was it a criminal case?"

"Yeah. It was crazy, actually." We reach the Subway and Ten holds the door open for me. We walk in and I'm hit with the smell of baking bread and the closeness of the space. Every extra inch is taken up with booths, counters, and the pop machine. There's barely any line.

"Can you tell me the details?"

Ten is studying the menu above the counter but he answers while he reads the choices. "A guy was accused of identity theft. He paid off a nurse when he was staying at a hospital and she gave him patient social security numbers."

"Wow, so was he guilty?"

"Oh yeah. We found him guilty on all counts."

We've inched up in line and I order a turkey sandwich with cheese, cucumbers, and mayonnaise. Ten orders a BLT with chipotle sauce.

After we've paid, gotten our drinks, and found a table, I resume the conversation.

"Okay, so did the guy go to prison?"

Ten has already taken a bite, so he sort of nods and shrugs simultaneously rather than speaking his answer. After a sip of Coke he talks. "I'm pretty sure that's what the judge sentenced him too. All we did was decide whether or not he was guilty.

My brain slips into a Theta state as I contemplate this. "Doesn't that weigh on you though? I mean, a guy's fate was in your hands. What if you were wrong?"

"We weren't wrong. He was definitely guilty." Ten takes another bite of his sandwich and the corners of his mouth turn up as he chews. I notice his cheeks are slightly flushed, just a little bit of pink underneath his tan skin. I'll bet he was really cute when he was little.

"Okay," I say. "Sure. But there have been cases where someone has been sentenced to life in prison, or even death, and it turns out he's innocent." I open my bag of Cheetos for emphasis. "And what about our case? I keep thinking they'll settle, because why would they leave a 14 million dollar decision to a bunch of schmos like us? I just don't get the jury system."

With that I dive into my own sandwich. I try smiling while I chew like Ten did but I don't think I'm as effective at it.

Ten wipes his mouth with the one thin paper napkin that was included in his sandwich bag. "I suppose it is sort of screwed up."

"Don't get me wrong," I say as I fiddle with my straw. "I think it's an ingenious system and the foundation of our democracy and all that good stuff. But people are flawed, right? Everyone is flawed."

Ten blinks like I might be asking him a trick question. "Sure," he concedes.

"So the jury system has to be flawed too. For that matter, everything is flawed."

"No," he says. Ten pushes a chip into his mouth, chews it quickly and swallows. "That's a huge leap. Perfection is everywhere and some of it is created by flawed people."

I push my shoulders down and cock my head to the side. "Like what? Give me an example."

"My baby nephew. He's a product of my very flawed big-sister and her flawed husband, but when I held him for the first time, I thought, 'this is perfection.'"

How sweet. He likes babies. Does he also keep a dream journal? I bet his iPod is full of songs by Snow Patrol.

"How old is your nephew?"

Ten grins and the shape of his face changes yet again. "Two weeks. I didn't think a fleshy blob could be so adorable." He gets out his phone to show me a picture. "Here," he says, handing me the phone.

"I know all babies are beautiful, but you have to admit that this one is particularly amazing."

I look at the picture and see generic baby. But I nod my head and agree. "He's gorgeous."

Ten laughs. "I can't wait until he's a little older. I'm going to be the fun uncle who teaches him to play golf."

"Golf?"

"Yeah. I love golf."

I nod and look down. Then I take a bite of my sandwich so I don't have to say anything. But Ten sees right through me.

"What's wrong with golf?" he demands.

"Nothing," I murmur through chews.

He raises his eyebrows. It's a challenge.

I swallow my bite and take a sip of my drink. "Fine. I've just always thought of golf as something that old, white guys do while their wives are home making bologna sandwiches with Miracle Whip and Wonder Bread. Meanwhile, their kids are playing Frisbee in the backyard."

"I love Frisbee too!" Ten laughs. "But when I play golf I only speak Portuguese, and if I hear anyone playing NPR I take a swig of my Colt 45 and spit on them."

I burst out laughing. Maybe I underestimated this guy. "Really?" I wrinkle my brows together. "Portuguese?"

He laughs some more. "Hell, yeah." He becomes more serious. "My mom was Portuguese. She taught me some."

"Okay," I say, unsure how to respond. I'm about to ask him more about his mother but my cell phone vibrates in my pocket. I take it out and see that my dad is calling.

"Hold on," I tell Ten. "I have to take this."

I press the answer button. "Hi, Dad."

"Hi. Did I catch you at a bad time?" Dad always starts his phone conversations this way.

"No, it's fine. I'm just eating lunch with…I'm just eating lunch."

"Okay, well I'll make this quick. Aunt Natalie called. She's having everyone over tonight so we can watch your show together. Won't that be fun?"

At the mention of "my show" I bolt up from my seat. Ten stopped giving me his *don't I know you from somewhere* look days ago, but if he can overhear any of this conversation, I'm done. Ten's eyes widen when I stand up so quickly, so I just mouth "sorry" and walk over to the corner of the tiny restaurant.

"What do you mean by 'everyone'?"

"You, me, Jack, and Ian. Eddie is going to stay home with the kids since the show is on after their bedtime."

My heart suddenly feels like it's gained a couple of pounds and its pants are too tight. I have to focus on my breathing to make sure I do it correctly. Tonight is when Grant and I make out in the bushes. Tonight is where I make so many stupid, embarrassing decisions. Tonight is what I want to erase not just from my mind, but from its very existence.

"Robin, honey. Are you there?"

"Yeah," I peep.

"Great. So seven o'clock? I can't believe you're in the final five! It's so exciting. I wish I could just speed up time and watch it right now."

I rub my forehead with the palm of my hand. I can't remember ever doing anything that has made my dad this proud: not when I made honor roll, not when I won my high school swim meets, not when I played Laura in a college production of *Glass Menagerie.* Certainly there hasn't been much to make him proud in the nine years since I've been out of school. I can't disappoint him now. He'll be plenty disappointed in several hours anyway, but maybe my presence will dissipate his inevitable distress.

"Sounds good, Dad. I'll see you tonight."

"Bye, Honey."

I hang up and go back to the table where Ten has resumed reading. When I sit he closes his book and I pick up my sandwich, but I put it back down without taking a bite.

"Are you okay?" Ten asks. "You look kind of pale."

I look at my lunch. The grayish-brownish turkey was enticing just moments ago, as were the neon orange Cheetos. Now they're the last thing I want. "That was my dad. He wants me to go to my aunt's tonight for a family get-together. And I hate family get-togethers. But…" I look at Ten's face. His eyes are kind. I bet he's the sort of guy who has a lot of female friends; he's the buddy but never the boyfriend.

I won't bother this guy I barely know with my stupid problems.

"…but I'll be fine. It's just one evening, right?"

"Sure," he says. "If I can get through three jury duties in two years, you can get through one family dinner."

"But you're not through the third jury duty yet." I look at the clock on my phone. "We should probably get back." I put my sandwich and Cheetos into their plastic bag. "I'll take these and save them for later."

Ten has finished his lunch. He takes a final, loud sip of his soda. "Shall we?"

"We shall." I get up and so does he. When we're back outside the sun is out and the wind has died down. Ten looks at his watch. In the age of cell phones, what kind of a guy still wears a watch? It looks expensive, probably gold plated. Maybe it was a present, perhaps from a girlfriend.

"You know," he says. "We still have twenty minutes. Do you want to walk a little before we head back?"

We're standing face to face, me a little bit taller, him a little more mysterious than he was an hour before. I don't think, I just answer. "Sure. It would be nice to get some fresh air and exercise before we sit in a box all afternoon."

He smiles. Those dimples are kind of nice. Maybe he isn't the buddy type. Maybe a girlfriend did give him that watch.

We turn the corner, away from the traffic, and we walk.

§

Several hours later I'm sitting in my Aunt Natalie's dining room, the same place where our Christmas meal is consumed every year. Tonight dinner is lasagna instead of turkey, and we are a much smaller group than we are over the holidays. Since Ted and Monty live out of town, and no kids or in-laws are here, it's just the five of us.

That's more than enough.

"…and then she told me I had to leave by October 28th. After all I had done for her, taking care of the kids, cleaning and shopping. A thank you would have nice. But no, instead I get kicked out. Honestly, if Monty hadn't been so sick when he got back I would have just left right away, before the new daycare had even started."

Natalie has been going on for a while. She spent several weeks this autumn in Seattle, taking care of Monty's kids while he was in Ghana for work and Lucy was without daycare. But Lucy and Natalie didn't exactly get along during her stay and Natalie is still pissed. She scratches her splotchy, red neck with the hand that isn't holding her fork.

Jack is sitting across from me and I catch his eye. His face is neutral, like it's written in Swiss and I can't read it. "Well I'm glad Monty started to recover before you left," he says to his mother.

"Before I *had* to leave," she huffs.

"What was wrong with him?" Ian asks.

"The anti-malarial drugs he was on weakened his system. Then he caught a very bad case of flu on the plane ride home, which turned into bronchitis." Natalie's jaw looks like it's about to snap, "It was scary, and he shouldn't be travelling like that anymore, and I let him and Lucy know I think so."

"But he's okay now," says Jack.

My dad pushes his empty plate away. "Natalie, that was delicious, but I don't think I can eat another bite." He looks at the watch he's owned since long before cell phones were available. "Robin's show is about to start. I don't want to miss any of it."

"I'm recording it." Natalie smiles gently. "Don't worry. I don't want to miss any of it either. In fact, this fall the one thing Lucy and I could agree on was watching Robin's show together. We never missed an episode."

"And you guys would call me afterwards," I say. "It was great. Neither of you ever said anything judgmental. You were the only ones I can say that about." I give Ian an accusatory stare. He knows he's guilty of grilling me after every episode about all the "stupid" decisions I made.

"I just want to know where you learned such bad judgment, Robbie." says Ian.

"Hey!" Dad says. "Robin's in the top five. That's pretty damn good."

"I think so too," says Natalie.

I grin at Natalie in gratitude. I really did enjoy the calls from her and Lucy, but mostly because of Lucy. She would always ask me questions about what it was like to try and get along and survive with a group of people I barely knew. What was it like to vote someone out? She was genuinely interested. Everyone else just wanted to know the dirt about Grant, but Lucy never brought him up.

"You know," says my dad. "Recordings sometimes fail. I think we should move to the living room and start watching."

"Dad," I reprimand him. "Ian and Jack and I are still eating."

Ian shoves a bite of his food in his mouth. Then he talks with mouth full, deliberately being disgusting. "Done!" he says.

"I can take my plate with me," Jack tells me.

My shoulders sag as I release a puff of air. Better to get this over with, I guess. "Fine."

We get up and move downstairs into the rec room. There's a pool table behind us, a wood paneled bar to our side, and a newish flat screen TV mounted to the wall that we face. We sit on one of those wrap-around couches. Its body is like a C-shaped, overstuffed snake, and without arms there's no good place to lean my weight against.

I sit between Ian and my dad. Jack is at one end of the couch, and Natalie is at the other. Natalie turns on the TV.

Chapter 8

After they play reminder scenes from the week's previous episode, the tribal theme music comes on. There's a slow-motion shot of each cast member, and we're doing things like running on the beach, grimacing while lifting heavy things, or in Grant's case, emerging from the water like a sexy Poseidon. My shot starts with a close-up. I'm smiling and looking over my shoulder while my hair blows in the wind. I have to say I don't look half bad. But then it switches to me doing the crawl stroke during a swimming challenge. I'm panting and the water dripping from my face makes me resemble a drooling dog. Still, my family cheers when my name is scrolled at the bottom of the screen.

"Uhg," I say. "I hate the look I have on my face. It makes me never want to go swimming again."

"Are you crazy?" Ian hits me in the shoulder. "If it wasn't for your swimming skills you would have been kicked off a long time ago."

My jaw clenches. "That's not true," I say. The tribal credit music is reaching its climax with a crescendo of drums. Before I was on the show I used to love the theme song, but now it sets me on edge. I press my right fingernail into my palm. "My swimming has barely come into it at all."

"No," says Ian. He speaks with such authority, as though his watching the show makes him more of an expert on my life than me, who has simply lived it. "Grant knew from the first episode you were a good swimmer. That's why he picked you for his alliance. If you hadn't been in his alliance you would have been voted out early, like that guy who wore the straw fedora."

"Joel," I say.

"Yeah, that guy. You know, he sort of reminded me of Monty."

Jack laughs. "Didn't he get voted out because Bailey thought he was gay? Maybe we should get Monty a hat like his for Christmas."

Ian laughs back. "Just don't get *me* a straw fedora. No self-respecting gay guy I know would ever wear one."

Dad sighs loudly in exasperation. "Could you all please be quiet? I'm trying to watch this!"

Jack and Ian stop their talking and laughing, which shows that they do know how to be obedient. I press two more fingernails into my palm in an effort to quell my protestations. Ian's theory about how I advanced in the game is what I've been afraid of. If he thinks that's how it played out, probably everybody else does too. The world knows that I just rode on Grant's slimy coattails.

Relax, I tell myself. In an hour this ordeal will be over, and you can overdose on angst alone, in the privacy of your own bedroom. I relax my hand, stretch my fingers out, and focus on the T.V.

The first shot is of rain. We were all huddled under the fort in a damp, depressed lump. Then Henry emerged and went for a walk. The scene switches to a testimonial as Henry faced the camera. His hair was standing on end, his light brown beard was as thick as it most likely had ever been in his life, and his heavy eyelids were drooping. But his smile was a mile long.

"So it's been raining for two days straight. There is nothing to do but sit around and grow mildew on our broken down bodies. Finally I couldn't take it anymore so I went for a walk. I figured I was already wet and walking in the rain wasn't going to affect me much. Plus, my muscles were starting to atrophy. Moving felt good."

The camera switches to Henry walking around, but it keeps the voice-over of his testimonial.

"I'm walking through the woods when I notice, off to the side, a tree with a round hollow. I still don't know what possessed me to do this, but I decided to go over and stick my hand into that hollow."

Henry is shown stepping over twigs and under branches to reach the tree. When he got to the tree he reached into the hollow, and his hand emerged holding a little tan bundle.

"I'd call it intuition but I'm not sure I believe in such a thing. Anyway," Henry said, "What do you know? When I unwrapped the fabric there was a note and a small brown necklace."

Henry's note is shown on camera and his voice-over read it. "Play this idol and you are free. Voted out is something you won't be."

Then Henry's face is back for his testimonial. He laughed. "Who writes these things? Does somebody actually get paid to come up with these stupid little rhymes?" He shook his head. "Oh my God! I have an immunity idol! I'm safe for one more round of voting! This is huge!" He kissed the idol and then tucked it away.

More shots are shown of us complaining about how cold and wet we were. Then the sun came out. I went out with the scuba gear to catch some fish. Bailey cleaned up camp. Henry went off for another walk, and Grant and Klemi sat and cuddled on the cliffs above the ocean.

"It will be you and me in the final two," Klemi said, in her thick Puerto Rican accent. "I can't wait for everyone else to be gone. Then we'll finally have some privacy."

"Tell me about it." Grant pulled her in for a kiss, and she responded with passion. Watching on the couch I wish I could lunge through the television screen and beat them both up.

Ian shakes his head. "I can't believe that guy. He really fooled both of you, didn't he?"

Anger is walloping my insides but I have to keep it hidden. I just smile and shrug my shoulders. My dad speaks up. "Robin is a smart girl. She'll kick him to the curb sooner or later, won't you Honey?"

"She's not allowed to tell you anything," Aunt Natalie chides. "You two leave her alone."

I silently thank Natalie and we all continue to watch.

After Grant broke away from the kiss he looked down. Who did he see below but Henry, out for his walk?

"Did he see us kissing?" Klemi asked.

"Who cares?" Grant kissed her forehead, and the affection of that gesture bothers me more than their passionate tongue dance from before. "That guy is a freak. He'll be gone after the next challenge. There's no way he's winning immunity again so we'll finally get to vote him out."

Klemi stuck out her lower lip in a pout. "You said we were voting out Robin."

Grant winked at her. "You're right, Baby. We'll vote out Robin next, then Henry after that."

My family all lets out a collective groan and the couch practically shakes beneath their communal frustration. "I really hate that guy!" Natalie says to nobody in particular. Jack and Ian voice their agreement. Only my dad remains rapt, his eyes and his focus never leaving the television screen.

But then, Oh My God, they show the scene with Grant and me making out behind the trees. Only with some fancy editing it looks like we're doing more than just heavy petting. Grant was on top of me, then I pushed him away, then he whispered in my ear. I smiled and said okay. Then they used some earlier footage, but it looks like it just happened, and he was back on top of me and the scene fades, leaving the audience to believe I agreed to have sex with Grant on national television.

Cut to commercial.

I can't look at my dad. I can't look anywhere but my lap. My cheeks are burning and there's a big lump in my throat. It's so big I can't imagine ever being able to ever say anything again, ever.

Everyone is quiet for what feels like a month but it can't more than thirty seconds to a minute. By the time the Alec Baldwin commercial for travel insurance, or whatever it is, ends, Jack thinks of something to say.

"I think we should call Ted. He's got to be connected. With all the New York business contacts he has, I bet a few of them are in the mob. He could put a hit out on that guy."

"We'll call Ted after the show tonight." Ian says this with resolve. He turns to me. "You can give us Grant's address, right? It will make it easier for the hit-man to find him."

"That's not funny," I murmur. I force myself to turn in Dad's direction. "The editing… that wasn't what it looked like. I wouldn't do that, not on national television." I look up and across the room, at everyone. "You all have to believe me."

Dad swallows roughly and pats my knee. "Sure, Honey. I believe you. Anyway, you're a grown woman. You can make your own decisions about that stuff."

My chest rises and falls as I force myself to keep breathing. "Yeah, of course, but I wouldn't decide to do *that* on national television."

Natalie shakes her head. "Oh, Robin." She says my name like I'm a kindergartner who just peed her pants. "Aren't we simply talking technicalities here? You were awfully intimate with him. I don't care how good the editing is, you can't just make something like that up."

I hang my head in shame.

"Lay off her, Natalie." My dad raises his voice, which happens about as often as a heat wave in November. Natalie's eyes widen in surprise but she doesn't say anything back. The show returns from commercial. "And nobody had better talk while this is on. The challenge is coming up and I bet Robin does great." He pats my knee and eyes the TV once again.

But before the challenge they show Grant and me during our post-make-out walk back to camp. We ran into Henry, laughed, and walked away. Grant muttered, "That guy is everywhere," which I had originally missed but obviously the camera didn't.

Then comes a conversation with Henry and me, which I have tried and tried to forget. Because every time I remember I feel like hitting my head repeatedly until my brain surrenders and admits how stupid it was.

I was wading by myself as the sun set over the ocean, when Henry found me.

"You know Grant is two-timing you, right?"

From the couch I watch my electronic self react through squinted eyes. My physical reaction is the same now as it was then. My throat goes dry and my pulse is hammering in my ears. I don't want to believe it's true.

"What are you talking about?" I asked.

"I saw Grant and Klemi this morning, while you were fishing. They were together, kissing up on the rocks. He's playing both of you."

I shook my head at him. "You're making this up. You just want me to vote with you, against Grant."

Henry took off his glasses and rubbed his eyes with sandy fingers "Ouch," he said. He blinked a couple of times. I saw him tear up a little and I wasn't super clear on whether it was due to pain or emotion. "Look," he said. "I understand the whole 'shoot the messenger' thing. But think about it. Am I really so stupid? What do I possibly have to gain if it isn't true?"

All my emotions had risen to the edge, into the danger zone beneath my skin. A pinprick would have caused them to come flooding out, like water from a de-thawed, pipe.

"Stay away from me," I said. I even poked his sunburnt shoulder with my index finger. "I know you're desperate. You know there's no way you're staying. You're just doing whatever you can to buy yourself some time."

"You're wrong!" he said. And he dug his hand into his pocket and brought out his immunity idol. "I found this, this morning. I have immunity. So I'm not going anywhere. The only reason I'm saying anything at all is because you're the only person left who I can stand. If you and I vote together we can get Grant out. Then maybe we'll have a shot. But if we don't, well, Grant is lying to you. And he will win. So if you think you're safe, think again."

My dad speaks to Ian, Jack, and Natalie. "See! I was right! Robin's not going to be taken in by that guy. Right, Robin?"

"Dad, you're the one who yelled at everyone not to talk. Just watch the show."

The show cuts to the immunity challenge. What they don't show is the sleepless night I spent, unable to keep my eyes off of Grant and Klemi as we all slept together underneath the shelter. Were they inching close to each other? I couldn't tell in the darkness but I couldn't look away. And I couldn't quiet my doubts.

I woke the next morning more tired than I've ever been. They show me struggling around camp and I remember how every muscle ached.

How my head throbbed. How my throat felt like it was lined with felt. I was aware of every single nerve in each one of my toes and all I wanted was a tall glass of water and a soft bed in a dark, quiet room.

I was seriously considering just quitting the game.

Then we got to the immunity challenge and Joe Pine explained our task. We had to walk on top of a log maze with a bowl of rice balanced on our heads. If ever our feet, the bowl, or the rice were to fall to the ground, we had to go back to the start. First person to finish the long, complex log course won immunity.

Here's the thing. The top of my head is amazingly flat. I discovered this at ten years old, back when I was convinced I wanted to be a super model. I spent hours in my bedroom, walking around with books on my head because I'd heard that's how models trained themselves. I never once dropped the books.

I also have good balance. I just do.

So I knew that if ever there was a challenge I could win, this one was it. I knew if ever there was a challenge I had to win, this one was it. Suddenly my doubts about the game disappeared and were replaced with unwavering confidence. I was no longer thirsty or in pain. I was practically laughing as the five of us stood on top of the logs, balancing our bowls, ready to race.

Ian notices the look on my face, and says, "Robbie, you look so happy! Did somebody say something funny right before you got up there?"

"Just watch," I say.

Joe Pine yelled, "Castaways ready, and go!"

It was like I was back in my childhood bedroom, listening to New Kids on the Block while doing dance moves with Encyclopedia Britannica balanced upon my head. It was that easy.

"Robin's off to an excellent start!" Joe yelled. "She's leaving everyone else in the dust!"

I turned each corner with ease, the bowl never threatening to waver from the flatness of my head. I hear Joe behind me. "And Grant's bowl is down. He has to go back!"

I smiled and kept on. "Klemi's fallen!" Joe yelled. "She has to start again as well."

I started to think I was being too confident, and I slowed down for the final stretch. But Bailey and Henry never even got off the ground, so I was all by myself when I reached the finish line.

Joe waved his hands in the air. "It's over before it's even begun! Robin wins immunity! This has got to be the easiest victory ever won in *Holdout* history!"

My family is cheering and screaming, jumping up and down in their seats. I can't help but smile at my victory, as Dad and Ian hug me from either side. Dad's phone rings.

"It's Ted," he says. He speaks into the phone. "I know! She was amazing, wasn't she?" Dad hugs me again and hands me his cell. "Ted wants to speak to you."

One ear is listening to Ted saying the nicest things he's ever said to me. "You were incredible!" he shouted. "I had no idea you had that in you!"

I thank him for the backhanded compliments, but my other ear is listening to the TV as I watch Joe Pine put the immunity necklace around my neck. I'm beaming, and as the camera pans across my tribemates' faces my victory feels even better compared to their defeat.

It's good I enjoyed that moment, because it all went down hill from there.

Chapter 9

Jack had asked me to keep his current living situation on the down-low. "I have enough to deal with right now," he had said. "I don't need my mother interrogating me."

So after the show ended we each drove back to my apartment alone, in our respective cars, which was a relief. By nine o'clock I needed a few minutes to get a hold of myself. My incredible high of winning the immunity challenge was followed by such a ghastly low, like diving from the rim of paradise into a tub full of ice-water and slugs. And the only thing worse than living it, was watching my family relive it for me.

When I walk into my apartment Jack's already in the kitchen, drinking a glass of water. I give him a silent look of complaint and he responds. "I'd have done the same thing." He's referring to my actions at Island Assembly at the end of tonight's episode. "Of course, my life is a mess, so I wouldn't take that as a compliment. But I do understand why you did what you did."

I reach into the freezer and grab the gallon of chocolate ice cream. "I'm glad you understand, and I do take it as a compliment, even if I shouldn't." I step next to Jack, slide out the silverware drawer and grab a spoon. "But I'm afraid you're the only one who will get it. My dad and Ian certainly don't." I stand and shovel ice cream into my mouth.

"They just don't like seeing you hurt." Jack takes another spoon from the drawer, and I hold out the ice-cream container for him. He digs in.

"What about the rest of the world? What will be their excuse?"

Jack leans back and tilts his head to the side. "Robin. What did you think would happen when you went on a reality show? I don't mean to sound harsh, but I can't understand why you're so surprised and offended that people are judging you."

I lick my spoon and place the ice-cream container down on the counter. "I'm not surprised. But you can't understand what it's like until you've lived it."

"Yeah." His voice is soft, sympathetic. "I keep thinking the same thing when I feel like people are judging me." He throws his spoon in the sink and refills his water glass. "I'm picking Mikey up from school tomorrow, so I'll be working before and after that. It's going to be a long day. I think I'll read and go to bed." He kisses the top of my head, sort of like how my dad used to.

"Yeah, I'm pretty tired too."

I read in bed for a while. I worry that I'll have trouble falling asleep, but hours later I wake, my lamp still on and my book fallen to the side. I switch the light off, throw my book to the floor, and slip back into a dreamless sleep.

§

The next morning I'm running late. I park my car at the courthouse and I'm scurrying upstairs, trying not to spill the coffee from my travel mug. I'm just about to reach security when I hear a voice behind me.

"Robin!"

I turn around. Ten is walking up to me, smiling broadly. He must have skipped shaving this morning, and he looks sort of rugged.

"So it is you!"

"Huh?" It takes me a moment before I realize. That's the first time he's ever called me by name.

"You're Robin from *The Holdout*! I thought you looked familiar!" He hits his head lightly with the palm of his hand. "I had been going crazy trying to remember where I knew you from!"

"Shhh!" I grab his arm and pull him off to the side, away from the security line.

"What?" Ten sees my urgent expression and responds to my intensity, speaking in a raspy sort of whisper. "It's not a big secret, is it? Because I don't think you're going to be able to keep people from realizing who you…"

"Well I'm going to try!" I speak in a soft, hushed yell. Each word is a tiny exclamation point. "I don't want anyone to know."

Ten's face falls. "Oh. Why not?"

After an exaggerated sniff, I exhale through my mouth and scold him with my eyes. Inside, I'm as embarrassed as I was back in ninth grade, when I asked Donny Romano to the Sadie Hawkins dance after he had already said yes to Mindy Maloney. I don't want to be a big joke. I hate being a big, tall, blonde joke.

"Never mind." My terseness makes Ten recoil. "Just don't tell anyone."

Ten's shoulders droop and his eyes scurry away from me. For a brief, irrational moment I'm tempted to step in closer, touch my fingers to his unshaven cheek, and smile at him until he smiles back.

But of course I don't do that.

I walk away, and he follows but remains a few steps behind. We don't talk in the security line or on the elevator ride up, and it's like yesterday's friendship was just a figment of our imagination. Now we're back to reality.

§

Once I'm in the jury box and the trial resumes I relax a little. So far nobody else has recognized me. Maybe nobody else on the jury watches the show. It doesn't have the rating numbers that it had a few years ago.

I massage the sides of my nose. These fake glasses are starting to pinch. With a quiet sigh I settle into my chair and my mind begins to drift. I know I should be paying attention to the testimony, but I can't help but replay the final part of last night's episode over in my head.

§

After the challenge, the first scene they showed was of us getting back to camp. Henry tended the fire, Bailey went off to relieve himself in the woods, and Klemi decided to bathe in the ocean. Meanwhile, I pulled Grant aside.

"We're voting out Klemi tonight." I stared deep into his eyes, looking for some sort of flicker that would betray him, but saw nothing but the warm brown depths I had grown to trust.

Grant squeezed my hand and I hated myself for heating at his touch. "What about Henry? Don't you think we'll look better for the jury if we stay loyal to our original tribe members?"

I shook my head hard. "No. Henry found a hidden immunity idol. It has to be Klemi."

Grant raised his eyebrows in surprise. "Henry has immunity? Are you sure he's not making it up?"

"He showed me the idol."

"Wow." Grant scratched his head and looked around in thought.

I braced myself as I asked the next question. "Were you kissing Klemi earlier?"

"What?" Grant was still holding my hand, and he tugged and squeezed as he returned my gaze. "Did Henry tell you that I was?"

I nodded my head yes.

Grant sighed. "No. Klemi and I were up on the rocks. She told me she wanted to talk strategy and I went along because I need her vote when she's on the jury. But once we were up there she started in about how homesick she is. So I gave her a hug. When we broke apart I saw Henry on the beach below, staring up at us."

I bit my lip and peered into his face, looking for some sort of a tell. Aren't people supposed to twitch when they're lying?

Grant released my hand. Then he tenderly tucked a loose strand of hair behind my ear. I wanted to believe him like I wanted to believe in Santa Claus until I was twelve.

"Robin. I promise. You and me—final two. And after the show is over, it will still be you and me. Okay?" He used his fingers to gently tilt up my chin, and his eyes implored me to affirm his promise.

And then, instead of saying yes, I stepped in, grabbed his face and pressed my lips firmly against his. I kissed him hard, like I was Al Pacino giving Fredo the kiss of death in *The Godfather*. I broke away first but I kept his face in my hands.

"I know it was you, Grant. You break my heart and you're going to pay."

He laughed. So I laughed too. Maybe I'm too pathetic to really sound tough but I still don't understand what was so funny.

Then there was a testimonial from Grant. He was sitting in the same place on the rocks where he had been earlier that day with Klemi. Shirtless, his posture presented all his best angles for the cameras. His brown eyes shone, and his adorable mop of dark curls swayed gently in the breeze.

"I always knew they'd find out eventually. But who knows? Maybe Robin's dumb enough to believe what I tell her. Most people will believe anything, if they want it to be true. So when I tell Robin that she's special to me, she won't doubt it." He suddenly turned thoughtful, and rubbed the back of his neck while he looked off in the distance. "Robin could easily win this game. So as soon as I can I'll get her out, and when she's on the jury, I'll have her vote." He turned back towards the camera. "Because I'll be sitting next to Klemi. And no matter how much Robin might hate me, she'll hate Klemi even more."

The scene switched again.

Bailey was lying down under the fort, taking a rare rest in the middle of the day. Henry came in and sat down beside him.

"Have you talked to Grant?" Henry asked.

Bailey kept his arm over his eyes as he spoke. "He said to vote out Klemi."

"Of course he did." Henry reclined himself down, so he was closer to Bailey. "But I bet he told Klemi to vote you out."

"So?" Bailey's response was gruff. "Grant has to say that. It has to be either Klemi or me."

The camera zoomed in on Henry's geeky face, on the straight-toothed smile that his parents no doubt paid thousands of dollars to correct. "But that's the thing, Bailey. It doesn't have to be you or Klemi. It could also be Grant."

Bailey's chin trembled ever so slightly as he considered this.

"You don't know for sure what Grant is going to do," Henry continued, "and you won't, not until tonight. But if you and I vote for him, we'll at least have a tie. Think about it. The person you'd be most likely to lose against is Grant. So why not just vote him out?"

"Hmm." That was Bailey's only response. At that he turned over and pretended to fall asleep. Henry got up and walked down to the ocean, where he had a testimonial.

"I did what I could," he said to the camera. "I'm definitely voting for Grant. I have no idea what Robin and Bailey are going to do, but at least I know I'm safe for tonight."

Then they showed the five of us walking and carrying our torches to Island Assembly.

It was dark when we got there, and as always, there was a fire burning in the pit at the center of the set. We all rested our torches against the wall and had a seat.

Joe Pine was perched on his stool. Everything about him was shiny, from his gelled hair to the buckles on his safari shirt. "And now the members of our jury." Joe said all their names as one by one, the six most recently voted out cast members walked in, each giving us a reproachful look as they entered. "Including Beth, who was voted out during the last Island Assembly." She looked so clean and made-up, barely recognizable. But when she narrowed her eyes and scowled at me I could tell it was obviously still her, and that her makeover hadn't changed her personality.

We were all sitting around the large fire: the jury on their own separate bench off to the side, the five of us in the middle of the set, and Joe on a stool that faced us all.

"Klemi," Joe said. "I have to say, you look pretty relaxed. How confident are you that you'll be staying tonight?"

Klemi rolled her eyes and wiggled her shoulders back and forth seductively. "I'm pretty confident, Joe. Nobody here likes me. So I'm the perfect person to bring to the final three because supposedly I can't win." Then she leaned over, met Grant's eye, and winked.

Joe did a double take. "Grant. Did Klemi just wink at you?"

Grant shrugged his shoulders. "She's just joking around."

Henry shook his head and laughed. Joe noticed. "Henry, what's that about?"

Henry looked at Joe squarely across the fire. "Joe, I happen to know that Grant has been double dipping. In the last twenty-four hours I've caught him both with Robin and with Klemi."

The heat from the fire was making me flushed. But Henry's words burned me.

Grant, however, remained cool. The light bounced off his tan skin and he radiated calm. "You 'caught' me? Yes, I was walking with Robin. Yes, I was sitting with Klemi. How is that double dipping?"

Henry answered simply. "It's double dipping because you had your tongue in both of their mouths."

Grant smiled in his endearing, crooked way. He batted his eyes. He cleared his throat. He looked down. "Um," he said. "I have grown close to a couple of people here. I won't deny that. But I don't think of it as playing people. And I won't deny that the hardest part of this game, for me at least, is separating my head from my heart."

I wanted to yell, *What the hell does that mean?* But I reminded myself that a million dollars is at stake. I kept my cool.

Besides, Joe asked my question for me, albeit in a more polite way. He flashed his talk-show host grin and the firelight gleamed as it bounced off his teeth. "What does that mean, Grant?"

Grant's face was so defenseless I had to tell myself to question his sincerity. "It means," he said, "that I have a job to do here and that job is to win. But it's not always easy to do my job because my emotions get in the way."

Joe leaned forward, his elbow resting on his knee. "But you said you had grown close to a couple of cast members. Just how close are we talking about?"

My breath caught in my throat as I waited for Grant's response, but Klemi spoke before he could answer. She flicked her hair over her shoulder. "Joe, flirting is simply a part of the game. But that's only true for the people who know how to flirt. If Henry doesn't understand that, it's because he doesn't know how to talk to girls." She smiled smugly. "It's the one thing he couldn't learn to do at school."

Henry sniffed as the wind blew smoke into his face. "Okay," he said through a cough. "So I'm not beautiful. Girls don't like me much. This isn't news. And I don't see how it changes anything."

"Bailey," Joe said. "What do you think? Have you been flirting to get ahead in this game?"

"Of course not. I don't need to. Can't say the same thing about Klemi."

Klemi leaned over and addressed him. "Really? You think I don't know how to do anything but flirt?"

Bailey's chest rose. "I know you don't."

Klemi glared at Bailey with her claws out, ready to shred him like a scratching post. "Everybody thinks I am empty-headed because I'm pretty. I'm sick of it!"

Henry answered her. "No, everybody thinks you're empty-headed because the inside of your skull contains nothing but air."

Beth and other members of the jury laughed out loud, though they'd been instructed not to make noise. Klemi fumed and Joe shifted the focus.

"Robin, you've been awfully quiet. What's your opinion? Have you been flirting to get ahead, and if so, do you blame Grant for doing the same?"

I looked at Grant and he looked back at me. He was trying to communicate something, as if we were sitting alone again on the beach and confining all our most intimate secrets. But the silence only floated between us, awkward and unpleasant.

I didn't even recognize the sound of my own voice as I answered Joe. It was deep and nasal, like I was a smoker with a sinus infection. "If I flirted, it wasn't to get ahead. I tried to be honest with everyone, including myself."

Klemi rolled her eyes and let out a harsh laugh. Joe questioned her with his eyes.

"How can she be so naïve?" Klemi demanded. "I would feel bad for her if she wasn't so dumb."

I shot Klemi a look full of arrows. "What's dumb about being honest?"

"Hello!" Klemi's accent made the simple word sound glamorous. "Anybody home? This is a game for a million dollars. Nobody wins by being honest."

"Well, I'm going to try. And I don't see what's wrong with making friends. That ought to be part of it."

"Okay," Joe said to me, "but what about Grant? Will you be mad if he's been flirting with Klemi?"

A headache was beginning to form. "What do you think?" Joe's face went blank and I continued. "Of course I'll be mad! I don't care if it's real life, reality TV, or a reconnaissance mission to the moon; if I find out a guy has been two-timing me, I get pissed off!"

I don't know what Joe was expecting me to say, but that wasn't it. He raised his eyebrows and said, "Well with that, it's time to vote. Just remember, you can't vote for Robin because she has immunity."

"Joe," Henry said. "I also have immunity because I found this." Henry got up and handed Joe the idol.

Joe looked it over, checking its authenticity. "Okay," he said. "This is an immunity idol, and it can be used one time only. Since he is presenting it tonight, Henry is also immune. That means only votes for Grant, Bailey, or Klemi will be counted. Robin, you're up first."

I got up and walked to ballot box, where a camera was facing me. I wrote down "Klemi" in large letters, and showed my ballot to the camera. I spoke in a stage whisper. "At long last, it is time for you to go." Then I folded the ballot, put it in the basket and walked back to my seat. One by one the other cast members came and voted, but the only other ballot they showed in the edited version was Henry's.

His ballot said "Grant" in large, block letters. "You are a liar and a cheat. I will be glad to see you gone."

Once we were sitting down, Joe said, "I'll go tally the votes." He quickly returned with the woven basket that contained our ballots.

"Remember that all votes are final," he said. "Once the last ballot has been read, the person voted out will be asked to leave Island Assembly immediately." He reached into the basket. "First vote, Klemi." Joe held up the ballot with my writing. The camera showed Klemi rolling her eyes. "Second vote, Bailey." Joe held up a ballot written with long, girly strokes. It had to be Klemi's. "Third vote, Grant." Henry looked over at Grant on the reading of his ballot and raised one eyebrow. "Fourth vote, Grant." Grant's eyes widened a little when he realized that Bailey must have voted against him too, and Bailey just stared impassively ahead. Joe cleared his throat. "One vote Klemi, one vote Bailey, two votes Grant, one vote left."

Joe reached into the basket at a glacial pace. Every member of the jury was riveted, sitting on the edge of the bench with anticipation. As Joe unfolded the ballot and held it up, my stomach threatened to rise and rebel. If Grant voted for Klemi, that meant he had been telling me the truth. But if he voted for Bailey, if he would betray his original alliance, if he would keep Klemi after promising me she'd be gone, then he wasn't just lying to me about tonight's vote. It meant that he'd been lying to me about everything else too.

My heart was banging in my chest, a perpetual rhythm made more endless because Joe was moving in slow motion. Finally he opened his mouth to speak. "Fifth vote, Bailey." Joe held up the ballot. There were triangles and rainbows sketched all over it. My jaw dropped as I remembered Grant's earlier pledge. *"When it's our turn to vote out Bailey, I promise to draw rainbows and purple triangles all over the ballot."*

I didn't know if I should have been laughing or crying, running to him or running at him. He mouthed "Told you," and smiled, like his vote was an inside joke and a gift, not a betrayal at all.

A couple of the jury members audibly groaned, and Henry sat up, alert, trying to catch my eye. I ignored him.

"That means we have a tie," said Joe. "In this situation we revote. Neither Grant nor Bailey will vote, and you other three will only be allowed to vote for Grant or Bailey."

Everyone looked down. "Okay," said Joe. "Henry, you're up first." Henry got up, took the ballot basket from Joe, and walked towards the voting spot. He gave me an intense stare as he went. It wasn't necessary. I already understood. As long as neither he nor Klemi changed their original votes, mine was the only vote that counted.

Henry returned and sat. Then it was Klemi's turn. When she returned she sat next to Grant, and she pushed her shoulder against his. He didn't exactly pull away.

"Robin," Joe said. "You're up."

I needed one more message from Grant: some unspoken announcement that I could actually trust him, that his feelings were real, that I'm not a fool, ready to fall for the first set of warm eyes and strong biceps which promised to soothe me.

But Grant was looking at Klemi and he didn't hear my silent questions. I stood and walked back to the original voting spot, again facing the camera. I knew the drill.

Once there, the camera showed me lost in thought. Away from the heat of the fire the island air felt unusually dry and cool. I shivered as I contemplated my choices.

Bailey could be just as dangerous, I told myself. The jury likes him, and if the last challenge is about endurance, he could win. I chewed on the inside of my cheek. *Maybe I could win against Grant, and if he's cheating on me, there would be no better revenge.* The pen was sitting before me, ready to write someone's name on a blank ballot. It was begging me to pick it up. *But what if he isn't cheating on me? If I vote him out, will that be it?*

Finally, I picked up the pen with the intention of writing down Grant's name. I tried, but the letters wouldn't limp out.

Don't be an idiot, I told myself. He's a liar and this is your chance to get him out.

I closed my eyes, willing myself to do what was necessary. Then, suddenly, I could hear my brother Ted's voice as clearly as if he were standing right there, speaking into my ear. "Don't ever let things fester," he said. "Unresolved situations are like poison, and they'll kill you if you don't figure them out." He had learned this at some point in business school and it became his mantra. How many times had he told me this? As older brothers go, he hadn't told me much. But these words of wisdom were the one life lesson he had taught me.

I knew it was a mistake but it felt as inevitable as puking after a night of break-up binge drinking. I wrote down my vote, put my ballot in the basket, walked back, and handed it to Joe.

I sat down, determined not to make eyes with anyone: contestants, jury members, Joe, or the camera. Joe pulled my ballot out of the basket.

"Twelfth person out and sixth member of the jury," he held up my ballot for all to see, "Bailey."

§

I shift in my seat and look at the clock. They've been showing a videotaped deposition by some guy who worked in the shipyard where the yachts had been stored. He keeps saying such damning things about how the yachts were treated that I start to wonder if I missed something and he's actually a witness for the defense.

But no, because at the end of it, the lawyer gets up and says, "Thank you, your honor. The prosecution rests."

Everyone in the jury box shifts and looks at each other with excitement. Then the judge looks at the clock, and says, "Well, then this will be a good time to recess for lunch. We will resume at 1:15."

We get up and file out in our normal, orderly fashion, through the side door, into the hall, and into the break room where our bags are stored. Before anyone can say anything about lunch, and before I have a chance of making eye contact with Ten, I grab my purse and race to the elevators.

I'm in such a hurry that at first I don't notice I'm sharing an elevator with plaintiff/bad boy Silas Smythe. The jurors were told at the beginning of the trial not to speak with anyone involved with the case. So I just face forward and intently watch the numbered lights come on as we pass each floor.

Silas clears his throat. I ignore him. He clears it again, louder this time, and even though I'm trying not to, my head swivels towards him. He smiles at me like we're standing in a crowded bar and he's caught my eye from across the room. He flicks his floppy black hair off his forehead and for a moment I think he's going to offer to buy me a beer.

He has to know I'm a jury member. He's been sitting in the courtroom every day for over a week, so surely he's had a chance to memorize all twelve of our faces. And if not, well, the bright orange "Juror" badge I have pinned to my sweater should be a dead giveaway.

But I can't look away from him. His bright blue eyes are so shiny, like empty chlorinated pools in the middle of summer. I kind of want to dive in even though I know they can't be natural, or real. Then the elevator reaches the bottom floor and the doors open to the lobby. Silas holds his arm out and says, "Ladies first."

I return to reality and step onto stable ground. Then I start to fume. Does Silas watch *The Holdout*? Is that what that was about? Or, does he think if he lays on the charm I'll vote to give him all his money back? Either way, I want to hurt Silas Smythe. Charming, good looking guys like him need to understand what the world is like for everyone else.

I go outside and walk around the block, unsure of where I'm headed. I'm hungry, but I don't want to go anywhere I might run into someone I know. Maybe if I wander around I'll find a hidden coffee shop that sells dry sandwiches and overpriced pastries. Or overpriced sandwiches and dry pastries – that would be fine too.

The wind is making my cheeks tingle and the exertion of walking is a relief. Then my phone rings. I grab it from my purse and see that it's Lucy calling. If anyone is going to say anything that might actually make me feel better about last night's episode of *The Holdout*, it will probably be her.

"Hi," I say. "How are you?"

"I'm good," she responds. "Did I catch you at an okay time?"

"It's perfect. I'm on break during jury duty right now."

She squeals. "Jury duty? Seriously? Oh, I'm so jealous. I've always wanted to be on a jury. What's it for?"

If anyone else had told me they were jealous that I had jury duty I would have thought they were being sarcastic, but I know Lucy's sincere. "Federal court. Civil case. It's about yachts. That's all I can say for now."

"Yachts, huh? Yeah, I'll want to hear all about it." She laughs. "Hey, Monty and I watched your show last night. Fantastic job in the immunity challenge! And that Island Assembly was intense! I can't believe how composed you were. I could never have been that stoic. I probably would have started crying or something stupid like that."

"You never know," I tell her. "It's hard to say what you'd do until you're actually in the situation."

"I suppose," she answers. "So did they edit much out, or was that mostly it?"

I hug my sweater around me, wishing I had brought my coat. The smell of baking bread is lingering in the cold, November air. I follow the scent, hoping to be led to a bakery. "That was mostly it," I say. "But they made it look like I had sex with Grant and I didn't."

"Oh!" Lucy's voice raises a notch. "I wasn't actually asking about that. But that's interesting, because we did sort of assume that you did, you know, have sex with him."

"Great," I say, flooding the word with sarcasm.

"Oh Robin, who cares? I mean, what if you did have sex with him, even then, so what? He's hot and for all you knew he seemed like a good guy. Most women in your position would have fallen for him too."

Lucy doesn't come off as the "easy" type, but if that's what she thinks, perhaps there's more to her than meets the eye. I step over a discarded Styrofoam container of leftover food, nearly smudging my boots with tomato sauce. "Thanks, but it's still embarrassing."

She sighs "I understand. Monty wants to hire out a hit on that Grant guy. I told him you can take care of yourself, but I worry he still thinks you're a kid."

"Ian and Jack were talking about getting Grant killed too. Funny that they all want to hire somebody else to do it."

"Maybe they don't want to get their hands dirty?"

I laugh. Then I spot the bakery I had been hoping for. As I enter and stand in line, I lower my tone. "You know, I had to sit through the whole episode with Ian, Jack, Natalie, and my dad."

I expect her to laugh at the awkwardness of it all, but she doesn't. Her tone changes, instantly more intense. "So Jack was there?"

I press my lips together. I had forgotten that Jack isn't really speaking to Lucy lately, and she hasn't been included in the dramatic loop of his life.

"Lucy, I have to go. I found somewhere to eat lunch, and it's almost my turn to order."

"Oh. Sure."

I start to hang up, but she says, "Wait. Can you just tell me – is Jack okay? I haven't talked to him in weeks. He hasn't returned my calls and I've been sort of worried. Do you know if everything is all right?"

"I guess he's okay. You know. Not great, but okay."

"Did something happen?"

"Um." I look to the ceiling and silently groan. "I don't want to get in the middle of anything, Lucy."

There's silence on her end as she's processing what I just said. "I…um, uh…" she's stuttering and I feel like an awkward clod who just ran over her foot, causing her unintentional pain. "All right," she finishes. Her cheerfulness sounds forced. "Sure. I guess I'll just try calling him again."

"It was good to talk to you," I say, and I hope she knows I'm sincere. "Can I call you later this week?"

"Of course. We'll talk then. Good luck on jury duty."

"Bye."

I hang up, order my food, and lament on how lame I am. I didn't even ask her any questions about herself.

I sit down with my lunch: creamy tomato soup, and a crusty, buttered roll that is neither overpriced nor dry. I stir the soup half-heartedly with my spoon.

If Monty and the rest of my family still think of me as kid, perhaps it's because I haven't given them any reason to see me as an adult. And unless I pick myself up and finally get a grip, that's not going to change any time soon.

Chapter 10

After jury duty gets out, I get in my car, but instead of driving directly home I take a detour to my favorite thrift store and comb the aisles for abandoned treasure. I find a purple taffeta brocade coat and a bunch of bright colored t-shirts. I snatch up anything that is solid-colored in a man's extra large, because the more fabric I have to work with the easier it is to turn it into something else. I also pillage the jewelry aisle, find a bunch of rhinestone jewelry, and add that to my stash.

When I get home I throw all of the clothes into the washing machine in the basement. I eat dinner and sketch while it washes and I continue my sketching while my stuff dries. But by then I'm standing in the laundry room, waiting anxiously for everything to be done and ready.

Back up in my apartment, it's after ten when Jack comes in. I've cut and ironed the purple taffeta, and I'm pinning it up, with a plan to turn it into a belted blouse with short, puffed sleeves, a scooped neckline, and tiny, shiny buttons.

"Hey," Jack says as he comes in.

"Hi." I hold up the fabric and my sketch. "Do you think Lucy would like something like this?"

Jack is still taking off his jacket. But he comes over to get a closer look.

"Um, maybe?" He holds my sketchbook in one hand, and handles the fabric with the other. "I'm not really an expert at women's clothes but I'm pretty sure she plays it safe with how she dresses."

"This is too much for her?" I look it over. Maybe it's not conservative enough.

"I don't know." He hands me back the sketchpad and sits down. "I mean, it's really pretty. But I can't tell you whether she'd wear it or not."

I bite my lip. Should I start again, or finish and sell it on eBay? Then I could work on something more traditional looking for Lucy next.

"What prompted this?" Jack asks.

I pin the tucks in the sleeve as I answer. "She called me today to talk about last night's episode. She was super-nice, as always, and when I mentioned you, she told me how concerned she is because she hasn't heard from you in so long. So I told her I didn't want to get in the middle and instead of getting mad, she just said she'd try calling you again. I felt bad, so now I'm making her a blouse."

"Sorry." Jack rubs the back of his neck and closes his eyes.

"What are you sorry about?"

"You feel bad, Lucy feels bad, and I…" He stares at his shoes. "It's just all my fault."

"Why don't you just call Lucy? I'm sure you'd both feel a lot better if you did."

"Because Jessie called me today." One half of Jack's mouth tiptoes into a smile. "I think we might be able to patch things up. We talked about getting a new, bigger place together, where Mikey could have his own room. And she agreed that we could wait a while to get engaged. But if she found out that I called Lucy, she'd be furious."

I accidentally stick a pin into my pinkie finger, and the pain stings. "Jack," I exclaim, perhaps more harshly than is warranted. "Lucy is your best friend. Plus she's your family now. You can't just cut her off to make Jessie happy."

Jack's jaw sets into a frown. "There's a conflict of interest here." He tugs at the edge of his shirt, trying to loosen his collar. "I can't make everyone happy. Lucy's all the way in Seattle and her life is with my brother. I mean, I can call her and tell her I'm fine but she's not going to like what I have to say after that, so it's probably best just to let it go."

I've stopped pinning the sleeves, and I just stand there, sucking on my pinkie, unsure of what to say.

Jack stands up. "I'm not staying. I just came by to get my stuff, and then I'm going back to Jessie's." He comes over, gently takes the pinned up fabric from my hands, and delicately places it down on my sewing table. Then he hugs me, harder and tighter than he's ever hugged me before. He speaks into the top of my head. "I also came by to thank you. I owe you big time."

I pull away. "Don't be silly. All you did was sleep on my couch. It's no big deal."

"I still really appreciate it." He starts to gather up his loose belongings and puts them in his duffel bag. I watch.

"Jack, are you sure about this?"

His head snaps up as if my question had startled him. "Yeah, of course I am. I love Jessie."

"Okay, but the other day you said you didn't know if you loved her or not, so I thought I should ask."

Jack goes back to his task of packing. "You have to meet her. Once you do, you'll see how great she is, and you'll understand." He zips his bag and stands up straight. "Some time next week, maybe? I'll give you a call."

I nod. "Sure. Sounds good."

He walks to my door and I follow. I'm already feeling lonely and he hasn't even left yet.

"Take care of yourself," I say.

"Jessie and I will be taking care of each other." He smiles.

"Right, of course."

"You take care too, Robin. And I'll call you."

He exits, and I close the door after him. Then I dead bolt the lock, which will keep everyone in the world out but me.

I go back to work on my blouse, but as I do my mind drifts. Last night's episode ended with my vote at Island Assembly, but the real drama was only just beginning.

§

Henry, Klemi, Grant and I walked back to camp in virtual silence. But once we arrived and set down our torches, I immediately pulled Grant aside and led him down to the shore.

"What the hell!" I demanded. "Why didn't you vote out Klemi?"

"Because." His voice was calm in contrast to my intensity. "I don't want to be sitting next to Bailey when the jury votes. He could win. But Klemi was right when she said that nobody liked her."

"Nobody likes Bailey either."

Grant sighs and looks up at the dark, starry sky. "Robin, come on. Bailey is the underdog. He's seventy years old, crusty, and no-nonsense. He's worked hard for everything he has. Anyone sitting next to him will look silly and over-privileged in comparison."

I pretended like the same thoughts hadn't occurred to me as I crossed my arms over my chest and jutted out my chin. "You've really considered every angle, haven't you?"

"Of course. Haven't you?"

I breathed deeply to keep myself calm. "You wouldn't look silly and over-privileged if you had some tragic story about your parents' death, would you? Or what if everyone thought you blamed yourself for your sister's addiction? What if we thought that nobody, including your grandparents, loved you? Then you'd be sure to win."

Grant didn't even flinch. Either I was spot-on or I was the biggest bitch in the world. I had no idea which.

"So have you been flirting with Klemi to get ahead in this game?"

"Yes." Grant replied without blinking, without apology.

I could feel tears start to form. I looked away, knowing I had just lost the staring contest. "What about me? Was that about getting ahead too?"

"No." He reached to touch me but I stepped away. "Okay," he said. "Since we're being so honest, I'll just tell you now that I'm voting you out next."

I stared at him with widened eyes.

"Robin, it's what I have to do. I can beat Klemi and I can beat

Henry. Neither of them deserves to win and the jury knows it. But I'm not so sure I can beat you." He grinned like a car salesman. "You should take it as a compliment."

"What about your original claim that you'd rather go to the end with someone you can trust and respect?"

His face was lit by the glow of the moon and the ocean waves crashed behind us. The evening air was warm with the sand smooth and cool beneath our feet. It would have been so romantic if it wasn't for everything about him being completely wrong.

"I lied," he said simply.

"Well, I didn't." I stepped in closer, and whispered. "You're voting me out?" I shook my head. "Not a chance. I will destroy you before I let that happen."

He laughed. "You don't scare me. You could have voted me out tonight and you didn't even have the nerve to do that."

Then he patted me on the head. "Enjoy your last two days here, Robbie. Because you're next to go."

§

On Friday I'm out of coffee, so I stop at a convenience store on my way to jury duty. I fill a Styrofoam cup with French Roast, mix in a hazelnut creamer, and secure the black plastic lid, hoping it will stay and the coffee won't spill out and burn my hand. I stand in line to pay. There is fruit in a basket by the cash register, and the apples look good, but I'm wondering what the chances are that they're not mealy, when my eyes wander over to the magazine stand. And there I am, on the cover of *Alright Magazine*. There's a photo of Grant in the middle, and I'm on one side; my hair is in a messy pony-tale and I'm wearing only my bikini bottoms and my grey hoodie. Oh, and I'm frowning. Klemi is on the other side of Grant, looking resplendent in her skimpy bathing suit and a superior, sexy smile. The magazine has laid out each individual photo to give the impression that Grant and Klemi are looking towards each other, happy, and I'm off on the side, like a pouty woman scorned. Underneath the pictures is the caption:

Sex, Lies, and The Holdout: Who Will Win Grant's Heart?

I grab a magazine as if it's the only one, and not simply on the top of a large stack. I grab it like I can make it all disappear simply by hiding it underneath my jacket. I reach the cash register to pay for the coffee and the magazine and I've forgotten about the apple. Then the clerk looks down at my photo, and she looks up at me.

"Oh my God!" she squeals. "You're Robin from *The Holdout*! I heard you were from around here. This is so exciting!"

I feel my cheeks blaze as everyone in the store turns their attention towards me. "It is her!" A customer cries. She walks over to me and I see that we're around the same age. "I love how great you are in the challenges. Every week my boyfriend and I bet on who's going to win immunity and I always pick you."

"Thank you," I say as I shrink down into my coat. All I want to do is flee this scene to the safety of my car.

"That Grant is such an asshole!" The cashier cries. "You're going to vote him off next, right?"

"Why didn't you vote him off last time?" My other fan grabs my arm. "I thought you would. If Grant wins it will be all your fault."

"Yeah," I say, removing my arm from her grasp. "I'm sure you're right."

"So is he a good kisser?" The cashier wants to know.

I laugh uncomfortably. "Um, I'm running sort of late, so if you don't mind, I'd like to pay for my stuff and go."

The cashier shakes her head. "Not until you sign this for me." She grabs another magazine and a pen. "Make it out to Tonya."

I end up signing a half dozen more magazines, and fielding several uncomfortable questions. I would have made my exit sooner, but I don't want Twitter to be buzzing with how rude I am. It's the last thing I need.

So I'm seriously late when I finally get to jury duty. I run up to the break room where I know everybody will be waiting, and I'm ready to make my apologies as I scuffle in. It's 9:07 when I open the door, and the eleven of them are all sitting around the table, each in their usual spot. "I am so sorry to be late!" I cry. "Were they ready for us? Have I held everyone up?"

At first nobody says anything. They all just look at each other and then they look at me, and I worry that it's worse than I thought. That the judge had said starting time was actually 8:30 and I'm fatally late. Then Two holds up *Alright Magazine.*

"It is you. It is TOTALLY you!" She laughs in her loud, braying sort of way and rubs at one of her heavily made up eyes.

"Yes, it's me." I sit down in my chair, place my coffee cup on the table, and put my jacket on the back of my chair. Luckily my copy of the magazine is hidden in my bag. But I haven't even had time to read the article yet.

Six speaks next. "We had no idea that we're on a jury with a celebrity! Why didn't you say something?" In this moment she reminds me of my Aunt Natalie, proud and affectionate.

Four is in the chair next to me, and her comment isn't quite as enthusiastic. "I'm surprised they chose you for jury duty. How can you be anything but a distraction?"

I don't know how to answer that, and luckily I don't have to. Tommy the clerk comes in.

"Is everyone ready?" He asks us all. He isn't really looking in my direction any more than he usually does, so I guess not everyone is aware of whom I am.

We all stand. And, speaking of people not looking at me, Ten avoids my eyes just as he has ever since I yelled at him. I try to fling him a smile, but he's not up for catching one. So we all file out, and as we do I ask Seven if this is the first time the clerk has come for us, or if he tried before when I wasn't there.

"Don't worry," Seven tells me. "The judge must have been running late too."

This morning's witnesses require a translator, because they are the owners of Potenza, the Greek yacht company, and they don't speak English. The testimony takes a while. However, the gist of it is this: Potenza says that the Smythes didn't take proper care of the boats. Potenza had outlined how high-maintenance these boats are, that they require at least ten thousand dollars worth of varnish a year to protect them, and that they should be stored somewhere that isn't on flat land, or in a leaky warehouse, or in the harsh sunlight but not in the water, which is exactly how the Smythes stored them for months at a time. At one point a Smythe shipyard had received a bunch of boats, but nothing was done with them. They just sat outside, their beautiful varnish jobs slowly decaying under the rays of the sun and their hulls becoming compromised without the proper supports and weight distribution.

The ex-college frat boy/defense lawyer asks his witness, "Why are you here Sir, when you have employees that could have travelled and testified on your behalf?"

The man in the witness stand is huge and bald, and he looks like he sweats a lot. He's stuffed into his suit, and I'm guessing he's a lot more comfortable in shorts and bare feet, out by the water. He starts yelling in Greek. The translator, a meek woman who is half his size, tries to keep up.

"My honor is stake," she says for him. "These boats are my life and my livelihood. This case is an insult to my name so I must defend my name and my boats. I make these boats by hand and I put my blood into them. How dare they say what they say! How dare they accuse me of building a deficient boat! My boats are top of line, best in the industry, and everybody knows this."

I would laugh at the ridiculousness of a sweet, mild-mannered woman expressing such anger on this thunderous man's behalf, as he continues to yell behind her. But I hold my tongue because it's not appropriate to laugh when you're on a jury, like how Beth and the others did towards the end. It helps nothing.

Besides, the generic white-haired lawyer for the plaintiff speaks up.

"Objection, your honor. Improper characterization. It is not Mr. Speros' job to summarize the testimony made by the plaintiffs, nor should he be able to quantify the superiority of his boats in relation to other boats."

The translator whispers to Mr. Speros, and I'm assuming she is translating the objection for him. The defense lawyer pushes his wire-rim glasses up on his nose and gives the judge his sardonic smile.

"Your honor, the witness is merely answering my question in his own way. This is an emotional issue for him, and he is treating it as such."

The judge looks down and her eyes appear closed. Is she asleep or is she just thinking? Silence surrounds us and we can literally hear the large wall clock clicking as we all wait for her answer. The lawyers seem as unsettled by her as *The Holdout* cast was by Joe Pine.

Pained that they might need to repeat themselves, the lawyers make eye contact with each other in a rare moment of camaraderie. Even Tommy the clerk is squirming a little in his seat off to the side. Then the judge's head rises up sharply. She addresses the defense lawyer. "That may be. But in a court of law it is our job to look past the emotions of a case and to examine the facts. Sustained."

The defense lawyer wilts and the plaintiff lawyer glows, and the testimony continues.

Damn. This judge has got it going on. I hope someday I can be as self-possessed as she is. Maybe thirty years from now, when I'm around her age, I'll be able to take my time in answering a question, and once I do, the men who asked it will follow my directives with no complaint.

Later we break for lunch. As we file out of the courtroom and into the break room I lunge forward and tug on Ten's sleeve. He stops and turns around, so I pull him aside, around the bend of the wall. We stand by a big picture window that overlooks downtown Des Moines.

"I'm sorry," I say. "I didn't mean to yell at you the other day. I was just embarrassed, self-conscious, and all the other things that make a person feel bad about herself."

At first I'm worry that he's holding onto his resentment. Then he smiles, his face transforms, and my senses relax. He speaks in a hushed, conspiratorial voice. "But you should be proud. After all, you're on the cover of *Alright Magazine*. How many people will ever be able to say that in their lifetime?"

I can't tell if he's being sarcastic or not, but if he is, it's a gentle, teasing sarcasm, and I almost want to step in closer to him. I almost want to get a stronger whiff of his Ivory Soap scent, and to touch the soft fabric of his oxford cloth shirt that must be standard issue for all real estate agents. The one he's wearing today is blue, and the cloth clings to his torso, accentuating his flat stomach and broad chest.

"Yeah, about that. Would you do me a huge favor?"

He wrinkles his nose. "What?"

"There's a copy of *Alright Magazine* in my bag, but I haven't even gotten to read it yet. And I can't face more questions about the show until I do."

He nods solemnly. "You want me to go in there, get your bag, and bring it to you?"

"Yes. And my coat. And find me downstairs. I'll take the elevator down now, and I'll walk around to the south door, and wait for you there. Okay?"

He arches an eyebrow. "Anything else?"

I do step in closer, but only by a millimeter. "Have lunch with me? I found a great bakery the other day. We could go there."

He looks out the window, down at the tiny, ant-like pedestrians below. Then his gaze is back on me. "You should go get the elevator now. I'll wait until after they leave to go in and get your stuff. So it might be a few minutes. Is this bakery close by?"

I nod and grin. "Yeah. And the service is quick, especially if you get the soup."

"I love soup," he says.

"Yeah, me too."

Then neither of us can think of more to say, so we go our separate ways. But I'm still grinning. I know he'll find me again soon.

§

We make it to the bakery and sit down with our food. I ordered the same creamy tomato soup and buttered roll from last time, and Ten has a half turkey sandwich and a cup of chicken wild rice.

I pull out the magazine. I start to read the article silently to myself, but Ten protests. "No fair," he says. "I got your stuff for you, so you're reading that out loud."

I sigh and give a quick glance around the bakery. Nobody seems at all interested in me, so I clear my throat and begin to read.

"The path to love is a complicated one, as anybody who has been watching this season of 'The Holdout' would know. Grant Zane has set his sights on two fellow contestants, Robin Bricker and Klementina Silvera. After last week's contentious Island Assembly, Bricker confronted Zane about his intentions. The end result? These former lovebirds are now promising to vote each other out.

'Grant's heart was broken,' says a source close to Zane. 'He totally dug Robin, and knowing she would vote him out really hit him where it hurts.' Meanwhile, Silvera is playing it cool. Though Silvera says she typically stays out of the world of wild hook-ups and dating drama, perhaps the chance to be with Zane was too good to turn down.

'I wasn't just using him to get ahead,' said Silvera in an exclusive interview with Alright Magazine. 'I have real deep feelings for Grant.'

Fans online seem stunned but fascinated by this love triangle, and many would say it actually does make some sense. 'Klemi is the sort of girl that any guy would want to be with,' said one online fan. 'But Grant and Robin have so much in common. I can totally understand their connection. If I was Grant I wouldn't know who to pick.'

What does the future hold for Grant Zane, Robin Bricker, and Klementina Silvera? Silvera clearly has a major crush, but she's not ready to sacrifice a million dollars for Zane's love. 'You'll just have to watch the remaining episodes,' says Silvera. 'I promise there are more surprises to come!'

What do you think? Will Cupid's arrow make any lasting impressions on these 'The Holdout' paramours? Join the conversation on Twitter. #Alright #HoldOutLove"

I stop reading and look at the surrounding photos and their captions underneath. One picture is of Grant and me kissing in the bushes. Below it is a quote from Joe Pine, *"Grant and Robin have an undeniable attraction to each other. I could sense the heat between them from the beginning."*

"Well, that isn't terrible," Ten says.

I lower the magazine. Ten is eating his sandwich and chewing while he talks. At least he manages not to be disgusting about it. He keeps his food off to the side of his mouth, unseen.

"It's all right," I say.

Ten laughs. "Ha ha. Get it? It's all right, and it's from *Alright Magazine*? I bet you didn't even realize when you said that…" His voice fades out when he realizes I'm not laughing with him.

I hang my head in my hands.

"What's wrong, Robin? It's not like they said anything bad about you. In fact I think you come off pretty good."

I'm looking down at the table as I answer. "I'm just so embarrassed."

"Why?"

I raise my head to respond. "Because. I was there to win and to prove how competent I am. Instead I fell for a guy. And he didn't even turn out to be nice."

"Well, of course not." Ten takes a sip of his water and I wait for him to elaborate.

After a moment I ask. "Why of course not?"

Ten uses his finger to trace the beads of moisture on his water glass. "Women never fall for the nice guys in these situations. They only fall for the nice guys when they've made a conscious decision to find one. The rest of the time they go for the bastards."

The sunlight is streaming through the window and it bounces off Ten's watch. I look from his wrist to his face. "Do you have a girlfriend?"

If he's thrown by my question, he doesn't show it. His face stays the same, a medley of brown, and he shakes his head no.

"But," he says, "I have a little sister. We watched the show together the other night, and I told her that you and I are on this jury together. She's dying to meet you."

I swallow my surprise. But what rises back up is worse. It's humiliation. "I didn't have sex with Grant, you know. It was the editing. They made it look like we were about to do it, but I had actually pushed him away."

Ten gives me a sideways sort of look, and nods gravely. "Okay."

I can't tell if believes me. Whatever. "Hey. I feel kind of silly asking you at this point, but what's your name?"

Ten laughs. "Nick."

Nick: a good, sturdy, nice name for a good, sturdy, nice guy. "Nick is a great name. But don't be offended if I still occasionally call you Ten."

"You call me Ten because you think I'm perfect?"

"No. Because you're juror number Ten."

He gives me an exaggerated eye roll. "Couldn't you have humored me on that one?"

I giggle. "Sorry."

He smiles and adjusts himself a little. He takes another drink of water, and I start in on my soup.

"So," he says. "Would you be willing to meet my sister? She's sixteen years old and your biggest fan. It would mean a lot to her, and she'd be very impressed with me too."

"Oh," I stammer. "Sure."

"Thanks."

He doesn't suggest a time or place. I assume that's coming later. But awkwardness descends upon us.

I do a little math in my head. "If your sister is only sixteen, how old does that make you?"

"Thirty," says Nick/Ten. "I was fourteen when she was born."

"Oh." I nod. "There's a big age difference between my brothers and me too."

"Yeah, I know."

It takes me a moment to realize that he's not stalking me.

"Right. You know a lot about me because you watch the show."

Ten/Nick shrugs his shoulders. "Hey, just to be fair, I'll tell you anything about myself that you want to know."

I reach out, grab his wrist, and turn his watch so I can see its face. "Maybe some other time," I say. "We need to finish our lunch and go."

He doesn't recoil at my touch and I don't pull my hand away super fast. Without looking down at his watch he responds. "We have plenty of time."

Chapter 11

This weekend I decide to kill two birds with one stone. I stop by Jack's restaurant to meet Jessie, but I also tell Nick to swing by with his sister. When I arrive on Saturday night the place is hopping and I'm lucky to find a table. There's no way Jack or Jessie will be able to chat for some time. So When Nick and his little sister Andrea arrive we sit and order drinks and food.

I end up having more fun than I thought I would. Andrea mostly asks questions about the filming of the show, and she also wants to know about the challenges. She barely mentions Grant at all.

I ask her about school. Turns out she's on the swim team like I was when I was her age. Unlike me, she's also in National Honor Society and Student Council.

I look at Nick's beaming face. His brotherly pride is pouring out. "Your parents must be so thrilled!" I say.

Andrea flips her long brown hair off one shoulder and her cheeks turn a little pink. "Not really," she says.

I knit my eyebrows together, and Nick can sense my question.

"I'm sure she would be proud, but our mother died when she was four and I was eighteen," says Nick. "Breast cancer."

"God, I'm sorry."

"You mentioned on *The Holdout* that your mom died when you were young too." Andrea's wide brown eyes overflow with compassion.

"Yes," I say. "In a car accident." I dip a calamari in marinara sauce, but I put it on my plate instead of in my mouth. "I was only two, which is probably a better age to lose her at than four. I have no memories of her at all, except from stories and pictures, so I don't really know what I'm missing."

Andrea and Nick nod. "I don't know if that's better," says Andrea.

"Losing your mother sucks. Period." The force of Nick's words are like a sudden strong wind, the kind that makes you drop your stuff and go scurrying after it. But I can't disagree.

"Yes." We meet eyes, and I see something, a connection between us, that I hadn't detected before. Usually when people want to talk about my mom something inside me clenches up and it becomes difficult to breathe like a normal person. Not now. Still, I change the subject because I don't want them to think I'm feeling sorry for myself.

"But my father is great. He did a really good job, given the circumstances."

"I wish I could say the same about my dad," says Andrea. "He's always been very distant. So when I was nine I asked Nick if I could live with him, and he said yes, thank God."

"Don't you guys have an older sister too? The one who just had a baby?"

Nick straightens his posture. "Yeah. She sort of went through a bad girl stage for a while. After our mom died she dated a lot of guys who played guitars, and she crashed on a lot of people's couches. She's settled down now, but she wouldn't have been a good bet for Andrea back then."

Andrea turns to Nick. "You were all I had."

His cheeks pinken. "It's not like you're any trouble." He nudges her, shoulder to shoulder. "Actually, she's the one keeping me in line."

I look from her face to his. The resemblance is uncanny. I bet teachers never had any trouble figuring out they were siblings, despite the age difference. Brown hair, brown eyes, tan skin, wide, warm smile. Completely un-extraordinary, except you can't stop looking at them.

"So what if I want to go on *The Holdout*? What would be your advice?" Andrea asks me this in an official, job interview sort of voice. How can a kid like her be so composed, so together, when I'm nearly twice her age and I haven't even figured myself out yet?"

"I'd say don't do it."

"But…" Andrea's face falls. Clearly that wasn't what she wanted to hear. "There's the chance to win all that money! A million dollars would pay for college, and then med school."

"Andrea plans to cure breast cancer," says Nick.

"There are other ways to pay tuition." I pop the calamari in my mouth and chew as I consider how to elaborate. "Look, being on the show just wasn't what I thought it would be. I'm sure you'd be great, but if I had it to do over, I'd stay home. It's not worth it."

Nick takes a gulp of his beer. "Has *Alright Magazine* been hounding you?"

I address him. "I've gotten some calls, mostly on my cell, and usually when it's turned off during jury duty. So that hasn't been too bad. But just knowing everyone is judging me, all the time…" I look back at Andrea. "It's not something I'd recommend."

Andrea nods seriously and I worry that I've ruined her impression of me.

"Hey!" I say, my voice up an octave from where it was before. "What do I know? You're young, and you have all sorts of adventures ahead of you. I'm sure you'll be great, no matter what you do."

Andrea's expression doesn't lighten. "That's a pretty broad assumption."

Despite myself I start laughing. "How old are you? Because I'm thinking there's no way you're only sixteen."

Nick starts laughing too. Finally, Andrea's grim face turns to a smile. "Shut up," she says to Nick.

"I didn't say anything!"

She pushes him, he pushes gently back, and the three of us go back to having a good time.

§

Later I walk them to their car. Andrea gets in the front seat, whips out her cell phone, and is oblivious to the rest of the world. Nick taps my arm.

"Thanks," he says. "I really appreciate it."

"It was fun," I reply.

Nick looks over his shoulder, sees that Andrea is still looking down at her phone, and then quickly goes in for a kiss on the lips. It's so sudden I don't have time to pull away, and it's over before it began. Still, I'm left with a tingly sensation, like how your skin feels when you jump into the swimming pool after sitting in the hot tub. I kind of like it even though I wouldn't have expected to.

I also wouldn't have expected such a bold move from a motherless real-estate agent who's been his younger sister's guardian since he was twenty-three. Hasn't he learned the consequences of taking risks? Maybe he was sick the day they covered that in motherless, over-responsible big brother school. But I can't imagine that Ted and Ian ever missed a day, or a lesson

He takes a step back from me. "See you Monday, Robin."

I open my mouth but words don't come, so I give him a meek little wave instead. He grins, gets in the car, and drives away. I walk slowly back to the restaurant, dragging my feet. Meeting Jessie is not high on my list of things that I want to do. I think it comes somewhere between balancing my checkbook and bleaching out my toilet bowl.

I pull open the heavy door and re-enter. After being outside in the cold evening, the restaurant air feels hot and sticky. I head back to the bar, pushing up the sleeves of my sweater as I go. When I get there I find Jack leaning against the edge, with a beer in one hand. His other hand is stroking Jessie's shoulder. She sits on the stool next to him. There must have only been one stool available, so he gave it to her.

Jack sees me and waves. "Hey!" He nudges Jessie and she turns around. Her hair is bobbed now, shorter than it was when I saw her here months ago at my going-away party. She smiles in a reserved, unhappy sort of way and my stomach flips and sinks. This is going to be even worse than I thought.

"Hi!" I say, holding out my hand. "You must be Jessie. It's so nice to meet you. I'm Jack's cousin Robin."

She gives me a limp-wristed shake. "I know who you are. I watched the episode of *The Holdout* where Jack visited you. Of course, I watched it alone, because Jack was sleeping on your couch at the time."

Jack squeezes her shoulder as if what she said was endearing. My hand drops to my side and I try to stay upbeat. "But you're planning to move in together now, right? That's so exciting. Congratulations!"

Jessie shrugs. "I suppose. It's not as exciting as being engaged, but I have to take what I can get."

Jack chuckles. I would too, except I don't find anything funny. "How was your dinner with the guy from jury duty?" he asks me.

"Good," I say. "His sister is so cute. She's like how I wish I had been at her age."

Jack turns to Jessie. "Robin is on jury duty right now. She's been going down to the courthouse for nearly two weeks to sit and listen to a case about yachts."

"How awful," says Jessie. "It's too bad you couldn't get out of it."

"Actually, I don't mind. It's been sort of interesting. I like learning about how federal cases work, and…"

My voice trails off as I realize she isn't listening to a word I'm saying. She's looking around the room, waving at a friend, and then she grabs Jack's arm. "There's Michelle," she says to him. "I have to go say hi."

Without as much as a goodbye she gets up and goes after Michelle. Jack just stands there, watching her walk away. Then he turns back to me. "I think she needs to talk to her about something important," he says apologetically.

"Sure." I take out my cell phone and look at the time. "Hey, I should get going anyway. It's late and I have to be up early tomorrow. I promised I'd go to the gym with Isobel."

Before Jack can respond, a person from the bar comes up to us. "Aren't you Robin, from *The Holdout*?" he slurs. He's standing a little too close.

I step back. "Guilty," I say. "Thanks for watching the show, but I was just on my way out."

He scratches above his ear and pulls down his shirt. "Yeah," he says, continuing his train of thought rather than responding to what I just said. "You're the snotty one. You're mad because that guy likes the hot girl better." He leans in and I can smell the beer and nachos on his breath. "On behalf of all the men in America, I'm going to tell you something. Bitches like you need to get the hell over it."

I'm sure I would be angry. But I don't have the chance, because in the space of a second Jack has the guy by the collar of his shirt.

"That's my cousin you're talking to," he says, his face growing red with anger and exertion. Around us conversation dies down as people rubberneck towards this sudden conflict. "And this is my restaurant you're standing in. So I'm going to tell you something. You need to leave. Now."

Jack releases him, and the guy stumbles backwards a little. One of his friends sees what's going on and comes over. "Let's go," he says to his friend. He speaks to Jack. "We don't want any trouble."

"Good," says Jack. "Leave right now and they're won't be any."

The two of them make their exit and I look at my cousin with new respect. "I didn't know you were a badass."

Jessie has seen the drama from across the room and she scurries over, elbowing past people to get to Jack. "What's going on?" she demands. She sounds angry, like someone took the last piece of pizza while she was in the bathroom.

"You just missed seeing your boyfriend get tough."

She broadcasts her doubt as she looks to Jack. "Really?"

Jack plays it off, puffing on his knuckle and rubbing it against his shirt. Then he attempts a ghetto-rap voice. "That was just Jack Bricker every day."

I laugh but Jessie doesn't. "Sweetheart," she says, "You need to be more careful. What if that guy had tried to beat you up?" She's talking to him with a gently scolding, preschool teacher voice. "Do you even know how to fight?"

I rush to save Jack as he just saved me. "He could have totally taken that guy, Jessie. Seriously, he was awesome."

Jack smiles his thanks, and I leave as quickly as I can. Once I'm outside I breathe a sigh of relief. Now I can go home, go to bed, and sleep in nice and late. Isobel and I aren't going to the gym until noon.

§

On Monday morning I wake up eager for the day. I dress myself in one of my newest creations from last week, a top I like too much to sell on eBay. It's a layered tunic made from both black and gray jersey, with a silky pink ribbon woven throughout. I put it on over tight black pants and my high black boots, but I don't wear my fake glasses and I let my hair hang loose around my shoulders. People have recognized me from the show and the world didn't stop, so maybe it's time to own who, and what I am.

I enter the courthouse with a spring in my step, and I'm debating with myself about what I'll say to Nick when I see him. Do I acknowledge the kiss, or do I play it cool? I still haven't decided when I approach the desk to check in, but instead of wishing me good morning, Madison, the jury clerk, tells me to go home.

"Did they settle?" I ask, alarmed.

Madison shakes her perfectly coiffed head. "I can't say. But unless you hear otherwise, show up here at the same time tomorrow."

When I'm back down in the lobby I see Nick walking towards the elevators. For a moment I consider pretending like I don't see him, but I kind of want to see him, sort of how I want a big snowstorm on Christmas or ghosts on Halloween. I walk purposefully towards him, with a smile fixed on my face.

"Hi!" I say.

He doesn't smile back. "Hi," he says, without expression, like I could be anyone on the jury.

"We've been told to go home," I tell him. "I think they might be settling."

"Oh." He looks at his watch. "Wow. I guess I can go into the office today."

Really? He has a chance for a day off, and going into the office is the first thing on his mind. Well, as long as he's being responsible... "You should probably check in," I tell him, "just so Madison knows you were here."

He nods and walks away. Huh. I don't know what I was hoping for, but it wasn't that. Why wouldn't a guy who kissed me two nights ago smile when he sees me today? Maybe he's having second thoughts.

Maybe my lips were unappealing. Maybe the girl who gave him that watch called him on Sunday and said they should get back together.

I button up my coat in anticipation of protecting against the cold, even though I parked in the underground garage. Now I'm doubting this top I wore. Maybe it's too much.

On my way down to the car I contemplate what I'm going to do with my day. I could start applying for jobs. Or, I could go online and scour university catalogs to find appealing graduate programs. Whatever. The one thing I won't do is worry about Nick. After the year I've had, I have no more room in my life for mixed messages and insincerity. Maybe it's a good thing if the trial is settling. It can just be done, and I won't have to deal with any of this anymore.

Yet, if they settle, that means I spent two weeks listening to and thinking about this case, and at the end, I don't get my say.

I go home, feeling as conflicted as a platypus: part-duck, part-otter, and as mixed up as a semi-mammal can be. Do I want to be land-based and quacking, or do I want to be sleek, dark, and swimming away from conflict? I'm pretty sure I'm still warm-blooded, but there have been some moments in the last few months when my blood ran cold. So, like the clothes I design, I'm just a motley conglomeration of parts that don't fit together, and even a little decision like whether I want to still be on jury duty has left me exhausted.

It doesn't matter though, because on Tuesday it turns out that the trial is still on, and I get out of the elevator and onto the fourteenth floor. I walk towards the jury room with my head down and I nearly run into Silas Smythe. In the process my foot trips over his, and I stumble. He puts a hand on my shoulder to steady us both.

"Whoa," he says. "Are you okay?"

I straighten myself up and look around. Four is approaching and she saw my interaction with Silas. Her hair is back and her forehead is crowded with strict, distinct lines. I can see them from here, and they all shout disapproval. I bet she's a hallway terror at the middle school where she works. My pulse starts to sprint.

I make eye contact with Silas and point to the Juror badge pinned to my coat. Then I shake my head no. Silas gives me a guileless smile and saunters off.

"What was that about?" Four demands. "You know that you're not supposed to be talking to him, right?"

I bite the inside of my mouth to temper my response. "I tripped, and he steadied me. I didn't say anything."

Four purses her lips. "But he talked to you. I wonder if we should report it. Do you think they'd declare a mistrial?"

Four starts walking, her strides wide with purpose. I follow. "A mistrial? After two weeks and what must be millions of dollars from both sides? All he did was save me from tripping and it's not going to influence me. That would be ridiculous."

Four pauses and purses her lips. "Justice is never ridiculous."

We reach the door to the jury room. Four has her prox card handy, so she beeps us in. I open the door and hold it for her. And I'm laughing. "I really wish you were right about that."

Most of the other jurors have arrived already. Immediately my head turns towards Nick's spot at the table. He's reading his book and he doesn't look up. Not even a nod hello. I know he heard us come in.

So that's how it's going to be.

Four starts telling the room why she's so late. Luckily she doesn't mention reporting me and Silas; her mind has already moved onto something else. "I had to go in and make more sub plans," she says. "And I had to leave the grading key for the test on twentieth century presidents. Can you believe that most of them don't know who FDR was?"

Most of us shake our heads ruefully, except Twelve, who can't be long out of school herself. Her face goes blank, so I'm guessing she managed to graduate without learning her twentieth century presidents. It's too bad she didn't have Four as her teacher.

In a couple of minutes we're summoned, and our entrance routine has become old hat. After lining up in our customary order we wait to hear "All rise for the jury," and then we walk in, pausing in front of our chairs until the judge tells us to be seated. The whole time Nick avoids my eyes. Now that he's sitting behind me I won't know if he's looking at me or not, but I think I can feel him glance at the back of my neck.

The trial resumes, and I sit there, wondering how much longer it can go on. Is there really anything left to say about yachts?

Then after around an hour or so, the ex-frat-boy defense lawyer concludes the cross examination of his expert witness, and I'm not sure I hear him right but I think he says, "Thank you your honor. The defense rests."

But I did hear him right, and after that everything happens really fast. Closing arguments are made, and the judge gives us instructions about how to proceed with deliberations. Then we're sequestered into our jury room. They bring us lunch because we're not allowed to go out, and they make us put our cell phones in a basket, which will stay with the security guard who is stationed outside the door.

The first thing we have to do is elect a foreman. Nine points to One, the guy who is always wearing a suit. "Heck," Nine says. "You're already sitting in the right spot, and you look the part. Why don't you do it?"

"That sounds good to me," I say. And it does, because as long as Four isn't made foreman, I'm happy.

One blinks from behind his large, square-rimmed glasses. "I can be foreman if that's what everyone would like.

People nod and voice their assent. Four sounds particularly enthusiastic, but her smile is vacant, like she's an actress who just heard someone else's name announced as winner at the Academy Awards. I know she had her sights set on being foreman from day one. She probably started rehearsing her foreman acceptance speech on the morning her jury summons arrived in the mail.

"Well," One says. "Why don't we start by giving everyone the chance to say what they think at this point? Let's start with juror number twelve and go backwards."

Twelve's mouth drops open and her eyes widen in shock. "You want *me* to go first?"

Six turns toward her. "If you don't want to go first, Dear, that's okay. We can come back to you." She looks over at One. "That's okay, isn't it?"

One nods in a nearly imperceptible way, and then he looks directly at Eleven. The one smoker in the group, Eleven is fidgeting and tapping his hands together. He sighs. "Okay, well I'm mixed. I think the Smythes sort of got screwed with these boats that fell apart too easily, but I also think they didn't store them right."

Next it's Ten/Nick's turn. All heads turn to him. He brings the tips of his fingers together and stares at them like he's never seen them do that before. "This case seems pretty one-sided to me. If you sell a bad product then you should pay. Potenza's boats didn't live up to their promise. I don't care how they were stored. Boats that expensive shouldn't just fall apart and sink."

I take in a deep breath through my nose and suck the insides of my cheeks. Then I bite my lip and curl up my toes inside my ancient black boots. I have to wait my turn.

Nine agrees with Ten. So does Eight. She owns her own boutique in a wealthy section of town, so she knows about consumer issues. Seven, who hardly ever says anything, speaks so softly that I have to strain to hear.

"Well," she says, "I'm not sure how I feel. It seems like a two-sided issue to me."

I nod and relax my toes a little. This I can work with.

Six goes next. She lays her palms down, flat on the table, and inhales like she's about to do yoga. "I also feel sort of mixed. I don't think the boats were built correctly, but it also seems to me that there is something fishy about the Smythes. I just don't trust them, but I also don't trust Potenza. At one point I wrote in my notes, 'greed, greed, greed.' That's what this is all about."

There are murmurs of agreement, and I grip the side of the table. *Play it cool, Robin,* I say to myself. *The pushy people never make it to the end. Don't get voted out for being too opinionated.*

Five, a twenty-something who hasn't spoken more than a few words a day for the entire two weeks, smiles when everyone looks at him. "Well, I agree that both parties are pretty greedy. That's capitalism for you." He smiles again to punctuate his statement.

He sits for two weeks listening to a trial, and that's all he has to say? He'd do great on *The Holdout*. His only quality that doesn't fly under the radar is his red hair. Oh well. Now it's Four's turn, and I'd bet cash money that she has a lot to say.

She sits up straight, giving us a textbook example of perfect posture. "Well, I think we need to look at all the evidence. It strikes me as odd that the Smythes had expert witnesses that examined all the boats, but Potenza's experts only examined one warehouse full. And I also don't understand why we didn't meet yesterday. If they were close to settling, then that says to me that one or both sides were nervous. So I think there is a lot to consider, and we need to go through all the information, step by step."

I squeeze my hands together. Finally I get to speak. *Keep it simple,* I tell myself. *Don't be too aggressive.* One looks at me, signaling that it's my turn. Then all eyes are on me, even Nick's. I pretend it isn't unnerving.

"Okay," I say, making a conscious effort to keep my voice steady. "I think Potenza is getting a bad rap. The judge said that in civil cases the burden of proof is on the plaintiff's side. With all the doubts about how the boats were stored and the damage that was done to them, I just don't see absolute proof that these boats were irregular or damaged upon receipt. For that reason, I completely disagree with most of you." I look directly at Nick, and he raises his eyebrows at me. A battle line is drawn in the sand.

Two laughs her braying laugh, which could be a response to the obvious tension between Nick and me. "I guess I'm still sort of unsure," she says. "I don't really understand how anyone can be completely on one side or the other. Unfortunately, I think it's going to take a while to figure it all out."

Great. If my mental tally is correct, so far we have three people who are on the Smythe's side, four people who think it's "mixed," two people who have no opinion at all, and me. That's ten people, and there's one left to go… who am I missing? I look to my side. Of course. I forgot about Four. But I'm not really sure what she thinks, because in all her opinions, she didn't really say anything.

One has heard everyone now (except for Twelve, but I don't

think she'll care if we just skip her) and he scribbles on the notepad in front of him. His tie is still secure at his throat, and he does look very official, like he's the head of our family and we're all meeting about grandpa's will.

He clears his throat. "Well, I believe that the Smythes did not treat these boats well, and that they are in the wrong and should have to pay."

One, who avoided everyone's eyes while he was speaking, now looks across the table at me. "So I agree with you," he says. "Even if nobody else does."

Bam! Somehow, I just managed to get on an alliance with the foreman of the jury.

Chapter 12

That evening I plan to watch *The Holdout* at Isobel's apartment. The only way to avoid watching again with Dad or Ian is to claim a prior commitment.

"I promised Isobel," I tell Dad on the phone. "She's having people over and it's going to be a get-together with a few friends."

"That's okay," my Dad says. "Because we'll be there for the live filming of the reunion show this weekend. That's what I'm really excited to see!"

Dad is referring to the season finale, where all the cast members gather once again, this time with styled hair and makeup, in a theater in New York. Joe Pine will read off the final vote and the winner will at long last be revealed. Friends and family of the cast members are invited, even flown out for free, so I put my dad, Ian, and Ted on the list. In retrospect I should have included Jack, since he was the one to visit me on the island, but I had to give them names before the filming even began.

Later, sitting in her apartment, it's like Isobel can read my thoughts. "Hey," she says. "How's your cousin?"

"Okay. But he's back with his girlfriend and I don't like her."

Isobel wipes at her runny nose. "Of course he's back with her. Guys always go back to the crazy ones. Too bad. He'd actually be kind of cute if he wasn't such a mess."

I raise an eyebrow at her. The last thing she needs is another guy with commitment issues, and nobody knows this better than her.

She changes the subject. "The reunion show is next week, right?

Is your family all going to be there, even Ted?" Isobel asks me this as we sit on her couch. She's in flannel pajamas decorated with pink and white cupcakes, and she has a pastel purple fleece blanket wrapped around her arms and chest. She reaches a hand out from under the blanket to blow her stuffy nose, and I see that even her Kleenex fits the girly, Easter-egg color theme she has going on.

"I think so. Unless he gets too busy with work." We have the television on, but it's on mute, and I watch a commercial for Papa John's Pizza with one eye. It's good that I ate already and that Isobel has no appetite, because once tonight's immunity challenge is shown, neither of us will want to look at food.

Isobel simultaneously coughs and huffs in indignation. "How can Ted be too busy with work? It will be the weekend. Worse case, he comes out Sunday morning and goes back Sunday night, which is what you'll have to do if you're still on jury duty."

"I'll be done with it by then." I stretch one of my socked feet out and place it on her coffee table. "We started deliberations today."

Isobel coughs again and sniffs a thick, wet sniff. "Good. So pretty soon you'll actually be able to talk about your life again." She gestures towards the TV. "And in a couple of hours, you'll be able to tell me everything about *The Holdout*. Sorry I couldn't have people over to watch tonight."

I shake my head. "Don't worry about it. This is better." Then I remember myself. I put my hand atop her flannel-covered knee. "But I'm sorry you're sick."

"Yeah, me too. Believe me, this is one cold you don't want to get. It's nasty."

The commercials end, Isobel un-mutes the television, and the opening credits commence. Even though I know what's going to happen, my stomach is full of pins and needles.

Tonight the credits are a little different. Joe Pine's voice comes on, and it is imposed over a bunch of shots from throughout the season. He gives a run-down of the major events, and the order in which people got voted out.

"Now," Joe says, "Only four remain. Klemi, the vixen." There's a shot of Klemi sunbathing on the beach, then she's arguing with Joel, and then she's kissing Grant up on the rocks. "Henry, the genius." They show Henry starting a fire by using the lenses of his glasses, they show him winning the immunity challenge that was based on knowledge, and finally they show him finding the hidden immunity idol. "Grant, the golden boy." Several clips are shown in quick succession of Grant dominating in the physical challenges, whether he's running, lifting, balancing, or throwing. Then they show him kissing Klemi, and after that he's kissing me. "And Robin, the enigma." But instead of showing a montage of my more memorable moments, they only show one. It's when I was on the beach with Grant. "I know what it's like to be lonely," I told him. They use an extreme close-up of my sandy face, and it looks like I'm about to cry.

Seriously? Did they have to make me seem like such a pathetic victim?

Isobel can read my resentment. "They were just trying to make you out as the likeable one."

"I won challenges!" I say. "And I played a very strong social game, despite falling for Grant! Why couldn't they show that?"

Isobel shrugs her shoulder as Joe Pine's voice continues its broadcast. The screen is divided into four, and the faces of Grant, Klemi, Henry, and me each command our own quadrant, sort of like a tribal Brady Bunch. "Tonight, four remain, but only three will survive for the final Island Assembly, where a jury of their peers will vote to decide… Who will endure? Who will persist? Who will become…the holdout!"

"Only we don't find out how the vote goes until this weekend," I say.

"I know!" Isobel says with a sniff.

After the extended credits are over Henry, Grant, Klemi and I are shown walking back from Island Assembly. Then comes my confrontation with Grant, the one where I threatened to destroy him, and he laughed and called me "Robbie."

"What a dick." Isobel's nasal voice condemns him and I surprise myself by laughing.

Next comes a conversation between Henry and me. "Why didn't

you vote him out?" Henry stood over me, his weight evenly distributed on both his feet, spine ramrod straight and chest out, as aggressive as he'd ever been. It was the morning after Island Assembly, and he and I were alone at camp. I didn't know where Grant and Klemi had gone, and I didn't care.

I was crouched down, scraping the soggy remains of rice from the bottom of our one cooking pot, and I kept my focus on the white mush. "I had to hear it from him," I murmured. "It may sound stupid, but I couldn't wait a week to talk to him about this. I had to know that he was cheating on me, and manipulating me, and using me. I had to know now."

Henry pushed his large glasses up on his nose and grimaced. "Well, I hope it was worth it. Because now he's going to win. Last night was our one chance to get him out. Even if he doesn't get individual immunity today, we still won't be able to swing more than a tie at tonight's Island Assembly."

I bit my lip in thought. "Why not?" I pushed the pot away, stood up, and wiped my hands on my thighs, which were clad in my grubby grey leggings. "Henry, there are three of us and only one of him. There's still a way around this."

A line of confusion appeared above Henry's glasses and in between his eyebrows.

I placed a clammy hand on his shoulder. "You could convince Klemi to vote for Grant." Henry shook his head no, but I grabbed his arm in urgency. "No, listen. Klemi is shrewd. She knows that Grant can win. Appeal to her sensible side. Tell her she has a better chance to win against you and me than she has with Grant."

Henry pinched up his face. His chin, which was covered in wispy auburn whiskers, set in tension. "But she's so annoying. Why can't you do it?"

I reached back and tugged on my messy ponytail. "Because she won't trust me. Klemi will think I'm just bitter because Grant chose her over me."

"Unless…." Henry's mouth hung open a little as he focused his thoughts. He pointed at the air, as if his finger was a pencil that could cross and dot his brilliance. "What if, she doesn't think that? What if Klemi thinks that Grant chose you?"

I took two steps away from Henry and plopped down in the damp, dirty sand. I knew what he was suggesting, but I didn't know if I could pull it off.

Henry sat down next to me. "Robin, this is far from over. Grant never chose Klemi over you. He just knows that you have standards and Klemi doesn't. But what if you make Grant think that you're still into him? Then we can convince Klemi that he actually likes *you* better, AND we can get her to vote him out."

I inhaled, filling my entire chest cavity with oxygen and blowing it softly out. "I don't think I can do that."

"You have to," said Henry. "Because if you don't an asshole is going to win."

I turned and looked him. Nice as he was, Henry was surely the sort of guy who spent his teenage Saturday nights in his room with a flashlight and a comic book. I bet he fantasized about large busted gals who avenged evil while wearing leather and heels, but when it came to real women in real life, his confidence waned.

But he's not in high school anymore, so I should treat him like the man he's become.

"Robin, have you thought about what you could do with a million dollars?"

I sighed. "Of course I have. I could go back to school, this time for a useful degree. I could help my dad with his retirement. There are all sorts of reasons why I want this money."

"Yeah, me too." Henry's bird-like nose had a tiny bit of sand on it and I reached to brush it away. He blinked in surprise at such a familiar gesture. "I could pay off my student loans, and I could start my business."

"In what?"

He raised his voice a little in excitement. "I want to develop a protective shield against radioactivity and environmental pollution, mostly to benefit third world countries."

"Oh." I understood about as well as if he'd been speaking in gibberish, but he had me at "protective shield." Grant would probably use the money to build his own child-labor plutonium plant.

At that moment Grant and Klemi walked back into camp. Klemi was holding a piece of parchment and she was waving it around.

"Guess what!" She sing-songed in her Puerto Rican accent. "We got tree-mail." She unrolled the parchment and started to read, glowing because all the cameras were on her.

"Congratulations final four,
But as for challenges
There is still one more.
Don't worry about strength
Don't worry about skill
The only thing you now need
Is the ability to kill."

Klemi lowered the parchment and addressed us. "What do you think that means? Will it be a hunting challenge?"

"Hunting takes skill," said Henry. "Usually the last immunity challenge has to do with endurance."

"But what do they mean, 'the ability to kill'?" Klemi put her tiny hands on her golden-brown hips, which were bare save for the string of her bikini.

Henry wove his fingers together and pulled them apart, ala Doctor Evil. "We have to balance our body weight on a platform that will slowly crush the skull of a capuchin monkey." His eyes twinkled. "The last person standing will kill the monkey and win immunity."

Klemi missed the irony and her jaw dropped. "That's terrible!" she gasped.

I coughed and stood up. "I have something to say to everyone."

Grant, who had entered the shelter and was about to lie down, propped himself up on his arms. Henry and Klemi turned their heads in my direction.

Now was the moment that my college acting classes could finally come to good use. I closed my eyes and remembered my professor's instruction. "Feel the moment, Robin. Observe your surroundings to forget yourself, and only then will you truly be alive and in character."

I thought it was a bunch of pretentious BS at the time, but what the heck? Maybe my old professor would be watching and she'd be sorry she didn't cast me in more roles.

"I want everyone to know how bad I feel about last night." I looked up towards the sky, squeezed my eyes shut, and fought against tears to will them to come. Then I lowered my head and walked over towards Grant. "But I especially want you to know, Grant, that I'm sorry. I'm sorry this game got between us, I'm sorry for accusing you of lying, and I'm sorry for ever trying to hurt you."

Moments before, Grant must have been hoping for a nap, because he looked half-asleep now. He blinked in surprise as he searched for something to say. But I didn't give him time to respond. Confident that Henry, Klemi, and the rest of the world could see, I moved in and kissed Grant on the lips. I placed my palm on the back of his neck, separated his lips with my own, sucked, and twirled my tongue to the best of my abilities. And I was good; I know this because he started kissing me back.

So right before I forgot myself and let myself enjoy it, I pulled away. I addressed Klemi and Henry. "Maybe I'm not cut out for this game, but I can't just turn off my emotions. I have no idea how I'll vote tonight, so don't ask me. I'm done with strategy." Then I pivoted on the pads of my feet, back towards Grant. "But I don't know how to be done with you."

I sniffed, wiped away my "tears," and concentrated on my breathing. My acting professor would have been so proud, because I was working against the emotion instead of towards it. "I can't do this anymore," I said in a voice choked with anguish. "So if you all don't mind, I need to be alone." I looked at Grant. "I can't talk to you until after the insanity of this game is over."

And I stumbled off, hoping Henry realized that I just gave the performance of a lifetime.

The show cuts to a commercial. I look over at Isobel, ready to receive high praise for my performance. Isobel and I had the same acting professor in college, so I'm hoping for some deep appreciation of my work, but all I get is the image of her head against her couch cushion, mouth open and gently snoring. Poor thing.

My phone vibrates. It's a text from Ian.

"Wow, Robbie, wow. Does he buy it?"

I text back. "You know I can't tell you."

He replies instantly. 'Oh come on. You won't get in trouble."

He's probably right, but it's more fun to torment him. "Just watch the show, Loser."

He texts back. "I'm going to call you 'Robin the Enigma' from now on."

The show returns from commercial with an establishing shot of a clearing. There's a table with four covered plates spaced evenly apart from each other. It's the final immunity challenge.

"Welcome, castaways!" The look on Joe Pine's face was gleeful, malicious almost, and he was nearly bouncing on the tips of his toes.

"This can't be good," Henry mumbled under his breath.

"Castaways, please take your place behind each of these four plates."

We followed his instructions. I stood between Henry and Klemi, with Grant on the end.

Joe's smile gleamed with anticipation. "Today, for your final immunity challenge, you will be experiencing some of the finer delicacies of this region. There will be three rounds, three delicacies. And in each case, the delicacies are still alive."

So that's what they meant by the ability to kill. We'll be killing our food as we eat it. Okay, I thought. With a million dollars at stake, I could eat some disgusting, living, thing. It couldn't be that different from eating Pop Rocks and I used to do that for free.

Joe continued to explain. "Now, because they're unfamiliar, you may have trouble enjoying these dishes as much as the natives do. So the last person to swallow down their food for each round will be out. And the first person to finish the final round will win immunity, and a guaranteed chance to sit before the jury and argue why they deserve the million dollars and the title of the holdout. Worth playing for?"

We all nodded. As if there was a chance any of us would say no.

"You can uncover your first dish."

I lifted the lid. Underneath was a rolling, squirmy bug with a ton of tiny little legs. It was brown and white, and it crept and crawled around the plate. And I was going to eat it.

I gulped down my fear and observed my competitors. Klemi looked unimpressed, like she was trying to stifle a yawn. But she always looked like that. Past her Grant's head was down, and his mop of brown curls hid his face. What wouldn't I have given to know what was running through his mind right about then? That information would have almost been worth a million dollars. Almost, but not quite.

Next to me, Henry was nothing but transparent. There were already beads of sweat on his forehead, and underneath his sunburn his skin was slightly green.

I caught his eye. "Stay strong," I whispered. "One of us has to win this."

He made an affirming fist in response but I wasn't convinced.

"You okay, Henry?" Joe asked.

"I'm excited, actually." Henry smiled through his apprehension. "At Princeton we used to eat our lab experiments for fun, so this is nothing to me."

Joe laughed and spoke to all four of us. "Well, your first dish is beetle larvae. Remember you must get all of it down. If any portion of it is spit-out, then you are eliminated. Show me your clean tongue when you've finished. With a million dollars on the line, you may begin."

I popped the larvae into my mouth. I could feel it crawling around, so I gritted my teeth and forced myself to chew. My mouth and throat were competing to see who could gag faster, but I kept chomping down until it was soft enough to swallow. Then, just when I thought I could show Joe my tongue, my stomach revolted and some of it came back up. So I had to fight my gagging response once more, only this time I wasn't swallowing live beetle larvae, I was swallowing dead, purified beetle larvae with a side of bile mixed in. And believe me, it tasted nothing like Pop Rocks.

But I got it down and showed Joe my tongue. "Robin is in!" Joe shouted. And in the next moment, Klemi stuck her tongue out as well. "Klemi's in! This is now between Henry and Grant!"

I turned and watched Henry with my fists clenched. His chest was convulsing like a swan's neck, and if I thought he looked green before, now he resembled Shrek's skinny, nerdy cousin. But through pure determination he managed to swallow the last of it, and he stuck out his tongue for Joe to see.

"Henry is in! That means Grant is out. Grant, I'm sorry, but have a seat."

Grant spit out the last of his beetle larvae, shrugged his shoulders, and sat on the bench opposite of us. "I've always been a picky eater," he said, grinning as if he just betrayed yet another charming tendency. Before I realized what I was doing, I responded to his boyish magnetism, and smiled at him. He smiled back.

I told myself that was okay. We're both just acting.

Our next dish was brought out and Henry, Klemi, and I each uncovered it.

"Shipworms," stated Joe. "They're a member of the clam family."

Just looking at it made me want to puke. A super long, super wide, super-alive gray noodle was slithering around my plate, leaving shiny slime in its wake. I've always been disgusted by slugs, and this thing was like five slugs on steroids.

Joe gave us the go-ahead. I picked up the shipworm between my fingers, and brought it to my mouth. My brain was telling my lips to part, but my teeth rebelled by staying clamped shut, which caused my jaw to tighten and tremble.

Open your mouth! I yelled silently to myself. *You think a seagull pooping on your head is a funny story? Being unable to stomach a shipworm is something you'll never live down!*

The shipworm was twitching in my hand, angling itself towards and away from my face. Finally I closed my eyes and released my jaw. I shoved the shipworm in all at once, and it tasted like a mold, grapes, and sour cottage cheese. Only it was slithering around my mouth. I tried to just swallow it down without chewing, but that only made me gag, and then I was puking up everything, including the beetle larvae from the last round.

I knew it was over. I kept my face down, hiding my burning tears of frustration. I heard Joe yell, "Klemi's in! Henry's in! Robin, you're out. Have a seat on the bench."

I wiped my eyes, rinsed my mouth with the water they had mercifully supplied, and sat down on the bench next to Grant. I kept a respectable distance between the two of us, but Grant scooted an inch closer to me. It was just enough for him to reach his sneaker out to touch my own. When our sneakers met so did our eyes, and his face was a warm invitation to respond.

As if.

I mean, yes. Our kiss from an hour ago was sizzling in my memory and I could feel the corners of my mouth turn up. I could also feel my pulse quicken and my skin temperature rise, but not by much. But it was all only because I'm such a good actress. And I'm sure Grant was acting too; he doesn't know how to do anything else.

The final plates were placed down in front of Klemi and Henry, and the lids were raised. This time an egg was revealed. From where I was sitting I could see feathers and the beginning of a beak sticking out. The rest of it was marbled brown and white, almost pretty if it was something else.

"Your final dish is duck embryos." Joe beamed, knowing he didn't have to eat it himself. All he had to do was stand there like a God in a blue safari shirt and commentate.

"You can do it, Henry!" I shouted. I looked at Grant, daring him with my eyes to offer Klemi similar encouragement, but he said nothing.

Henry danced in place, punching the air like Rocky. "I got this!" he shouted.

Joe laughed. "I'm impressed with your confidence. You both may begin."

Klemi calmly placed the egg in her mouth. She may as well have been chewing gum. She was slow and steady, bored even, but she never wavered. Maybe this challenge was made for her. I bet Klemi has been in a lot of situations where she had to swallow foreign, living substances.

Henry, on the other hand, ate with the same sort of frenzied resolve that he most likely used while presenting his master's thesis on wormholes in 2 + 1 dimensions. He'd swallow, start to stick out his tongue, then he'd heave forward, clamp his mouth shut, and start again.

This all took place in the space of two to three seconds. I was sure that Klemi was going to win, when all of a sudden she yelled out, "Eww! I bit down on its beak." She heaved as she said this, and whitish, brownish, feathered mush came spilling out of her mouth like lava from a volcano. Meanwhile, Henry made his final, brave swallow and stuck out his tongue.

"And Henry wins immunity!" Joe yelled. I jumped up, leaped over to Henry, and gave him a double high five. I knew I was probably over-doing it with my enthusiasm, especially after my declaration that I was done with strategy and playing the game. But I couldn't help myself.

Joe placed the immunity necklace around Henry's narrow neck. "Henry, you're safe tonight at Island Assembly. As for the rest of you, I have nothing for you. I'll see you tonight."

Now, on the edited television version, the tribal music begins and we all start moving in slow motion. The camera zooms in on Henry, glowing in triumph, Klemi pouting and wiping her mouth, and Grant's face, fallen, as he watches me link arms with Henry and walk away. It's probably just sweat, but it almost looks like a tear is falling from Grant's eye.

I had no idea that happened. But it doesn't change anything now.

The show cuts to commercial. Right on cue, my phone vibrates with another text from Ian.

"Which is more disgusting, a shipworm in your mouth or seagull poop in your hair?"

"I'm now ignoring you for the rest of the show," I text back.

"LOL, Robbie. Have a sense of humor."

I push the phone away. If any living witness to my seagull poop incident doesn't send me a mocking text for puking up a shipworm, it's because they're not watching the show tonight. So on second thought, I sit up, grab my phone, and turn it off.

When the show comes back from commercial, they show a series of interactions and testimonials.

Klemi was wading waist-deep in the ocean. Henry, with his arms protectively shielding his bare, pink chest, approached her.

"Have you thought about who you're voting for?" he asked.

"Robin," she said, without even looking in his direction. Then she must have stepped on something sharp. "Ay!" she said, and she leaned over to pick it off her foot. In the process she revealed some major cleavage, and Henry's jaw dropped, his eyes widening as he stared. When she stood up straight, his head snapped back.

"Umm…" he stuttered. "You should vote for Grant. Robin won't tell us who she's voting for and there's no way to know if Grant is lying. Either of them could be voting for you."

Klemi sucked on her bottom lip as she thought. "Why do you care?"

"I want Grant out. He'd win against any of us. But if we vote him out tonight, it's anyone's game."

Klemi nodded and turned away. "I'll think about it." She waved her hand at him dismissively and Henry took his cue and walked off.

Then there's a testimonial by Grant. He was leaning against a boulder, wistfully looking off into the distance. "I have no idea what Robin was pulling this morning with that kiss. She's probably trying to play me. But nothing that she says or does is going to change how I feel or how I vote. If she still wants to talk to me after the game is over…" he shook his head and sighed. "This game is screwed up. I never thought Henry would win the final immunity. Now I have to choose between Robin and Klemi." He shrugged. "Oh well. She's just one girl. There are more people like her in the world. And I'm here to win a million dollars, not to fall in love."

Cut to Grant and Klemi walking along the shore, holding hands. "Tell me the truth," she said. "Are you using me to win this game?"

"Yes," said Grant. There were no lines of conflict or tension on his face; apparently telling Klemi the truth came easy for him.

Klemi stopped, released his hand, and gave him the evil eye.

"What?" he demanded. "You're doing it too. I like you, okay?

And I hope you like me. But we're both using each other. I thought you understood that."

Klemi crossed her arms across her chest, but Grant reached out and clasped her waist, pulling her towards him. "Come on," he said. "We're having fun. And…" he kissed her lightly on the lips, "…one of us is going to win a million dollars."

Klemi relented with a smile and kissed him back.

Fade to Robin the enigma, facing the camera for a testimonial. My hair was pulled back as neatly as could be, and I had washed up in the ocean earlier that day. Even my hoodie was cleaner than normal, and I almost looked like a Noxzema commercial. I was holding my torch, ready to go to the final Island Assembly.

"I've had a lot of time to sit and think today. And this is what occurred to me: you can steal love and you can steal justice, but neither will be worth anything if they're not given to you willingly." I raised my eyebrows and smirked. "Ironically, learning this lesson has only made me more likely to try and steal both." Cut to a long shot of our foursome setting out, shadows with torches, as the sun sets behind us. My testimonial continues, only as a voice-over.

"This game has changed me in ways I didn't expect. I thought I was coming here for a fun adventure and a chance to win a million dollars. But being on *The Holdout* has finally taught me how to fight. Maybe I'm getting voted out tonight and it will be my turn to go. But I'm not going down without a struggle."

Such brave words. Too bad I didn't live by them sooner. I glance over at my lifeless phone. Who is texting me now, ridiculing my bravado? What tweets will be sent and how much fury will they contain? Are people going to accuse me of being a whore for trying to convince Grant I was still into him, or will they indict me for being an idiot and not seeing through him sooner? Eventually I'll turn my phone back on and find out.

On TV we walk into the penultimate Island Assembly.

"Welcome, castaways," said Joe Pine.

We sat on our bench and the jury entered. The fire burned with enthusiasm in its pit, making me feel like my skin could blister just from being nearby. Joe perched on his stool like the Thinker statue and commenced with the necessary dialogue. I could only focus with half my attention span. Between my ears there was ringing and I said little to nothing as Joe interviewed us. Only Henry was happy to answer Joe's questions.

"Henry, any idea who will be going home tonight?"

"Well, it's obviously going to be Robin, Klemi, or Grant. I could say any of them and I'd have a 33% chance of being right."

"That's it? You can't do better than a one in three projection?"

Henry blinked several times, keeping the rest of his face still. "I could," he said finally, "but I'd hate to ruin the surprise."

Joe cocked his head and smiled with his lips pressed together. "Okay, well I for one am anxious to find out. Let's vote." He gestured for Henry to go first. One by one, we each walked to the ballot basket. When it was my turn I scrawled "Grant" in huge letters, making them take up all the space on the paper. Then I went back and took a seat on the bench, keeping my eyes down as I did.

"I'll tally the votes," said Joe. He brought out the basket, and lifted out the first ballot. "First vote, Grant." Joe held up my ballot. "Second vote, Grant." Joe showed us Henry's ballot. By now I could recognize everyone's handwriting. "Third vote, Robin." The ballot Joe displayed was in Klemi's loopy scrawl, with a frowny face dotting the *i*. "Two votes Grant, one vote Robin, one vote left."

My heart was pounding in my ears and the ringing grew so loud that I looked around to see if other people could hear it too. Unintentionally I glanced at Grant and he gazed back at me. He didn't smile and in his eyes I saw defiance. That's when I knew for sure. When it came time for him to choose between Klemi and me, it was barely a choice at all.

"Fourth vote, Robin," said Joe. "We have a tie."

Chapter 13

But until we clarify the first item we can't proceed. I think we need to send the judge a written message with our questions. Also, we need a projector. That way I can show the list up on the screen, and we can check off each item as a group." Four grabs a sheet of paper and a pen. "Does anyone mind if I compose the note to the judge?"

We all nod our heads, and murmur things like "That's fine," or "Sure, knock yourself out," and Four starts writing. I rub at my temples and the joint in my jaw. There's a dull pain behind each.

"Okay!" says Four, and she reads off what she wrote. We've been at this for three hours already today and we haven't gotten anywhere. When we all approve the letter, Four steps outside and hands it to the security guard.

Eleven is fidgeting in his seat. "Does anyone mind if we take a break while we wait for the judge to reply? I could use a cigarette."

If Eleven is going outside to smoke then we all have to go outside with him. There's no such thing as alone time anymore.

"I would love to take a break," says Six. "Some fresh air would be lovely."

The group collectively looks over at One, our foreman. "Sure," he says. "Let's do it."

So the security guard chaperones us onto a service elevator. We load, ride down, and unload like we're in a tedious clown car, and he guides us down a back hallway to a door that is normally locked. Stepping outside onto a tiny patch of grass, adjacent to the street, we all collectively inhale the cool November breeze, except for Eleven, who inhales poisoned air instead. I pretend to be interested in hearing Twelve tell Four, Six, and Two about her honeymoon plans, but I subtly look around for Nick. He's over talking to Five, and as I approach I hear snippets of their sports conversation. But they both turn to me when they notice my presence.

"Hey!" I say.

At least Five smiles when he sees me. "Hi! I watched your show last night. I'd never seen it before, but since I know somebody who's on it now I thought I'd take a look. It was intense!"

"Thanks," I say.

He gives me a thumbs up. "You were great! Eating that bug. Wow."

"Yeah, it was pretty disgusting."

I glance down at my shoe and scuff in it the soft dirt. There's a stretched out moment when I wait for Nick to acknowledge me or give some sign that he doesn't suddenly, inexplicably hate me. All he has to do is say something.

"I watched it too."

My eyes shift from my foot to his face. "What did you think?"

Nick shoves his hands in his pockets and scrunches up his shoulders. Then, in a soft, nearly intimate pitch, he says, "I think your life is pretty complicated."

Oh. So that's what this is about. Sure, it had occurred to me that having my baggage aired on national television might scare off potential suitors, but I was hoping it was something else. Something easier to fix. "Everyone's life is pretty complicated," I reply. "And anyway, you knew that before."

He pauses before he answers, his eyes clinging to mine. "That wasn't meant as an insult, Robin."

"So I'm supposed to be flattered?"

He keeps his tone spongy and calm, like an NPR announcer. "It was just an observation. You asked me what I thought and I told you."

Five moves his head back and forth, between Nick and me, following our exchange. I sigh, knowing I can't do this here. I probably shouldn't do this at all. If only there was some over-the-counter pill I could take that would counteract my hurt feelings. I'd call it

Thera-Blue.

Eleven must have finished his cigarette, because the security guard motions for us to start walking. I turn around to go and Five walks ahead. Nick and I are now out of earshot of everyone else. I pivot step in front of him and throw away any subtly I might possess.

"Do you regret kissing me?"

He pauses, sighs, and shakes his head no.

I cross my arms over my chest. "Then why are you acting so weird?"

"Because I'm weird." He nervously rubs his thumb's fingernail with his index finger on the same hand. "My life is weird. I don't know how to handle something like this."

I knit my eyebrows together. "Something like what?"

He looks past my shoulder, and sees that everyone has gone inside. The security guard is holding the door open for us and we need to move.

Fingers straight, he drops his hand to his side. "Look, I like you. But can we wait until after jury duty to have this conversation?"

Standing there face to face, my eyes are directly across from his forehead. Absurdly, it occurs to me that were I ever to take him to a wedding I couldn't wear heels. But I never wear heels anyway. "Sure, why not?" I punch him jokingly in the shoulder to show there are no hard feelings and I move out of his way so we can walk together inside.

But before I do, he reaches out, grabs my hand and squeezes for the briefest of moments while simultaneously staring into my eyes. My heart flutters as our fingers touch. Then we let go and the moment is over.

"I'll also give you a detailed rundown of my thoughts about the show last night," Nick says.

"Thanks, but no."

He gives me his crooked smile and his voice turns gravelly. "What? You were great."

We're inside now and the security guard has closed the door behind us. We catch up to everyone at the service elevator.

Nick addresses the group. "Who all watched *The Holdout* last night? Wasn't Robin great?"

"Oh my God," says Two. "I was saying that before. It was the best episode of *The Holdout* ever. Dude, I thought she'd freak out at the end! That's good television."

"Thank you?" I offer.

Six pats my shoulder in her maternal way. "You were very impressive. I really don't know how you didn't crack from all the stress."

"I thought I did crack."

"Only sort of," says Two. "I mean, you didn't go all…" she shakes her head violently and bugs her eyes out. "…crazy, crazy. You know?"

"Sure."

"I thought she went a little crazy," says Five to Two. Then he talks to me. "But you weren't terrible. I mean, it was sort of justified."

Nick is laughing, and I kick him in the heel as a thank you for bringing up the show. The elevator arrives and we get on.

Two, Five, and Six continue to debate my sanity but I only sort of listen. I know what my mental state was. I remember all too well.

§

After Joe read the final vote they turned off the cameras. "We need to set up the fire challenge!" Joe yelled. "We have a tie." He sighed, exasperated that his workday had been extended, and addressed the cast. "Just a moment, you guys. We need to set up the challenge." He condemned us with his voice, since clearly we were to blame for this inconvenience.

The crew came out with piles of sticks and rocks. They formed two large circles with the rocks and put the stick bundles in the middle of each. A foot or so above each fire pit they stretched and tied a thin rope between two stakes. We sat and watched.

I was next to Grant, close enough for him to hear my whisper. "You have no ethics at all, do you?"

He whipped his head towards me. "You can't be serious. I said I was going to vote you out. I didn't lie. You're the one with no ethics, pretending to still be into me so I'd change my vote."

My voice shook though I was hissing. "But it wasn't a lie in the beginning! Unlike you, I didn't make up my feelings just to get ahead in the game."

Grant rolled his eyes. "What show do you think you're on? This isn't The Bachelor. If all you're doing is looking for a boyfriend than you're playing the wrong game."

"Okay," Joe yelled. "We're set. Let's go!" Everyone sat up straight again, the cameras turned back on, and Joe resumed. "Tonight, as a tie-breaker, you will perform in a challenge." Joe waited for the weight of his words to sink in before he continued. "Robin. Grant. You will both be tasked with starting a fire."

Inside I could already feel flames and they were scorching me. Nothing would feel better than to win and see Grant's torch snuffed out.

"The first person whose flame burns through the rope above their fire pit gets to stay. The loser will be out of the game. Understand?"

Grant and I nodded. Cameras followed us as we went and knelt in front of our prospective pits. They had provided us with flint, tinder, and kindling. This should be easy enough, I thought.

"You never had a chance in this game without me," Grant mumbled. "You're dead weight. And you sure as hell don't have a chance against me. You're nothing but a joke and you should bow out now."

Hearing him voice my worst fears switched me into fuming mode. "Shut up!" I yelled. Everyone — cast, crew, and Joe Pine, all stared at me.

"He was saying mean things to me under his breath," I explained. "He was trying to undermine me."

Grant laughed his charming, nice guy laugh and innocently widened his teddy-bear eyes. "All I did was wish her luck. I said, 'may the best castaway win.'"

My anger spiraled out. "That is such a lie! He is such a liar. He told me I was dead weight."

"No I didn't! I would never say that. She's the one who's trying to shake me."

"Okay, okay." said Joe. "Robin, Grant, your only course of action here is to compete and win. Are you ready?"

We nodded. The challenge began.

I picked up the sticks and formed them into a teepee shape with the tinder in the middle and kindle on the outside, using the strategy I learned years ago in Girl Scouts. Once everything was in place I grabbed the flint but it slid through my fingers because my hands were slick with sweat. I took a deep breath, wiped my hands on my leggings, and picked up the flint again. I could literally feel the cords in my neck bulging. I scrunched my shoulders and leaned into where a big piece of thin bark was sticking out. I bit down on my lip as I rubbed my flint together – one, two, five times before a flame ignited. Quickly I brought down the flame to make contact with the bark and it caught fire. My teeth released their grip on my lower lip and in doing so I could taste blood. But it didn't matter.

I allowed myself to look over at Grant. His sticks had caught fire, but he had kept out a piece of bark to fan the flames. Why hadn't I thought of that? I hastily took off my t-shirt and used that as a fan.

"Is she allowed to do that?" Grant asked Joe.

"She is," said Joe.

Grant and I both furiously shook our arms, up and down, up and down, willing our fires to grow higher. At one point a stick of mine fell, so I reached in to replace it. As I did I singed my hand, but I pushed away the sensation of smoldering flesh.

And then there was a gust of wind. Although it seems implausible, I swear this is true: the same gust somehow managed to simultaneously extinguish my fire while it caused Grant's fire to flourish. While my flame struggled to be anything more than smoke, Grant's flame leaped and jumped, giving birth to several little baby flames, which then quickly conjoined into one, rope-destructive fire that was a force to be reckoned with.

"No!" I yelled as I saw my flames turn to ashes.

Meanwhile, Grant's blaze burned right through the rope above it.

"And Grant wins the challenge!"

My bloody lip was throbbing and my hand was screaming for a splash of cold water. But neither was as painful as the smug look on Grant's face as he laughed in victory.

"That is so unfair!" I heard myself yell, but I don't remember making a conscious decision to say it. "It was the wind. He got lucky with the wind."

Joe remained unchanged. "I'm sorry, Robin. But it's time for you to go."

I brought my smarting hand to my lips and sucked on it. Tears were streaming down my face, and suddenly I became aware that I was clothed only in my sports bra and leggings. With a thousand washings the shirt would still stink like old cheese, so I tossed it into the dead fire pit and grabbed my torch.

I sniffed as I walked past everyone, trying to regain my composure. "Now you really can't give up," I said to Henry.

"You're a sore loser, Robin," said Klemi.

I didn't dignify that with a response. My heart felt like it was being squeezed through a garlic press, and I turned to the jury so they would understand. "Grant is a bastard," I gasped. "I hope you all just saw what really happened here. He doesn't deserve to win."

"Robin." Joe's voice was strict, meant to quiet me down. He gestured for me to approach and holdout my torch. I did as ordered, but I was a bloody, burning, shirtless, crying wreck.

"Robin, the tribe has decreed. You're out."

He snuffed out my torch. This was my cue to leave quietly with my head held high. But I couldn't follow the script. I tried to stay silent, like the stoic, levelheaded lady I had set out to be, but my physical and emotional injuries came shrieking through even as I struggled to repress them.

"No," I said to Joe. "They didn't decree anything. I got two votes. Two votes! How am I out?"

"Robin." Joe said my name like I was a disobedient child and he was the disciplinarian.

I didn't recognize my own arms as I swung them wildly and pointed to the jury. "I never received a vote from any of them!" My voice was coming from the bottom of my stomach, and it was deep, like a pool of quicksand. "I never got any votes at all, until tonight. And it was a tie, and the wind helped Grant win." Behind me Grant was snickering and I thought my brain would explode, leaving a mealy, bloody residue all over the pristine bamboo set and Joe Pine's unwrinkled shirt. All the hunger, thirst, sleep deprivation, loneliness, and stress erupted inside of me and came out in one huge clump of crazy. I threw my torch brutally to the ground and grabbed the front of Joe's blue safari shirt, pulling him towards me. "Explain to me how anything was *decreed*, Joe. Explain it to me now. There was no majority. I want a do-over and I'm not leaving until I get one!"

Joe blinked rapidly and gulped heavily. Was he worried that I might hurt him or that I'd muss up his outfit? I heard someone clear his throat, and then Joe was looking off to the side, over my shoulder, making eyes with someone on the crew. "No, that's okay," he said to the cameraman. "We're fine here." Joe put one hand on each of my shoulders and pushed me back with vigilant restraint. "There are no do-overs, Robin. And *I'm* decreeing it. You're out."

I sighed and looked up. A mass of stars occupied the sky, and here I was, less than a millionth of a blip in the immense universe. Recited lines from college acting classes jogged through my mind: star-crossed, the fault is in our stars; it is not in the stars to hold our destiny but in ourselves. I already knew about destiny and what a bitch she can be. Although my face was tilted upwards, tears were streaming down, and I understood it was time to go.

"Fine," I whispered. I turned back one more time and met eyes with Henry. He gave me a sad smile and a wave. "Good luck, Henry."

Then I walked away.

§

Back in the jury room Four has gotten her projector. She says she uses one just like it in her classroom at school, so she's operating it now and basically running the show. Our foreman doesn't seem to mind.

"Okay, so I think the judge's note answered everyone's questions, right? Now we need to decide if we agree with the first claim. Were the boats damaged upon receipt?" Four has the judge's instructions projected up on the screen, and she points to the first claim.

"Yes," says Nick. He's sitting at the table with his arms stretched out and his hands clasped.

I push my chair forward and lean over Five to talk to Nick. "How can you say that? They were obviously damaged by the way they were stored."

"Right," says One. His chair is back, and he sits at the head of the table, closest to the door, with his legs crossed. "The boats weren't treated well. I don't see how we can award the Smythes anything."

"You can't be sure about that," says Nick.

"It doesn't matter," I tell him. "In civil cases the burden of proof is on the plaintiff. If we're not sure then Potenza still wins."

Six shakes her head. "But that's far too simplistic. There was obviously something shady about these boats, and I don't believe it was only because they were stored incorrectly."

Four clears her throat. "Maybe we should vote on the first claim? Just to see where we all stand?"

My jaw clenches and I turn deliberately towards One. "What do you think, foreman? Should we all vote?"

He shakes his head as if coming out of a fog. "Oh. Okay."

We vote. Ten jurors vote yes, and two jurors (One and myself) vote no.

"So we're right back to where we were." Eleven taps his fingers against the table, then gets up and looks out the window.

Nick slaps the table and addresses me directly. "Look. If we say no on this, then the Smythes get nothing. We're done. Do you really think that's fair?"

"I don't think the boats were stored right."

Nick's normally pinkish cheeks turn a deeper red. He throws his arms up in the air. "I don't either! And we can give the Smythes next to nothing in damages. But come on, Robin. Look at the evidence." He grabs the exhibit notebook and flips through its pages. He stops when he finds what he's looking for, holds it up and points. "One of the boats that sank was sent directly to its final owner, and they stored it and maintained it flawlessly. Still it sank after only six months."

"Okay, that's one boat. We should make Potenza pay for all the boats because of one damaged one?"

"The other boats were damaged too," says Four. "The expert testimony proved it."

"Potenza had experts too," I say.

"Yeah, I didn't like their experts," says Two. "One of them looked like a drugged-out Nick Nolte."

"How is that relevant?" I demand.

"They were sleazy," says Six. "My gut is telling me to trust the Smythes' expert witnesses more."

"You can't go off your gut," I tell her. Six tilts her blond head to the side and smoothes her sweater over her large bosom. My mom would be her age if she was still alive. I make my voice as benevolent as I can. "This isn't about emotion, it's about the facts. That's the only thing we can base this off of."

From across the table Two chortles. She's wearing the same black hoodie that she's worn every day of jury duty, and her dyed red hair is pulled back in the same ponytail. "You're totally going off emotion," she accuses me.

"No, I'm not."

"Sure you are." She coughs and her voice sounds throaty. "You're still pissed that Grant beat you in *The Holdout*, and Silas Smythe reminds you of Grant. You're prejudiced."

I'm so shocked by what she says that a cloud passes over my vision and I have to rub my eyes to return to reality. When I do, I'm still sitting across from Two and I still want to throttle her.

"You have no right to say that to me. Just because you watch *The Holdout* doesn't make you an authority on how my mind works."

She lowers her eyelids without closing them all the way and smirks. "I have a right to say what I think, and that's what I think."

"Yeah, and just what is going on between you and Silas Smythe anyway?" Four asks from her spot at the projector, like she's the student council president addressing the class slut.

"Nothing! He saved me from tripping, that's all."

"You shouldn't have been talking to him. Period." Four brings her index finger and thumb together to draw a line in the air.

I look around the table for some sort of support, but I may as well be braless while running a marathon. One is practically asleep, looking off in the distance and then at his watch. So much for my alliance.

"Were you actually talking to Silas Smythe?" Nick asks me this. I squeeze my hands into tight little balls to keep my fingers from shaking.

"No. He talked to me." I can feel my chest contracting, or perhaps my organs are growing; it doesn't really matter because the effect is the same. I open my mouth and the words hobble out, bruised before they begin. "We were in an elevator together once, and he cleared this throat a lot and said 'ladies first' when it was time to get off. I didn't say anything back. The other time was in the hallway when he kept me from tripping. He asked me if I was okay and I didn't respond. It wasn't a big deal. "

Nick's mouth hangs open. "If he was trying to influence you at all, then that is a big deal."

"But it didn't work. I wasn't swayed by him."

"No," interjects Two, "you were swayed against him." She points an accusatory finger at me. "You think Silas was trying to use you in the same way Grant did. You're completely biased against Silas Smythe because of what he represents."

"That's insane!" I jump up from my chair because it's become impossible to stay seated. If I was the crazy, reactionary type I would pick up my chair and throw it through the window just to express my anger at being accused. But I settle for kicking my chair forward so it's flush against the table. "I am not biased, or prejudiced, or any of those other bad words like tainted, influenced, or swayed. I am rational and I base my opinions on facts. The facts. Period." I look at Four to see if that gets a response. She rolls her eyes.

Nobody responds. Nick just sits there, peeling the label off his water bottle.

Six stands and places a gentle palm on my shoulder. "Robin, I do think you should consider what we're suggesting. Sure, we don't know you very well, but we saw your show last night. What you said to Grant at the final vote does make me wonder if there's some truth to all of this."

I had no idea that jury duty would be so similar to therapy. If Six was my therapist, I would tell her that what I said to Grant is the one thing I don't regret.

§

After I got kicked off *The Holdout* the first aid team soothed my burn with aloe, put some ice on my lip, and had me swallow down a high strength ibuprofen with cold, sweet apple juice. Then I was taken to the hotel that housed all the cast-off jury members. The suitcase I had packed for after the show was waiting in my very own private room. I took my first hot shower in over a month, and the lavender scented bath soap and conditioning shampoo felt more luxurious than silk. I toweled off and put on my favorite old t-shirt and soft cotton pajama pants, both of which smelled like fabric softener and home. Then I ordered room service – a Cajun chicken sandwich, salad, and a coke. Plus a chocolate sundae for dessert, with extra whipped cream. I ate it all, and each bite was more delicious than the last. Afterwards I watched a captivating Spanish soap opera, until finally I couldn't keep my eyes open. Then I snuggled up, curled in smooth, dry linens, and closed my eyes while I lay atop a mattress as soft as a cloud. This was after a month of being hungry and damp, and smelling like feet.

But that night I didn't sleep at all.

I just stared at the darkness, with one thought running through my mind. "How can I make Grant lose?"

The final vote would be in less than twenty-four hours. Each jury member would get to ask the last three contestants one question. All I had to do was come up with the perfect, revealing question that would make Grant falter, flinch and forfeit. But what was it?

The next day I talked to Beth and Bailey.

"I'm not voting for him, but I think the others are," said Bailey.

"He played a good game," said Beth.

"But he's the one who got everyone to vote both of you out. We were in an alliance! How can you tolerate that?"

Beth shrugged her shoulders. "Who said I am? But look at the choices. None of them deserves to win. At least Grant had a plan."

In the air-conditioned hotel breakfast room, the skin on my arms formed goose bumps. I looked through the picture windows to outside. Being indoors no longer felt natural. I longed for sun on my face and sand beneath my feet.

Beth grabbed her tray like she was about to get up. "Besides," she said, "I feel bad for Grant. After what happened with his parents and his sister, he could use some good fortune. I bet Henry's been pampered all his life."

She cleared her dishes and walked away. But she had left me with an idea.

Show producers were still monitoring the jury members and use of the internet was strictly forbidden. So I went and stood in the first floor bathroom.

After only a couple of minutes a touristy looking lady walked in. I held up $100 and pointed to her phone. "Please," I said, hoping she understood English well enough to get my meaning. "I just need to use your phone for a few minutes."

She pushed her Gucci sunglasses further up her head and raised her eyebrows. "Are you one of the contestants from *The Holdout*?" she asked.

I bit my lip. "I can't say." Then I just stared at her phone.

She smirked. "Fine," she said, giving me her phone with one hand and extending her other hand to receive the money.

"Thank you!" I said, as I handed her the bill. "But this never happened, okay?"

She shrugged. "Whatever."

I smiled my appreciation and then turned away, trying to be stealthy about my quick Google search, which told me all I needed to know.

Two hours before the jurors were scheduled to leave for the final Island Assembly, we were ordered to go to hair and makeup. They spent a long time blow drying my hair and painting my face. When they finished I looked sort of like Beach Barbie, except my boobs weren't nearly big enough. I was wearing a black strapless sundress, which wasn't something I had packed but what the stylist chose for me. It kept creeping down and I kept pulling it back up.

On set we waited back stage for Joe Pine to call us out, one by one. "Are you going to freak out again tonight?" asked Beth. "That was pretty awesome when you grabbed Joe Pine by the shirt. Kind of made me like you again."

Joe called out, "Beth, Bailey, and Robin, voted out at the last Island Assembly." I walked onto the set.

Henry, Klemi, and Grant were sitting in their usual spot. I gave Henry a smile and a wave. I saw Grant's jaw drop as he took in my appearance. Who could blame him? I do clean up nice.

Joe spoke to the jury. "Tonight, at the final Island Assembly, the last three contestants will sit before you as you ask them your questions. It is now their job to convince you that they deserve the million dollars. But before we start with your questions, each contestant gets to make a brief, opening statement." He turned around. "Klemi, you're first."

Klemi flashed a rehearsed looking smile, lowered her shoulders, and stuck out her chest. "Okay. Well, you all know me. I don't lie. I tell it how it is. Maybe you don't always like what I have to say, but I didn't deceive anyone this entire game. I know I wasn't always the easiest person to have around, but *The Holdout* isn't supposed to be easy."

Then it was Henry's turn. He cleared his throat. "Well, I'm sure a lot of you are surprised to see me sitting here. I guess I'm also shocked that I made it to the final three. Part of it was luck, like when I found the hidden immunity idol. And, I know that for a while nobody was voting me out because they didn't see me as a threat, since I was so bad at the physical challenges. But I did do well in the challenges that weren't about speed or strength, and I like to think I played a good social game. I worked hard, trying to get people to vote out Grant, who was the game's biggest threat. I didn't succeed and I think that has more to do with you all on the jury than it does with me. So now you're left with a choice. You can award the million to Grant, the guy who worked against all of you, or to me, the guy who tried to work with all of you."

"Or they can award it to me," said Klemi.

Henry pushed his glasses up on his nose and kept his gaze forward, not on Klemi. "True, but I'm not really sure what you did in this game." He grinned. "But obviously, jury, if you think Klemi deserves the million, vote for her." Henry spread his hands to either side in a gesture of diplomacy.

"Okay," said Joe. "Grant, you're on."

Grant had been staring off to the side, watching the shadow of flames dance against the bamboo set. When he heard Joe say his name, he turned his head, and his eyes went directly to mine. He spoke only to me, ignoring everyone else.

"Robin," he said. "I'm sorry for hurting you." He sighed and his stare made me realize how empty I felt inside. "Since you left last night I've had time to think, and I truly regret my actions. This whole time I was playing a game, and I did what I thought I had to do to win. I never wanted to hurt anyone though, especially you." He looked away from me, and scanned the faces of the rest of the jury. "If you all think that what I did was unforgivable, then you should vote for Henry." Klemi let out a dramatic sigh of exasperation, but Grant didn't acknowledge her. "I don't want the million if that's how you all feel. But maybe you can absolve me for the mistakes I made, because you realize that I'm still young and stupid. Perhaps you can recognize that despite everything, I did play one hell of a game. If so, vote for me," he looked back and spoke with his bedroom voice, as if we were alone in each other's arms, "but only if you can forgive me."

Bile rose from my stomach to my mouth, and it tasted like fury. He waited until now to be reticent, and it was just one more part of his act.

"Okay," said Joe. "Time for questions from the jury."

We went in order of when we were voted out, so I was to be last. Each question was fairly tame, along the lines of "What was your biggest strength?" or "What would you do with the money?" or "Which action of yours do you regret the most?" Grant said he regretted hurting me and he even wiped a tear away as he spoke. You would think he was the one who majored in theater.

When it was Beth's turn she got up and stood before the three of them. "I don't have any questions but I do have something to say." She put her hands on her hips. With the lit torches that surrounded the set, the fire pit in the middle, and the candles flickering from every spare spot, she was illuminated by flames from every direction. It was like she was presenting a speech in hell. "Klemi," she said, "you're worthless. Nobody is going to vote for you so I'm not wasting my time saying anything more. Henry, you're a nice enough guy, but you're weak. I would vote for you if I respected you, but I don't. Grant, you're a liar and a cheat, and I don't buy the speech you just gave. Nobody is that young or stupid. But you are strong, and you did play a good game." She shrugged her shoulders. "So I guess you have my vote."

"Thank you," said Grant.

"Don't thank me," said Beth. "I could still change my mind." She sat down.

Then Bailey got up. "I do have a question, and it's for you." He spoke to Grant. "Does loyalty mean anything to you?"

Grant was sitting in a forward leaning position, his arms resting on his knees. The muscles in his biceps strained under the sleeves of his green t-shirt and his Adam's apple moved up and down before he opened his mouth to answer.

"No." he said. "Growing up like I did, loyalty isn't something I've had much experience with."

Bailey, who is a man of few words, nodded. "That's no excuse. You make me sick."

Wow. At long last, Bailey and I had some common ground. I studied Grant's face for a response to such strong words, but he remained as unchanged as a Twinkie that has sat on the pantry shelf for years.

Finally it was my turn. I stood with wobbly knees, knowing this moment would be one I would relive, over and over, both in my memory and on TV. So I had to get it right the first time. A dozen cameras were capturing my every angle, but the only pair of eyes I cared about belonged to Grant.

"So," I said. "You asked for forgiveness."

"Yes," replied Grant.

My heart was beating so strong I could feel it in my ears. "I could forgive you, except…" I breathed, in and out, in and out, to steady myself. "Except, this one thing is holding me back." I looked around. Jury members were perched on the edges of their seats, and even Joe was hunched forward, like he was prepared for quick action if necessary. Did they all think I was going to go crazy again?

"Grant, I told you before that my mother died."

He nodded.

"She was in a car accident when I was two years old. I don't remember her, and I don't remember the time shortly after she died, but my family told me that I wandered around for days, looking and calling out for her." I sniffed and swallowed down the dangerous emotions that were surging through me. "She was a good woman. She loved my brothers and my dad, and although I was something of a surprise, my dad says that she was thrilled to have a daughter. So she loved me, and even though I don't remember her, I remember the feeling of loving her back." I blink rapidly and stand up straighter, righting my posture. "And I mention this now because honestly, nearly thirty years later, I still feel like no matter what I do, I just can't let go of her." I pause, take a moment, and will myself to hold it together. "That's why I never really talked about her while I was still a contestant in this game. Using her memory to manipulate my standing in *The Holdout* wouldn't be worth a million dollars." Grant's mouth was slowly starting to drop, a gradual pull of gravity. "Some things are too painful to talk about, or too sacred to capitalize upon. But you wouldn't know about that, would you? A person like you, who has never suffered a day in his life, can't possibly understand someone else's pain, or how destructive a lie can be."

I paused. The only sound came from the crackling of the flames. I breathed deeply, preparing myself to deliver my next punch. "I guess what I'm saying is, while I would never use my mother's memory to get myself ahead in this game, I feel pretty good about using her memory to destroy you."

Grant started to speak, but I cut him off. "Wait." My voice was hard and strong. "Before you say anything, I want to tell you one more thing. You did play a good game. Your only flaw was that you underestimated me."

I pivoted and addressed the jury. "How many of you heard Grant's story about his parents dying in Iraq and his grandparents blaming him for his sister's disappearance?"

Beth, Bailey, and several others raised their hands.

"Well," I said, drawing my words out for emphasis, "it was all a big lie."

I turned back to Grant. Even with the orange-red flames illuminating his face, he was pale. "Don't try and deny it," I said. "I know everything. Your parents do work for Halliburton, but they're still very much alive, and their huge paycheck funded your education at St. Paul's prep school in Connecticut, where you excelled in every sport possible. Your sister is there now, and I hear she's breaking records in girl's lacrosse."

"Wait." Grant, now in a panic, held up his index finger. "How did you find…" His face fell and he looked to Joe. "She's not allowed to know this stuff."

Joe answered through suppressed laughter. "Maybe not, but there's nothing we can do about that now."

"You can't prove anything," Grant said to me.

"I don't have to. Because we all know I'm telling the truth, and that you're a liar."

The flames danced and jumped around us. I was expecting Grant to melt into a pile of deceit and regret, but he smiled instead. It was the same cocky "can you believe this" smile he gave me weeks ago, on the boat during the first few minutes of the game. "My parents are alive," he said. "They travelled a lot. That's why I was in boarding school."

"So why did you lie? I think the jury deserves to know."

Grant thought for a moment, looking off in the distance and sighing. He returned his gaze to me when he answered. "Why not lie?" His face hardened as he shrugged. "Seriously, why not lie? It's a game Robin. Who ever said I had to tell the truth?"

I sniffed, wiped my nose, and hoped my makeup wasn't running.

"But I really am sorry," said Grant.

"Yeah, I don't forgive you." I shifted my focus to Henry. "Henry,

I feel like I owe you an apology. I should have listened to you in the beginning. And I should have recognized earlier what a threat you really are." I grinned. "Of course, if I had, I probably would have voted you out, or at least tried to." I turned to the jury. "This guy is not weak. He may not be athletic, but he's strong in other ways. He managed to stand on his own, without an alliance, and make it to the final three. It wasn't luck that brought him here; it was strategy and pure determination. Personally, I can't think of anyone more deserving of the million dollars or the title of *The Holdout*. And he wants to use the money to invent some shield that will make the world a better place…so anyway Henry, you have my vote."

"Thanks, Robin."

I smiled at him one more time, and then I turned and sat back on the jury bench. Joe's mouth was hanging slightly agape, but I expect he was relieved that I made it through my little speech without physically attacking anyone. In a slightly higher voice than normal, he spoke to the camera.

"Okay, it's time to vote. Remember, tonight you are writing down the name of the person who you want to win *The Holdout*. Robin, you're up first."

I stood, prepared to make my final move in this game.

Chapter 14

One advantage of being in jury deliberations over the Smythe case is I'm not allowed to have my cell phone at all during the day. This gives me a built-in excuse for not returning calls or texts. When I pick up my phone on my way out of the courthouse I have a kazillion messages, mostly from friends and family, but a few are unfamiliar numbers. They're probably reporters, and while I don't delete them right away, I don't listen to them either. There are only two calls I want to return.

"Hey," I say when he picks up. "Is your family going crazy yet?"

"I'm going crazy," he replies. "Do you think I have a chance?"

Of course anything I say will be pure speculation. To cut down on potential spoilers, even us show contestants don't yet know who won *The Holdout*. We'll find out this week with the rest of the country, when the live reunion special is aired. But I've answered this question at least a dozen times before, and I answer it again because that's what friends do. "Of course. The only one who doesn't have a chance is Klemi. But otherwise I could see it going either way."

I hear him sigh. "I don't know. Sometimes I think yeah, I could actually win this thing, but then I have a dream where Grant gets all the votes and I realize I forgot to wear clothes to the reunion show."

I laugh. "I bet Tenzin would love it if you did."

Henry chuckles at that, and I get him to give me all the latest details about his new relationship. Tenzin is the first real girlfriend he's ever had, and he says it's going well.

"I can't wait to see you this weekend. Is your family going to be there?" Henry asks.

"My dad and my brother Ian will be. I'm not sure about my other brother. What about you?"

"Yeah. Everybody, from my mom to my third cousin once removed. It just makes the pressure to win more intense."

I sniff and wipe my running nose with my sleeve. "Don't worry. I voted for you, and I'd bet money that Bailey did too. You only need three more votes to win."

We wrap up our conversation as I enter my apartment.

"Take care of yourself, Robin. And try not to answer any calls from *Alright Magazine*."

"That won't be a problem. During deliberations I'm not even allowed to have my phone, so I'm missing any call that happens between nine and five o'clock."

Henry and I have been in contact pretty regularly since the show ended. It keeps us both sane, being able to talk about what happened and project how the votes might go. But our conversations have expanded beyond *The Holdout*, so he knows all about jury duty and my "complicated" personal life.

"Okay, well good luck with deliberations. Don't back down, because if anyone knows how to be a holdout, it's you."

It's probably just that my eyes are watery from congestion, but Henry's cheesy words of encouragement bring tears to my eyes.

"Bye, Henry."

Deliberations ended this afternoon without any sort of a verdict, but on the upside I managed not to throw furniture or grab anyone by the lapels after I was accused of being overly emotional and prejudiced. The downside is that we'll all be back at it tomorrow, and I feel like I'm getting Isobel's cold. Maybe tomorrow I'll grab Nick's water bottle on the sly and sneeze into it.

I take off my coat and my boots, and collapse onto my couch. I rest my feet upon my milk crate coffee table, but just as I've gotten comfortable, I realize I need a Kleenex. I get up and grab the entire box, and then I sit back down again. Once I've blown my nose and adjusted myself to my satisfaction, I make my other call.

"Hello?"

"Lucy! Hi, it's Robin."

"Robin. Hey, thanks for calling me back. How are you? How's jury duty?"

I cough away the tickle in my throat. "Okay. We're into deliberations now, and I don't agree with anyone except the foreman, but he's half-asleep most of the time. Meanwhile, most of the people on the jury have been watching *The Holdout* and they're accusing me of being irrational…" I pause to wipe my nose, and then I remember that during our last conversation I only talked about myself.

"…never mind," I say. "How are you doing?"

"Fine. I'm afraid I don't have anything nearly as interesting going on as you do though."

"That's probably a good thing."

"Actually, it's the reason I called. Hold on." I hear a young voice in the background asking for a banana. "Okay, but throw the peel away yourself this time," Then her voice comes back, full volume. "Do you have any plans for Thanksgiving?"

"Umm…"

"Wait. Before you answer, just let me tell you what I was thinking." I hear the sound of dishes being put away while she talks. "One of the classes I'm teaching is about the evolution of the American justice system. It occurred to me, what's more American than reality television?" Silverware is clinking into its drawer. "Nothing, except maybe for jury duty. So here you are, having immediate experiences with both. Well, it's fascinating." Plates are being stacked on top of each other. "And I'm wondering, if I flew you out, would you be willing to speak to my class about it all? You could stay for a visit, and celebrate Thanksgiving with Monty and me, and we could show you around Seattle. It could be really great."

In the distance a baby cries. "Hold on a minute," Lucy says, and I can tell she's holding the phone away. "What happened?"

"Nothing. He pinched me."

"Abby, that doesn't make it okay to pinch him back."

"But it hurt!"

The crying becomes louder, probably because Lucy has picked up the source. "Sorry," she says into the phone, loud enough that I can hear her over baby Noah. "So what do you think?"

"Umm…"

"I know it's sudden. But I was thinking; you have your reunion show this Sunday. What if we try and book a flight from New York? There would probably still be flights available that early in the week."

I cough again and look around my apartment, which seems dingy in the fading evening light. "I'd feel bad, having you pay for my ticket."

"Oh! I forgot to say that part. I have a small university budget for speakers and special supplies. I wouldn't be paying for it, the university would."

Noah's crying subsides as Lucy shushes him. I picture him in her arms, as she stands in their chaotic kitchen. It's so different from my silent, solitary life.

"Sure, I'd love to."

Lucy whoops. "Really? Oh, it's going to be great! And Monty will be so excited that you're coming."

It's hard to imagine he'll care. There have always been many miles and years that separate us, so we've never been close. But I smile and tell her that I'm excited too.

§

The next morning I wake up feeling like I have an extra liter of snot backed up in my nose. The pressure is so intense that it hurts to stand. I take some Sudafed, which always makes me loopy, and I wear my warmest sweater to combat the chills that regularly wash over me.

On my way out I run into Isobel. "Hi," I croak.

"Oh no," she says. "It sounds like you got my cold."

"Yeah, but that's not the worst of it." I take a big sniff. "Yesterday at deliberations, the jury accused me of being biased! They said I'm comparing Silas Smythe to Grant. Can you believe that? Now I have to go deal with them all again today."

Isobel pushes the outside door open and we walk towards our cars. "But Robin, you said yourself that Silas reminds you of Grant."

The fog in my head lifts for a moment as I realize she's right.

How could I forget that?

Isobel pats me on the arm before getting into her car. "Hang in there Robin. I know you'll get through this, and I know you'll do the right thing. And take care of that cold!"

I wave goodbye as she drives off, and it takes me a minute to realize I'm standing in the parking lot, dazed and high on cold medicine. I sigh and open my car door.

When I get to the courthouse I toss my phone into the security guard's basket, enter our deliberation room, and take my seat without making eye contact with anyone. I hang my head in my hands until it's time to resume our deliberations.

When everyone arrives, Four turns on her projector. "Shall we begin?" she asks. I lift my head as my sinuses silently scream in pain.

"Unless I'm mistaken," Four says, "we're still on the first item." She rolls her eyes and huffs a little as she looks in my direction.

The words burst out of my mouth like hot coals. "And unless I'm mistaken, you're not actually our foreman. You're just pretending to be." I barely realize what I am saying before all the heads in the room swivel in my direction and stare at me with stunned eyes. It's like I showed up to Island Assembly naked. And it's then that I realize: If this was *The Holdout*, I'm the one who would be voted out first. It would happen faster than a gust of wind could snuff out my torch.

Four arches an eyebrow and gestures over to One. "If he wants to sit at the projector, he can. Or for that matter," her nostrils flare, "so can you. I'm just trying to be efficient. Some of us have real jobs we need to return to, and I'm hoping to speed things along."

Four's cutting remark sends me way past the commercial break of detesting her. "I thought you cared about doing things right," I say, my voice hoarse and strained. "But now I feel pressured. I'm sure it would be easier for everyone if I caved and agreed that the boats were damaged, but I'm not going to change my mind just to appease everyone."

"Then you're simply being stubborn," remarks Nick.

My ears are clogged from all the congestion in my head, so maybe I didn't hear him right. Yet when I turn towards Nick his chin is jutted out and aggression is leaking from his face, like sap from a pine tree. Getting close to him right now would be sticky.

I ignore my wounded emotions and barrel on. I recite the speech I rehearsed on my drive here, though it hurts to speak and I can hardly hear myself. "Actually, I've been thinking about it." I look over at Nick. "I get what you're saying, about the boat that sank even though it was stored correctly. So I'll concede my stance and agree that all the boats were damaged upon receipt." I shudder a little, which always happens when I give in. I square my shoulders and raise my chin. "But I want to make two things clear: One, I don't think Potenza should have to pay any damages other than the original cost of the boats, and two, if anyone brings up my actions on *The Holdout* again, I'm walking out of here and filing a complaint with the judge. Are we clear?"

People nod. Six murmurs, "You sound really sick."

Two says nothing, and I deliberately keep my gaze from drifting in her direction. Four taps her pencil against the table and says, "Okay, so we can check the first item off as yes?"

Jurors two through eleven all murmur their assent, and then we all look to One. He pushes his glasses up on his nose as he opens his mouth to speak. "Fine," he says. "I won't fight common opinion."

We make our way through the deliberations and things move fairly quickly. There is still some argument about how much Potenza ought to pay, and I fight the effects of cold medication as I struggle through this last challenge of speaking coherently.

"The Smythes are at fault too. They damaged the boats by not taking care of them. So Potenza will pay to get their boats back, but they're getting back damaged goods that they'll have to refurbish. I refuse to concede that they should have to pay more in addition to that."

"Fine," Nick says. "I agree. But I think we should include money for the shipyard that was attached to the Smythe's claim."

My chest tightens, as do my fists. "Why?"

Nick sighs. "Because they're just a little shipyard, and they're not millionaires like the Smythes are. The people who own it got screwed."

I sneeze and it only makes my nose feel more clogged up. "But we don't know that the Smythes would give the money to the shipyard."

"It's the gesture," replies Nick.

"This shouldn't be about gestures."

"Wait, what are we talking about?" says One.

"We're discussing whether or not the shipyard should receive damages," says Four, pointing to some figures that are projected on the screen. She rolls her eyes at Two, and Two rolls her eyes back.

"Well, why would we do that?" One asks. "That makes no sense to me."

Inwardly I groan. He has to be the worst jury foreman in the history of the world. I know I'm not the only one who thinks so; every time he speaks, the rest of jury looks like they have sand caught underneath their bathing suits. The only person I've ever met who has less to offer than One is Klemi, and even she could write a dissertation about sand, bathing suits, and the crevices we struggle to keep clean.

We go back and forth. Everyone agrees with Nick, except for One, but his abstract, unprompted questions only serve to annoy people. Meanwhile I'm feverish and worried that the rest of the jury will start to change their minds and argue for more money for the Smythes, just to contradict One.

My head is swimming in some choppy waves. I should be curled up underneath my covers in the fetal position, not arguing about a civil case between millionaires. "Okay, okay. If we add in the amount of the claim from the shipyard, plus the exact amount of the boats being sold back at cost, how much does that come to?"

Nick takes the court-sanctioned calculator and starts adding figures. "Nine million, two hundred thirty eight thousand, five hundred fifty eight dollars and 79 cents."

That's over nine times as much as I could have won on *The Holdout*, and it's still only a drop in the bucket for both the Smythes and Potenza. Their lawyer fees alone were probably more. "Okay, can we all agree on that?"

Everyone is eager to be done, so even though other people thought the Smythes should get more and One and I thought they deserved less, we reach a consensus. Several minutes later One is reading out our verdict for the courtroom. Silas Smythe sits with his dad, and afterwards he stands and shakes hands with the generic, white-haired lawyer. Then, to my horror, Silas turns in my direction, looks straight at me, and winks.

My jaw drops as I look around. Did anyone see this? I don't spend long analyzing it; Silas is not worth my time. As soon as I'm out of the courtroom I grab my stuff and go.

Some of the jurors stick around and exchange email addresses, but all I want right now is some hot tea and then a pillow beneath my head. I take the elevator down and I'm halfway through the lobby when I hear my name called out.

I stop and turn around. Nick is coming towards me. He's smiling but his shoulders are tensed. "You left without saying goodbye?"

"I have nothing to say to those people," I tell him. "Accusing me of being biased because of *The Holdout* hit below the belt." *Even if they were right.*

He thinks for a moment. "I didn't accuse you, though."

"You didn't defend me either."

"So that's it?" Nick's eyebrows crease together. "I thought we were going to talk once the trial was over."

I feel a big sneeze coming, but I try to sniff it away. My eyes water and I cough instead. "I figured that deal was off."

"Why?"

"Because we argued so much during deliberations."

"So? The wonderful part of jury duty is after it ends, you can forget all about it." Nick narrows his eyes. "With three juries in two years, I should know."

A chill washes over me and I tug my coat closed. "It's like a game, then?"

He scratches the back of his neck and looks off to the side, out the window. "No. I don't play games unless it's *Candy Land* with my niece." I give him a feeble smile and he peers at me. "I'm not the kind of guy who uses people, Robin."

So now he's comparing himself to Grant, though I've never mentioned him by name. Or maybe he's implying that I'm the one who is playing games. Either way, he's not being entirely straight with me. But instead of pressing the point I just nod my head.

He reaches out and gently taps my shoulder. It's like I can feel his touch through my coat. "I'll call you then?"

I shrug my shoulders. "I'm leaving town this weekend, first for New York and then Seattle. I won't be back until the Monday after Thanksgiving."

"Then I'll call you tomorrow."

Part of me wants to gush and get excited at the prospect of continuing this – whatever it is we have. But I hold myself back, neither confirming nor denying his statement. Fool me twice and yada, yada, yada. "Bye," I say with a wave. Then I go home and bury myself under three different blankets in my bed.

§

I wake up several hours later to the vibrating of my phone. It's 8:30 at night, and when I grab my cell I see it's a number from yesterday's missed call list. It has to be the seventh or eighth time this person has called. I decide to pick up, and if it's a reporter I'm prepared to say "No comment, and don't call me again."

"Hello?" I croak.

"Robin? Is that you?"

I cough and wipe my nose. "Who is this?"

"It's… it's Grant. How have you been? I've missed you."

Chapter 15

The next day Nick stops by with a container of chicken soup and a DVD of the original *Twelve Angry Men*. "I was thinking we could watch it, and recast all the roles with members from our jury."

I'm standing in the doorway, in a ratty old sweatshirt, pajama pants, and fleece socks. On Nick's feet are thick-soled brown shoes, which make our height difference almost non-existent.

"I thought you were just dropping by to give me something," I whisper. Talking at full volume feels like swallowing a golf ball.

"I was." He holds out the soup container and the DVD, and I take them from him. "I don't have to come in." He looks over my shoulder, into my apartment, which is covered in stray Kleenexes, abandoned mugs of lukewarm tea, and discarded boxes of cold medication.

"My place is sort of a mess right now."

"I don't mind."

"You could catch my cold."

He shrugs. "I have an incredibly strong immune system."

I laugh and cough simultaneously. "All week you've been acting like you don't want to know me. Now you won't take no for an answer. I don't get it."

He sticks his hands in jacket pockets and hunches up his shoulders. "Okay," he concedes. "I'll just say what I have to say out here." An uneasy smile emphasizes the curves of his face, making his cheeks pinchable. "I like you. But I'm not good at starting relationships. Since I was eighteen I've had to be responsible, and Andrea has always been my first priority. So…" he shrugs. "I'm awkward. And, I know you have a lot going on, which makes me think it's not a good idea, spending time with you. But I enjoy hanging out." He looks away, around, down, and back at me. "When you get back, after your trip and your reunion show, will you call me?"

"Sure," I say, with as much power as my disabled voice will allow.

His smile fades, and a look of concern replaces it. "You should go back to sleep. If you don't get better, how are you going to answer Joe Pine's questions on TV?"

"It won't matter," I say breathily. "Joe will mostly want to interview Grant and Henry."

"I have a feeling he'll want to interview you too."

I bite my lip, not sure what to say next. "Thanks for the soup. And the movie." I hold it up. "Maybe we can watch it after I get back?"

"That would be good." He nods, like there's more to say but something is holding him back. "Oh, what the hell?" Nick mumbles. Then he steps in, smooth and slow this time. I have enough reaction time to move away, but I don't. I let him place one hand on that spot between my head and the back of my neck, and I don't mind when he pulls me near and his mouth meets mine. For a moment I forget about my clogged sinuses and stuffy head as I experience the warmth of his lips, the generosity of his touch, and the power of his confidence when there's no space between us. A tingle runs through me and my head feels light, and neither sensation has anything to do with this cold.

But then a sneeze breaks us apart and I turn my head just in time to avoid spraying him with snot. I nearly spill the soup in the process, but Nick reaches out and catches the container before it falls to the ground. "Sorry," I say as he deftly hands me back the soup. "Aren't you supposed to be the awkward one?"

"Normally, yes." Nick raises one eyebrow. "But that kiss just brought out my super powers."

"The ability to rescue falling soup containers in a single bound?"

"Among other things." His smile soothes me way more than my throat-coat tea. I almost relent and invite him in, but nothing so easy can be worthwhile.

"Thanks," I say. "I'll call you in a week or two."

"Good." He squints like he's trying to read me but I'm too difficult to decipher. "Are you okay, then?"

The question catches me off-guard. "What do you mean?"

"You know… your cold, the pressure from the show, our jury experience." He pauses. "Grant." Hearing Nick say his name is like having a brick dropped at my feet, and I'm startled by the thud. Nick clears his throat self-consciously. "I don't want to pry. I just wanted to know if you're okay, and that you're not, you know, hurt."

I tense up. "What would you do about it if I was?"

His brown eyes, which are usually in perpetual motion, stay still as they peer into mine. He answers me in a soft, hushed voice. "I'd try and make it better."

For a moment I'm sure he could make it better and for a moment I'm desperate to let him. But fear holds me back, rendering me paralyzed and mute.

He takes my silence as a rejection of his offer. "Take care of yourself, Robin." He waves goodbye and turns to go.

I find my voice. "I'll call you when I get back."

He turns around once more, and the look on his face confirms what we both already know: that call may or may not happen.

Then he walks away.

Hanging my head, I re-enter my apartment and chastise myself for being such a wimp. As I put the soup in the refrigerator for later, I notice my cell phone lying on the kitchen counter. I pick it up. No new calls. Grant hasn't called me back since I hung up on him yesterday, and the queasiness lurking around my digestive system is either a new symptom of this cold, or it's disappointment. I close my eyes and shake my head. Please let it be the cold.

§

Two days later I've arrived in New York with my Dad and Ian. My cold has subsided enough that I can breathe and talk without too much trouble, but my limbs still feel heavy and simple things, like walking a city block, are taxing.

Ted gets in late Sunday morning and meets us at the hotel for lunch. We sit at a table covered with a white tablecloth and lit by a dim chandelier overhead. I order a cheese and tomato omelet but all I do is pick at it. After lunch it will be time to report to the studio, where I will see Grant. My stomach is in knots.

Ted isn't eating much either. He's too busy texting.

"How can they expect you to work on a Sunday?" asks my dad.

Ted shakes his head while his fingers press the tiny keys. "You don't get it, Dad. Everybody works on Sundays."

Ian, for one, appears to be enjoying his lunch. He talks through a big bite of his hamburger. "Did you know that Robbie is flying to Seattle from here? She's visiting Monty for Thanksgiving."

Ted raises one eye. "Why?"

"Lucy invited me," I tell him. "She wants me to speak to her class about the American justice system."

Ted laughs. "You're kidding, right?" He puts his phone down and picks up his fork. "Why you? Was Kim Kardashian unavailable?" He takes a bite of his Cobb salad, chews, and swallows it down with a sip of his tonic water with lemon. But he's snickering the whole time. "Nice photo of you on the cover of *Alright Magazine,* by the way."

Ian pats my hand. "Don't be mean," he says to Ted. "She's going to compare her experiences from *The Holdout* to her recent jury duty."

"Sounds thrilling," replies Ted. "But I'm still surprised Lucy asked you, especially when her husband is this big time lawyer." He makes an exaggerated eye roll. "Oh. That's right, I forgot. Monty gave up law for what, philanthropy? What's that even about?" Ted's phone vibrates with a text alert, and he picks it up again to respond.

"I think he's still practicing law. He's writing policy…" I let my voice trail off when I realize that Ted isn't listening. I look down at my omelet. Its grey-white skin is covered with tiny beads of grease, the cheese has congealed, and the bits of tomato stick out like pin pricks of blood. I push my plate away.

"I should get going," I say. "I have a couple of things I need to do before I go to the studio."

Dad smiles at me. "Okay, sweetheart."

I get up and my father stands as well, giving me a hug. "You knock them dead tonight, okay? We'll be in the audience to cheer you on."

I sniffle. "Are you sure you're not disappointed that I didn't make the final three?"

Dad leans in and kisses my cheek. "Honey, I couldn't be prouder of you."

He's sweet, but still, I can't help but wonder: could he be prouder of Ted or Ian?

"Good luck tonight, Robbie. Be sure to wave to us." I smile my thanks to Ian, and glance over at Ted. He's still texting.

"Thanks for coming, Ted."

He looks up. "Oh. Yeah, you're welcome. What time does it start tonight?"

"Eight."

He sighs. "Okay, well I'm leaving as soon as it's over. I have an important 7:00 a.m. meeting tomorrow."

Ted's attention is now entirely on his phone. Ian and Dad have started talking about sports. I search my pocket for my room key and quietly walk away.

When I'm back in my room I lie on the bed and stare at the ceiling. Even with my eyes open, images of the last time I saw Grant, face to face, float through my mind.

We had checked our bags at the Kalibo airport, and we were waiting for our respective flights, which were to leave a mere twenty minutes apart. I was sitting in the crowded waiting room and Grant was standing, leaning against a window. He was freshly showered, wearing a light blue t-shirt and khaki shorts, but his hair was still too long and his curls stuck out in every direction. While still adorable on the outside, I now knew what lurked beneath. I tried to ignore him, but when the person sitting next to me got up, Grant took the seat.

"Well," he said, "if Henry wins, he'll have you to thank."

"That's not entirely true," I replied.

For a moment he sat silently staring at his thumbs. I leafed through my magazine without seeing any of it.

"I really am sorry, you know." He swiveled his body towards me, knees and chest and head had all invaded my personal space.

I didn't flinch. "I don't care."

He placed a hand on my knee. I picked his hand up and dropped it to his side.

"I'm trying to apologize. Doesn't that mean anything?"

I focused on an article in my magazine. It was about the pros and cons of dating a divorced man with kids. They had a checklist but I couldn't take it in. "What about your smack talk during the fire challenge?"

He sighed. "I was just trying to shake you, but it was all for the game, Robin. I didn't think anything that I did or said would have consequences outside of the game."

"I don't believe you're that stupid."

"I never meant to hurt you."

My fingers clenched, wrinkling the glossy edges of my magazine. "Oh, I see, but using me, that was okay?"

"You used me too," he said quietly. "Maybe not in the same way, or as much, but you did use me too."

The announcer came on, speaking Spanish, but I could understand that my flight number was being announced. I stood and grabbed my carry-on.

"Good bye, Grant."

He stood too. His rosy lips parted slowly, afraid to ask their question. "Am I ever going to see you again?"

I was not going to let in his clean-shaven charm. I stared at him, eye to eye. "You'll see me on the show."

Then I had to turn away, because if I kept his gaze my face might betray my emotions. The fact that Grant's eyes were filled with tears meant nothing to me. Nothing at all.

Now, lying on my hotel bed, I squeeze my eyes shut. I could invite him here tonight and he would most likely say yes. My body warms at the thought. I abruptly raise myself up, go to the bathroom, and splash some water on my face.

When I look in the mirror the face that stares back at me seems foreign, and I don't think she could scare a bunny rabbit. I square my shoulders. "Buck up," I say to my reflection. "You've come this far. Don't blow it all again."

§

The stage lights are blinding. We're sitting on a reproduction of the bamboo set that was used for Island Assembly. All sixteen of the cast-members are here, and we've been divided into four rows. The fourth row, raised up in the back, seats the first four people voted out, and it progresses on in that order. I'm sitting in a glorified office chair at the far right of the front. Grant sits next to me; Klemi is to his left, and at the edge is Henry. On a big screen to the side they play highlights from the final Island Assembly, including my entire speech to the jury.

Tonight, Grant is wearing black jeans and a charcoal grey shirt with a thin green tie. I can smell his after-shave from where I sit, and his curls have been cropped short. On screen, I watch a grubbier version of Grant asking me for forgiveness, and I see my tearful-self deny his request as I make my final pitch for Henry.

As the filmed flashback fades Joe Pine steps into the spotlight. He's wearing his usual safari shirt, but it's a darker blue tonight and his shoes look like they've never met a speck of dirt. None of us on stage do either. I could barely recognize myself when they were done with my hair and makeup. Tonight they've dressed me in teal and silver, and my hair is clipped back in a wide, shiny clasp. My blouse is thin and scoop-necked and my chest is adorned in a thick chain of turquoise. Maybe I'll get to keep the outfit?

The crowd cheers when they see Joe, and the steel guitar and drums play *The Holdout* theme song. Joe shouts over it all into his microphone. "Welcome to *The Holdout: Philippines* live reunion special! These cast members have had a long wait to hear the results of the final vote." He turns to Grant, Klemi, and Henry. "How nervous are you right now?"

Henry uses one finger to rub at his eye. He's wearing contacts instead of glasses, and his hair is clean and combed. He's also dressed almost all in black, save for the white shirt collar sticking out from his sweater. I sort of expect him to speak more deeply now, but when he talks it's with the same old tenor. "I've been more relaxed," he jokes with a squeaky, trembling voice.

Joe indicates the ballot basket he's holding. "Grant, Klemi, do either of you want to guess who will win?"

"I think Grant will win," says Klemi.

"I'd rather just have you read the results," says Grant.

The crowd cheers and Joe, enjoying the energy of the room, throws his head back in laughter. "I think the audience is with you on that. Okay. Let's find out who our million dollar winner is!"

Joe stands, smiling, and reaches into the ballot basket he is holding. Grant and Henry scoot their chairs towards Klemi, so the camera can get a good shot of the three of them. As Joe removes each ballot, he reads it first, and then shows it to the audience.

"First vote, Grant." There is a smattering of applause from the audience. "Second vote, Grant." More applause. I lean over to try and catch Henry's eye, but he's staring straight ahead. "Third vote, Grant."

Grant's grin is stretched so wide that he has to think he's won. Joe reaches for another ballot. "Fourth vote, Henry." Screams from the audience erupt, probably from Henry's family. "Fifth vote, Henry." More wild applause. "Sixth vote…" Joe pauses, and slowly holds the ballot for the audience to see. "… Henry."

Joe speaks over the cheering crowd. "That's three votes Grant, three votes Henry, one vote left." My stomach is twirling around like a ballerina, but then I realize: I haven't seen my own ballot yet.

"Oh my God!" I yell, and then quickly clamp my hand over my mouth.

Joe shoots me a cross-eyed look and I mouth my apology. He then reaches in, looks at the last ballot, and slowly holds up my writing for the world to see. "The winner of *The Holdout: Philippines*, Henry!"

The tribal music swells. Streamers fall from the ceiling, and the audience is chanting their approval. Tears come pooling to my eyes. I leap out of my seat, as happy as if I'd won myself. I jump up and down, cheering, and Henry does the same. Before he runs off the stage to be congratulated by his family, he hugs me, hard. "Thank you, Robin!" he says in my ear. I hug him back, so tight that for a moment I'm incapable of letting go.

But he releases me, and ventures down into the audience to receive hugs and kisses from his mother, his father, his girlfriend, and all his third cousins who tagged along. I sink back into my chair, smiling and wiping the tears from my eyes.

"Congratulations, Robin. You win."

I turn towards Grant. "Henry won," I say.

He speaks through a plastic smile. "My losing is your winning." The muscles in his face relax and his eyes widen. "I can't defeat you, and that only makes me want you more."

My fingers rub against the smooth silver of my bracelet as I try to form a response.

"Did you hear me?" Grant asks.

"Yes, I heard you."

"Robbie! Hey, Robbie!" Through all the music and cheers, I hear Ian's shouts. I can't see past the stage lights, but I wave in the direction of his voice. Doing so gives me a chance to interrupt the buzzing of my nerves.

Joe tells the television audience to stay tuned and we cut to commercial. Henry is shepherded back onto stage and we prepare for the cast interview. When the show resumes Joe starts questioning Henry about strategy, and they show clips of his greatest moments.

"Well," says Joe, "This has definitely been one of the most eventful seasons of *The Holdout* in our show's history. That was due in no small part to Grant." There is a smattering of boos from the crowd, mixed with claps and shouts of support. "Grant, tell us about your strategy of making people emotionally attached. How did that work for you?"

A self-deprecating smile creeps modestly across Grant's face, like he's a grade-school winner at a science fair. "Not so well," says Grant. "I didn't think about the endgame, or who I would hurt."

"So you still have regrets?" asks Joe.

"It's funny you should ask," says Grant. He hops off his chair, faces me, and nimbly lowers himself to his knees. A huge camera zooms in to catch the moment. "Robin," he says. "There are no hidden agendas now. The game is over and I lost. So I'm begging you for one more chance. I can't get you out of my mind, and if you say yes I will travel to Iowa and take you out on the most amazing date you've ever been on in your life."

Grant places a hand on hand on my knee. I'm torn between jerking my leg away or grabbing his hand to guide it further up my thigh. I do neither; instead I sit there, shocked and silent as the studio audience yells their directives at me. I look from Grant's teddy bear eyes to Joe's gleeful presence standing above me. I bet he wants me to say yes so they can hire a camera crew to follow us around.

"Um, I'll have to get back to you on that," I say.

There's a loud, collective "Ooh!" from the audience. Grant's smile dissolves and he returns to his chair.

Joe takes a step in towards Klemi. "Klemi, what do you think about this? Are you sad that Grant is now choosing Robin over you?"

Klemi leans back in her chair and crosses her legs. "Please," she says. "I went on *The Holdout* to win money, not to find love. The only thing that makes me sad tonight is that I didn't win."

Joe nods his head, talk-show host style. He sidesteps closer to me. "What about you, Robin? Why did you go on *The Holdout*? Was it to find love?"

I tuck a loose strand of hair behind my ear and take a deep breath. I don't trust my voice to answer adequately. "No, not to find love. But it wasn't just to win money, either. I guess I thought it would a once-in-a-lifetime experience, and I wanted an adventure, and all the self-discovery and challenges that come along with it."

Joe raises his eyes. "But what if part of that adventure is in fact, finding love?"

I weave my fingers together in my lap and try not to look at Grant, but I'm like a bobble head with a metal brain and he's a great big magnet. Grant is staring at me, waiting for me to respond.

I shrug. "What if it is?"

"So… you're not saying no to Grant?" asks Joe.

"I'm saying I have to think about it." My voice, which had been on the mend, becomes muddled with mucus. I clear my throat. "I can't think clearly on live television."

Joe chuckles like I've just said something hilarious. "What do you think about that, Grant?"

Grant spreads out his hands in surrender. "If it isn't a "no" then I can live with it."

A woman from the audience shouts, "I'll go out with you!"

Everybody except me laughs. "You've got a lot of female fans, wouldn't you say, Grant?" Joe asks.

"I suppose," Grant answers.

"Well, funnily enough, it's time to find out just how many fans you have." Joe turns to the audience and the cameras. "Every year we let our viewers vote on their favorite cast member of the season. This year it should come as no surprise that Grant was one of the top contenders."

The crowd applauds and Joe holds up a hand to quiet them. "However," he projects, "there is somebody else who also made a very strong showing. And my theory is that her popularity was due mostly to this moment."

The screen to the side lights up again, and it shows me grabbing Joe by the edges of his safari shirt. "Explain to me how anything was decreed, Joe. Explain it to me now. There was no majority. I want a do-over and I'm not leaving until I get one!"

The crowd goes wild.

My cheeks burn as I try to figure out if they're cheering for me or mocking me. But Henry is leaning over, giving me a thumbs-up, and I can hear my Dad and Ian shouting and clapping above the rest of the noise. It takes Joe a moment to calm the house down enough so he can speak. "One of the best moments in *Holdout* history!" he cries. "And even though you got blood stains on my favorite safari shirt, I have to agree with popular opinion. It was classic, and it's the reason why, this year, you are the fan favorite and the winner of $100,000!"

Next to me Grant brings his hands together in loud, strong claps. He winks and says, "Congratulations. You deserve it."

It almost makes me forgive him.

§

After the cast party, where we all got drunk and congratulated Henry a million times, after Joe Pine told Grant and me that we should both come back for *The Holdout: Saints VS. Scoundrels* (a season starring returning players), after I introduced Ian and my dad around and then hugged them goodbye, Grant pulls me out of the party room and into a dark hallway. I don't try and resist.

No words are exchanged. He pulls me close, we wrap ourselves around each other, and he kisses me like he needs to, just to survive. I let myself enjoy it for thirty seconds – okay – for a minute, and then I push him away.

"I meant what I said, about the date."

"I meant it when I said that I'd think about it." I lean in, and kiss him on the cheek.

He cradles my face in his hands. "So what does that mean?"

"It means that I'll call you," I say. Then I walk back to my hotel room, alone.

Chapter 16

The Seattle airport is sort of round, so I feel like I'm going in circles as I walk from my flight's arrival gate to baggage claim. There is a dull throbbing in the back of my head, a result of one too many celebratory cocktails from last night. I cringe a little when I think about Grant kissing me and about how I kissed him back.

"Hey! You're Robin from *The Holdout*!" A woman in her forties, pulling a pink suitcase on wheels smiles widely as she approaches. "I'm so happy you won fan favorite! I voted for you ten times!"

"Thank you," I say, and I give her a weak handshake.

"You really showed Grant in the end, didn't you?" She lifts her suitcase and plops it back down for emphasis. "But you'd better not let him take you out on that date. Fans all over the country will be sorry they voted for you if you do." She wags a finger at me and waves goodbye.

I wave back, thanking her once more, and my stomach sinks. What would she and the rest of the world think if they knew about my forbidden moment with the enemy?

When I finally get to the bottom floor to collect my baggage, I see Monty and his three-year-old daughter, Abby, standing off to the side, away from the heavy traffic. She's tugging on his arm, pointing in various directions, and each time asking, "What's that?" Monty says something, probably an answer, and they repeat the cycle. Then Abby points in what happens to be my direction, and Monty notices me and smiles in recognition.

"Hey!" he says, capturing me in a hug. "Can I get your autograph?"

"Ha, ha." I hug him back, but the embrace is quick and perfunctory. When we pull away I notice how thin he looks. Thin and a little pale.

"Fan favorite - that's amazing! Congratulations."

I glance down at my feet in shyness. "So you watched the reunion special."

"Of course." He grabs my carry-on bag and his eyes search for a baggage terminal screen. "But don't worry. Lucy recorded it. She's convinced that you'll want to see it for yourself, so be prepared. We're watching it again tonight."

"Okay," I offer feebly. Abby is staring up at me, and she tugs once more on Monty's arm.

"Daddy, who is that?"

He leans down to talk to her. "I told you. It's Aunt Robin, remember?" She shakes her head no.

Monty grins. "You know, I can still remember you at her age."

I smile and shift my weight. "Hi, Abby," I say. "I like your hair." Her curls are all pulled back with a bright pink bow. She smiles and buries her face in Monty's leg.

"She's a little shy," Monty explains. "It can take her a while to warm up to people."

"I totally understand."

We retrieve my checked luggage, take the elevator to the parking garage, and load ourselves into Monty's Subaru. "Sorry about the mess," he says, as he buckles Abby into the larger of the two car seats in the back.

I remove an empty juice-box and a Raffi CD case from the front passenger seat before climbing in. "No worries," I tell him.

He gets into the driver's side. "This is usually Lucy's car, and she's the one who takes the kids to and from daycare."

We exit out of the garage and enter the freeway. I lean my head against the seatback and close my eyes.

"Tired?" Monty asks.

"Exhausted. This has been a crazy week and I'm still getting over a cold."

"Well, we'll be sure to give you time to rest up." He pats my shoulder with one hand and his other hand confidently grasps the steering wheel. A silence descends inside the family vehicle and I wonder what we'll talk about for almost an entire week.

After a couple of moments I speak. "Ted and Ian say hi."

Monty uses his free hand to tap his fingers against his leg. "Really? I find that hard to believe."

"Why?"

"Well, not about Ian. But Ted hates me. He has ever since we were teenagers."

The polite thing to do would be deny it, but I hate to deny the truth. "You shouldn't take it personally. Ted hates just about everyone." Monty raises his eyebrows but stays silent. "You two went to the same high school, didn't you?"

"We all did," says Monty. "When I was a senior, Ted was a junior, Jack was a sophomore, and Ian... he would have been in sixth or seventh grade, I guess."

"What about Lucy?"

He turns his head towards me for a just a moment. "She was the same year as Ted. But I didn't know her in high school."

"Jack did though, right?"

"Only right before she was about to graduate. But they've been close ever since."

I answer quickly. "Until now."

Monty gives me a sideways glance. "I wasn't going to mention that. Lucy told me not to put you in the middle. But I hate to see her so hurt. Do you know what is up with him?"

I look out the window at the grey sky and the congested freeway. I should feel guilty for everything I'm about to say, but I've debated this with myself already, and I've decided to act in Jack's best interest. "Sort of. I haven't talked to Jack since he introduced me to Jessie." I turn towards Monty. "She's awful," I whisper, because it's too disloyal to say out-loud. "She talks down to him, and she's demanding and rude. Plus, she's the reason Jack won't return Lucy's calls. Jessie is convinced that Jack has romantic feelings for Lucy, and Jessie's making him choose."

With an eye roll and a shake of his head, Monty responds. "Okay, she sounds awful."

"You should talk to him and convince him not to marry her."

Monty laughs like I just suggested that low-fat cheese is as good as the real thing. "If I told Jack not to marry Jessie, he'd only rush to the altar more quickly." He taps his fingers some more. "Why is he with her, if she's so bad?"

"He's tired of feeling unloved."

Monty raises his eyebrows in question.

I look down and examine the denim that covers my knees. There's a small crusty spot that shouldn't be there and I pick away at it. "Jack told me a lot of stuff in confidence, so I'll just say that he doesn't want to be alone."

"No," Monty replies, gripping the steering wheel and rejecting the idea. "He doesn't know how to be alone. I spent years at it but Jack was barely out of diapers when he married Petra. Now he's diving into his second marriage without taking any time for himself."

"I think Jack would say that he's been alone for years, but he just happened to be married the whole time. Don't you think that's worse?"

Monty's response is silence, but I can tell from the concentrated line between his eyebrows that he's processing what I said. From the backseat, Abby pipes up.

"Daddy, are we almost home?"

He doesn't answer her. "Daddy!"

Monty shudders and comes out of his reverie. "Sorry, Baby. We'll be home soon."

§

When we arrive Lucy greets us with hugs and some delicious pasta, and I nurse my hangover with wine, marinara sauce, and garlic bread. After dinner they put the kids to bed and then we watch my reunion special. Lucy and Monty sit side-by-side, arms around each other on the couch, and I recline in the easy chair to the left of the TV. As we watch I feel mild embarrassment, as if the shirt I'm wearing has a small stain because somebody else spilled their grape juice on me.

Then we get to the part where Grant asks me out, and my embarrassment switches to the full on I-caused-this-humungous-purple-stain-myself variety.

"You're not going out with that douche bag, are you?" Monty demands. "I wish he were here so I could punch him."

I feel my cheeks flush as I prepare my response. But I don't have to say anything because Lucy snorts.

"Excuse me?" Monty pauses the TV as he addresses her.

"What?" she replies.

"Why did you snort?"

Lucy waits to answer, her face neutral, and then she spreads her mouth into a smile. "I think it's sweet that you're so protective. That's all."

He takes his arm off her shoulders and eyes her with suspicion, not quite buying her explanation. "Do either of you want anything from the kitchen?" he asks.

We both say no. Once he's out of earshot, Lucy turns to me. "Grant would totally kick his ass," she whispers. "Don't let them anywhere near each other."

I chuckle. "Don't worry, I won't."

She looks toward the kitchen, scoots in closer to my chair, and raises her voice just a notch. "He was so sick when he got back from Ghana. It was awful. I was worried for weeks, both while he was gone, and then after. Even now..." her voice trails off as she sighs. "He's not entirely back to normal. It's been a rough few months. I was starting to think we'd never get back on track. But does he seem okay to you, compared to how he usually is?"

I momentarily contemplate telling her no, he looks kind of pale and skinny compared to how he usually is. But why do that to her? "I don't know that I'm much of an authority, but yes, he seems okay."

Satisfied with my answer, Lucy gives me a grateful smile, but her expression turns to concern. "Are *you* okay?"

"Yeah, just tired."

"Do you want to go to bed? I can show you to the guest room."

I concede to my fatigue, and Lucy shows me to bed. That night I sleep a deep, dreamless sort of sleep. When I wake I forget for a moment where I am, then it all comes rushing back. Today is the day I'm supposed to be an expert on justice. Ted's right; the idea of it is hilarious. I bury my head in the covers, wishing I could stay in this spot all day.

§

When we arrive at the lecture hall it is nearly full. "Wow," Lucy says softly. "I know I don't have this many students enrolled in the course. You must be a big draw." She starts class by introducing me. Then I get up and face the auditorium full of college students. After being on television and knowing that millions of people are watching, you would think a room with a couple hundred post-adolescents wouldn't be so intimidating. But it is.

I begin by describing my experiences on both juries. It takes me around ten minutes to get through what I had planned to say. Lucy had told me to leave a lot of time for questions, so that's what I do.

"So you were on two juries within a year. Did you feel like justice was really served on either of them?'

I'm standing behind the podium and Lucy's students fill about three-fourths of the lecture hall. A student with spiky hair and huge, film canister-sized rings in his ears asks me this. I bite my lip before answering.

"Not really," I reply. "But I learned a lot. One thing I realized is there's no such thing as absolute justice. It's all subjective. But I was happy Henry won, and I thought that was just, even if I cheated a little to make it happen. Of course, Grant cheated too, but he did so within the confines of the game." I pause. Half the students are staring at me and the other half are staring at their phones, and I can't tell if I sound like an idiot. "Does that answer your question?"

Another student breaks in. "Wait. Did you just say that justice is subjective?"

I locate the source of her voice. She's sitting in the second row. Smooth black hair, tan skin, green eyes. Stunning. "Yes," I tell her. "That's what I said."

"But the whole point of the jury system is that it's not. Of course people are going to want different outcomes, but ultimately there has to be one clear verdict."

She's got to be twenty-one or twenty-two and majoring in pre-law. I bet she knows how pretty she is but would rather have people think she's smart. If I could see her closet it would probably be as neat as her appearance, every shirt ironed and hanging up in its color-coordinated spot. She probably labels her garment boxes.

I wish I had her confidence.

"Um, I don't claim to be an expert on this subject. I just happened to have had a unique experience." I shift my weight from foot to foot and grip the podium with damp palms. "But the whole time I was on the federal jury I kept wondering why these high-powered business men would leave a multi-million dollar decision up to a group of yahoos they found off the street. And when I was on the jury for *The Holdout* it occurred to me there was no way I could be impartial, since I was only there because the remaining contestants voted me out. So I have no idea if either outcome is actually 'just'," I make air quotes when I say the word, "but I can tell you this. We search for absolute justice because it *doesn't* exist, and not the other way around."

The pretty/smart girl responds with an arch of her eyebrow and we move on to more questions. Soon they're on to less philosophical subjects, like "How could you have had sex with Grant on national television?" (Nobody believes me when I tell them that was the editing.) But I'm surprised when the hour is up; time went by way quicker than I thought it would.

Lucy beams all the way from the lecture hall to her office and then to her car. Just as we climb in it begins to rain so she beams some more on the drive home, probably to make up for the sun's absence. "That was so great, Robin. You did really well."

"Thanks," I say, feeling incomplete in my response. I don't think I deserve her praise. If any of my blood relatives had been there they wouldn't give me such a rave review.

"I do have a question for you though." Outside the sky is dark from the afternoon storm and the windshield wipers are on turbo speed. It makes the space inside the car feel smaller. Lucy glances at me for just a second. "Do you really believe there's no such thing as justice?"

"I do. I mean, yes. I don't think there is any real justice, just like I'm pretty sure there's no such thing as being absolutely right."

"Huh." She keeps her eyes on the road.

"You're not insulted by that, are you?"

She laughs. "Of course not. It just makes me a little worried. Next you're going to tell me you don't believe in true love." We pull into the daycare parking lot. "You can wait here if you want," Lucy says. "I'll be right back."

She rushes out of the car and runs into the daycare building to avoid getting wet from the rain. It occurs to me she could use some help, carrying two kids and all their stuff, so I get out of the car and follow her inside. But that's the end of our conversation, at least for the moment.

The week goes by in a happy, complete-family sort of haze. Of course there are moments of stress, like when both kids are crying at once, or when neither adult remembered to pick up milk, or when exhaustion from their daily routine settles in. But Thanksgiving is great; Lucy wears the blouse I made her, several of their friends come for dinner, and there is lots and lots of food.

After the meal is over, the guests are gone, and the kids are in bed, the only thing left to do is digest all the turkey and pie. While Monty watches some football game upstairs, Lucy and I relax in the living room.

Lucy takes a sip of her tea. "So, are you going to let Grant take you out on that date?"

"I know I shouldn't." I tug on my hair, which has started to escape the elastic band that was holding it back. I scoop it up and secure it in a tighter ponytail.

"But you want to?"

My cheeks burn. "Even if I did, there's still no way. The world has seen what an ass he is. I can't go out with him and still maintain my self-respect."

"Maybe you're taking it all too seriously."

"Oh, I'm sure I am. That's always been my problem."

"Yeah, that was always my problem too." Lucy rolls her shoulders back and stretches out her neck. "It still is, sometimes."

"Really?"

"Sure."

I shake my head. "But you know you can trust Monty. I can't imagine ever trusting someone enough to marry him."

She laughs. "Trust isn't something that just magically happens, you know. At least it didn't for me. There was no magic moment when the clouds cleared and the angels sang."

"But that's what all the movies and TV shows say is supposed to happen," I joke, even though I'm sort of serious.

Lucy waves her hand dismissively. "You don't believe in that stuff, do you?"

"No," I say, aware that my answer would cause me to fail a polygraph test. "But growing up, sometimes I wondered if I missed out on an important piece of information that my dad, sweet as he is, neglected to tell me."

Lucy cocks her head and squints at me. "Okay," she says slowly, as if she's deeply considering what she's about to disclose. "I suppose there was one time; Monty and I had only been dating for a month, less even." She drops her arms and her shoulders fall back into place. "I had just found out I was pregnant and things were weird between us. So I tried to break up with him. I accused him of freaking out. He didn't get worked up or upset; he just took me back to his apartment and showed me a bag of Oreos he had bought earlier that day."

I scrunch up my face in confusion, and she waves her hands around expressively while she explains. "He hates Oreos and I love them, so why would he buy them if they weren't for me? Then he got all lawyer-like, claiming exhibit "A" was proof that he wasn't freaking out, and the defense rests, and he's innocent on all counts." She laughs and rolls her eyes at the memory. "He even started jumping around, like in a victory dance or something. The picture of it is still burned in my mind." Her smile fades and she meets my gaze. "That was when I knew. Even though I wasn't sure I could trust him, it was worth it to find out."

I smile. "I'm still waiting for a moment like that."

"Yeah…" She sighs. "But that's just it. Simply waiting for a moment like that isn't enough." Lucy reaches over and squeezes my knee. "Robin, you're gorgeous, and amazing, and I'm sure guys would be lining up to buy you Oreos and dance around their apartment for you, or whatever your equivalent of that is, but you have to be brave enough to let go a little. That's the moment you're waiting for, and you're the only one who can make it happen."

Chapter 17

December 2012

When I get home to Des Moines I sleep for two days. The relief of having the show over and the conversation changed is like the feeling of a bad headache going away. But on my third day back I wake up and remember I have phone calls to make and $100,000 to spend, invest, or stick underneath my mattress.

Figuring out what to do with the money is the easy part. The phone calls are a little more complicated. So I put off making them, and before I know it Christmas is here and I'm still alone. Jack can't say the same. He has decided it's time for the whole family to meet Jessie, but I only learn this through a text, probably because he didn't want to be talked out of bringing her.

On Christmas day I'm the last one to get to Aunt Natalie's house, so I'm greeted by a lot of noise, bustle, and sticky-handed hugs from my nieces and nephews. Everybody is dispersed throughout the house and entertaining themselves until it's time for dinner, so I make my way to the kitchen, carrying the pan of asparagus casserole that I was asked to bring.

And I walk right into a burning vat of tension. Jessie is standing by the sink, arms crossed and face scowling. Jack is fiddling with the food processor. Lucy is peering over his shoulder, but she looks my way when I enter. I say hi to everyone and put my casserole dish on the kitchen counter.

"Robin!" Lucy cries, "Good to see you." She comes over and hugs me. I return her embrace and make eye contact with Jack over her head. His expression is a cry for help.

"What's going on?" I ask.

"I can't get the food processor to work," says Jack.

Jessie huffs. "If the onions aren't finely chopped then the dish will be ruined."

"We have a model like this at home," says Lucy. "Let me try."

"I wasn't asking for your help," replies Jessie. "Jack?"

"I'll check the outlet. Maybe it just needs to be plugged in more tightly." He messes with the cord and Lucy takes his old spot, trying to fit the bowl into place. And then somehow in a surge of power the food processor spins and Lucy screams.

"Oh my God!" she yelps, and I can see her three middle fingers have been bloodied. Thinking fast, I grab her by the shoulders and move her quickly to the sink, where I stick her injured hand under cold running water. Even with the water on at full force I can see a lot of blood pouring out. I grab a dishtowel and, squeezing her fingers together, apply pressure.

Jack turns pale and rushes over. "Lucy, I'm so sorry. I didn't think it could turn on without its lid. Are you okay?"

Her face is screwed up in agony. "No! The tips of my fingers got cut off!" she gasps. "It really, really hurts!"

Jack and I look over at the food processor, which is splattered in red. "Are they still in there?" Lucy asks, keeping her head to the side. "Put them on ice so they can be sewed back on."

If any parts of her severed fingers are still around, they only exist now as pulverized flesh. "I think they're too mashed up, Lucy," I loosen the towel and examine her hand. All of her fingernails still exist, though shorter than they used to be. "But don't worry. Your fingertips will grow back."

She starts to say something, but then glances down and notices her mangled fingers and the now blood-soaked towel that was wrapped around her hand. Her eyes roll back and her whole body just wilts. Jack catches her and lowers her gently to the floor.

Enter Monty, his timing perfect and his eyes towards the refrigerator, as if he's simply going for a beer. When he finds a bloody, passed out version of his wife lying in the middle of the kitchen his head jerks back as if he's been slapped.

"What the hell?" he yells. He crouches down beside her and gently taps her cheek. "Lucy?"

"I accidentally chopped off her fingers," Jack tells him, his voice full of remorse. "But it's just the tips. They'll grow back."

Monty's face looks like it can't decide between showing rage or concern, his mouth twists and he bites the inside of his cheek as he inhales. Wanting to feel useful, I find a new dishtowel and wrap it back around Lucy's hand, applying more pressure. "She'll be okay."

"She'd better be!" Monty says this to Jack. "What the fuck, Jack? What is wrong with you?"

Jack stands. "I said it was an accident, okay? It's not like I was *trying* to cut off her fingers!"

Monty stands as well. "Yeah, well, you weren't trying hard enough not to!"

"Hey!" Jessie inserts herself into the conversation. I had forgotten she was there. "He said it was an accident. Lay off."

I didn't think it was possible, but somehow the tension in the room goes from half-volume to full blast. "Who the hell are you?" Monty asks with an aggressive squint.

Jack steps next to her. "Don't talk to her that way. This is Jessie, my fiancé."

Monty's mouth hangs open for a moment before he starts to laugh, then stops abruptly. He turns to Jack. "You are so screwed up."

For a moment Jack is a little boy, unable to defend himself against his older brother's taunting. His lower lip juts out, his eyebrows knit together, and his cheeks redden. Then he remembers himself, and the knowledge that he's actually the bigger, stronger person in the room must come to him with a start. He pushes Monty squarely in the chest, and Monty's face registers shock as he stumbles back. Monty catches himself, but just barely, and his unexpected vulnerability hangs in the air like a bad smell.

Then Natalie comes into the kitchen and her eyes bulge. "What is going on?!" She addresses both her sons. The two brothers simultaneously turn to their mother and shout over each other.

"Jack cut off Lucy's fingers!"

"Monty's being rude and arrogant again!"

"Stop!" Natalie cries. She looks down at Lucy, who is still lying passed out on the floor, and makes eye contact with me.

"Robin," she says, like I'm the only other adult in a room full of children. "Please explain what happened."

"Well," I cough. "She got the tips of her fingers caught in the food processer, and they were sliced off. Then she passed out."

As if on cue, Lucy groans a little and struggles to sit up. Monty kneels down next to her, putting his palm on her back to support her. "Are you okay?" he asks.

Her head wobbles as she tries to focus. "Yeah…" she says. "Did I pass out?"

Monty turns towards his mother. "We need to get her to the emergency room."

Natalie shakes her head. "On Christmas? You'll be there all day. And if the tips can't be sewn back on, all they'll do is wrap her hand and give her some Tylenol. We can do that here."

"We still should bring her in," he demands.

"Nuh uh," Lucy mutters, stronger now. "I don't want to miss Christmas. No emergency room …I'll be fine."

"Let's get her to the upstairs bathroom, where we can wash out the wounds and bandage her up." Natalie says, with enough authority that nobody argues.

Monty puts his hands under Lucy's arms. "Can you stand?"

Gingerly he helps her up and Jack looks on with a stricken face.

"I'm so, so sorry, Lucy," he says, tears caught in his throat. "About everything."

Lucy tilts her head towards Jack, and her mouth creeps out of its frown. "It's okay," she sighs, before turning away. Monty and Natalie take her upstairs and Jack grabs some paper towels to clean up all the blood. I help while Jessie just stands there.

"Jack, I think we should go." Jessie taps her shiny black shoe and it makes a clicking sound.

Jack doesn't respond; he just continues to wipe the floor.

"Jack, seriously. If this is how your family is going to act, then I don't want to stay."

Jack scrubs away at the beige linoleum, slowly making the streaks of pink disappear. "I just cut off my sister-in-law's fingers, Jess. People are bound to get upset about that."

Jessie throws out her hands in frustration. "It was only the tips!" Jack keeps his head down. "Fine." Jessie pulls at the edge of her red Christmas sweater and tucks her hair behind her ears. "I'm leaving. I strongly suggest you come."

She storms out of the kitchen and Jack looks past her. His whole body is slumped with defeat.

"I think you should stay," I tell him.

He sighs. "Of course you do," he replies. "You're not afraid of being alone."

He gets up, throws the wad of soggy pink paper towels in the garbage and walks away. I hear the front door open and close.

§

Somehow we continue with Christmas. By the time we all sit down at the table I'm starving, and as we pass around dishes of green beans, mashed potatoes, and my cheesy asparagus casserole, it's a challenge not to heap my plate too high.

When everyone has served themselves to their satisfaction, my dad proposes a toast. "To another year of health and happiness," he says. "May we always be so blessed."

He looks in the direction of Ian and Eddie's new daughter as he raises his glass, and we all lift our glasses and say, "Hear, hear."

Then Ted gets up and goes to the kitchen. When he returns he's carrying a tiny covered plate. "Speaking of health and happiness," he says, "what sort of family would we be if didn't honor our superstar?" He places the little platter in front of me. "Robin, this is for you, from all of us."

He's smiling broadly as he sits, and I look at all of them in question. Are they seriously honoring me?

My brothers and I rarely exchange gifts. "You got me a present?" I try not to gush. "That's so nice."

"Go ahead, Robbie," says Ian. "Open it up."

I lift the lid. Underneath lies a milky-gray and shiny shipworm, which is every bit as big and disgusting as the one I tried to eat on the show. The only difference is it's not alive. I laugh, ramming the sting of disappointment down, away from my unaffected facade.

"Do you know how hard it is to find one of those things in December?" says Ian. "Ted had to call around all over the place."

"So you're going to eat it, right?" says Monty. "Don't lose this chance to redeem yourself."

"That's right," chimes Ted. "Now you can prove how tough you really are. Show us you're not still the whiny little girl who cries when a seagull poops on her head."

Everyone is laughing. I look at the shipworm, and I know there's no way I can eat it. I know there's no way I should have to.

"That's not funny!" Lucy cries. Her bandaged hand is resting against the table, and her eyelids look heavy. "You guys should be ashamed of yourself!"

Monty and Ian stop laughing, but Ted still has on his smirk. Lucy uses her good hand to point at Ted. "You. I know about you. You cheated all the time in economics class. Nobody wanted to sit next to you, and when Mr. Simonson called you on it, you cried."

Ted's jaw snaps shut, but he opens his mouth quickly again, to defend himself. "I have no idea what you're talking about, but whatever; it was years ago."

"Oh no. You know." She leans forward, drawing out her words. "You know. And I know you know." Everyone at the table is a rapt audience member, including me. "You talk about being tough, Ted, but you were a big ol' crybaby in high school."

Ted's nostrils flare. "We didn't know each other in high school. You're thinking of someone else."

She shakes her head vehemently and curls spray from her head. "Uh uh. It was you. Like that time you asked that cheerleader to prom at a pep-rally; she turned you down and you cried. And that time you lost the track meet, I wasn't there but the next day everyone said you cried."

I'd give anything if this were true. I pass my eyes across the table, hoping to find another witness to back up these claims, and they rest on Monty. Every muscle in his face is fighting laughter. He can barely contain himself as he looks at Ted and then at Lucy, and back and forth again. He rests his hand on her shoulder. "Honey, maybe you should…"

She turns on him. "And you!" She emphasizes every syllable as she invades his space and he tilts himself back. "I should tell everyone the story about how you peed your pants on an airplane."

Nobody says anything; we're all waiting for her to go on. "It was in Africa," she says to us all. "He was on a little plane with super-bad turbulence, and Monty was so scared that he peed his pants, and everyone noticed the huge wet spot in his crotch when he got off."

Monty chuckles as he tries to deflect the situation. "If you all had been there you'd understand. It was really intense." Lucy snorts and he turns to her. "Fine, you're right," he says gently. "I'm not that tough. But we were only joking with Robin."

"Yeah," says Ian. "It's nothing to get upset about."

Lucy's head was beginning to droop, but she snaps back to answer Ian, and her voice gets thicker, like she's sipping peanut butter through a straw. "Of course you thin that," she says, slurring her words. She takes a sip of her wine. "It's easy to tay a joke when isn directed a you." She drops her head in her hands, and cries "Ouch" when it hits her injured fingers.

Natalie eyes Lucy and her half empty wine glass. "Maybe you should lay off the wine," Natalie says. "Especially since you're on codeine."

Lucy's mother, who had been looking at her daughter in concern, speaks to Natalie. "What? That can't be right. Lucy wouldn't take codeine. She doesn't like painkillers."

"Well, she took codeine today," says Natalie. "I should know. I gave it to her."

Lucy raises her head in a moment of lucidity. "You said it was

Tylenol."

"I said it was Tylenol 3. Which everyone knows, means codeine."

"Mom!" Monty yells. "Not everyone knows that. Obviously Lucy doesn't, or she wouldn't have taken it."

"Well excuse me for trying to help."

Monty slaps his hand against the table. "I can't believe this. What's next? Is someone going to bash her in the head and finish her off?"

"Don't feel well…" Lucy mumbles. "I think I need to lie down."

"Are you all right?" Monty asks, his anger turning to unease as he watches her struggle.

"… be fine. Eat dinner. Just need to lie down for a minute."

Monty starts to get up, but Lucy's mother stops him. "I'll go with her," she says, and she helps Lucy stand. "Come on; let's go into the other room."

Then Abby starts to cry. "Is mommy going to die?" she wails.

Monty shifts his gaze from his wife to his daughter and places a hand on her head. "No, no, baby. She'll be okay."

But Abby only cries louder. The noise spreads like a virus to her younger brother, and in moments he's crying too.

"Come on," Monty says with resignation. "I'll prove it to you both. Your mother is still alive, for now at least." He raises one eyebrow and smirks. "But I wouldn't let Uncle Ted anywhere near her; he might poison her pumpkin pie."

"Making jokes like that is only going to scare them more," Natalie scolds. Monty just glares at her as he and his father-in-law hoist the children out of their seats and take them into the living room.

Those of us who remain at the table hesitate to speak. But Ted breaks the silence.

"Obviously Lucy is strung out. I didn't cheat and cry all the time in high school."

"Seriously?" I can feel my body temperature rise. "That's what you're worried about? Who even cares, Ted?"

He gives me a twisted, condescending smile. "I was just trying to set the record straight. Don't get so excited." Ted turns to Dad. "Did you see the business section the other day? It sounds like a big merger is coming…"

I pick up the shipworm and throw it at my oldest brother. It lands with a moist smack in the middle of his face. The entire room is silent and he's motionless for a second, stunned, before he grabs a napkin and wipes off the slimy mess. When he turns to me I can see the rage shooting from his eyes.

"What is your problem?"

"I don't think your joke is funny. That's my problem. If you're so tough, you eat the shipworm."

"No." He throws the shipworm, balled up in his napkin, back at me. I duck and it falls to the floor. "I didn't sign up to be a sideshow spectacle on national television. You did. If you can't take some heat about that, then you're even weaker than I thought."

"Ted!" Ian reprimands him. "Lighten up. She didn't think it was funny. Let it go."

"Don't bother." I get up from the table. "I'm done."

I storm out, only making it as far as the kitchen before my dad catches up with me. "Robin!" he calls out.

I turn around. "I'm too old to be scolded, Dad."

"I'm not here to scold you." He limps closer to me. "Ugh. I think I might need a knee replacement."

I sniff, rub my eyes, and try to express sympathy even though I'm not in the mood. "That's too bad."

He places his hand on my shoulder. "Hey. Don't take it so hard. Ted doesn't know how to talk to you, so he makes up for it with stupid jokes. He was just being defensive."

I move away from my father, grab a water glass from the cabinet and I fill it at the sink. "Well, I'm sick of it. And it's not only Ted. You and Ian do it too, just not as bad."

I drink my water, aware that my father is staring at me. When I lower my glass I see his face, full of regret. "Sorry, Honey," he says. "It's just, well to be honest, none of us ever knew what to do with you. You were so young when your mother died. Of course Ted and Ian were young too, but you… you were barely even a person."

"I still feel like that sometimes, Dad." I gaze at the wall. It's covered in white and brown wallpaper, a pattern of spice shakers. I've always thought it was ugly, but right now it's the only thing I can focus on.

"I know. What you said, on the show, that you can't let go of her?" His voice cracks. I nod my head. "I'll always remember you then. 'Where's Mommy?' you would say, over and over. And every time the front door opened your face would light up, and you'd toddle over, expecting it to be your mother. Then you'd be so confused and sad when it wasn't her." He comes closer and turns me to face him. "Eventually you stopped. I guess a part of you simply accepted that she wasn't coming back, even if the other part would never understand. But Robin, Honey, that's what we have in common. I *still* can't convince myself that she's actually gone."

I close my dripping eyes and hug him. "Oh, Dad. I'm sorry."

He holds me tight but continues to talk. "No, Honey. I'm sorry. After she died, Ian tried to make everyone happy and Ted got angry. I could deal with that, but I never knew how to make it better for you."

We hug each other hard. Tears are wetting my cheeks, and I feel Dad's tears dampen my shoulder. After a minute or so, Dad sniffs and pulls away. With his shoulders squared, he leans down and looks me in the eye. "Don't listen to Ted. You're the strongest, bravest person I know. Your mother… she would be so proud."

My heart is flooding. "Do you really think so?"

Dad's eyes are lit up, and not just because they're watery. "Yes, I really think so." He kisses my cheek. "Come back and eat? You've got to be hungry."

I feel a gust of cool air as the outside door opens and shuts. Someone has come in.

"In a minute," I tell him.

Dad kisses me on the forehead and walks back into the dining room. I wipe my eyes and breathe deeply to calm myself. I know I can go back in and eat dinner like a rational, civilized adult, but I need another minute to get over the fact that I just acted like a child. I open the refrigerator door. Natalie stocks cherry juice for the kids as a holiday treat, and at the moment it sounds way more appealing than wine. I'm searching for the bottle when Jack walks in.

"Hi," he says, looking like he's taken a beating.

"Where's Jessie?" I ask.

Jack shrugs. "Does it matter?"

"Of course."

"We're taking some time," he says with a sigh. "I told her I had to come back here and she didn't like that, so I guess we're broken up." I listen as I continue to search for the juice. "I know it's for the best," Jack adds. "But now, on top of everything else, I'll have to endure some major taunting."

"Sorry," I tell him. "But at least you didn't rely on your drugged, wounded cousin to defend you, or throw a shipworm at Ted, then pitch a fit and storm out. That my friend," I say as I scoot beer and a big cheese-ball to the side of the refrigerator, "is worthy of some taunting."

"Huh?"

Behind the jug of milk I find a small, round, lidded plastic container, and I pull it out and open it. Inside are five more shipworms.

"What's that?" Jack asks, his face screwing up in disgust.

"You don't know?" Jack shakes his head. "They're shipworms and they're my Christmas present," I say, suddenly feeling the holiday spirit.

"That's pretty disgusting," Jack says. "Couldn't they have just gotten you a sweater?"

I study the shipworms coiled together in a moist, shiny lump. I raise the container to my face and take a whiff, but they have barely any odor. "You know, they're actually not so bad." I smile as I realize; maybe there are no do-overs in *The Holdout*, but at Christmas dinner? The jury is still out.

I grin widely at Jack. "This could turn out to be best present I'll ever get." Jack wrinkles his forehead in confusion. "You get to eat one," I tell him.

"What? No thanks."

I grab his arm. "Come on. You have the strongest stomach of anyone I know. Remember that boat ride, when everybody else was puking over the side and you just sat there, reading your book?"

Jack looks at me like I'm unbalanced. "I still don't want to eat a shipworm," he says.

I smile crazily at my unwilling co-conspirator. "This time we're going to win, Jack." I tug him towards the dining room, holding the shipworm container tightly in my hand. "Come on." When Jack and I enter the dining room conversation ceases and everybody looks up.

"Jack, honey," Natalie smiles. "I'm so glad you came back. Is Jessie here too?"

Jack acts completely normal. He grabs a plate and takes a seat, speaking as he does. "Nope. Just me. How are Lucy's fingers?"

There's a murmuring and a bustle as platters of food are passed to him, and I stand there, watching for a moment before I remember myself. "Jack!" I say. He looks up. "Don't stack your plate too high. You'll be eating a shipworm first." I hold up the container and then I turn to Ted.

"You bought six?"

"I had to," he answers, scowling. "They wouldn't sell me just one. Half a dozen was the lowest they'd go."

"Well, it's perfect." I walk closer to the table. "Because we're going to have a shipworm challenge. Right here, right now."

"I already told you I'm not eating one of those things," Ted says, his voice rigid.

"Fine," I reply. "Then you forfeit and you lose. And I'll have bragging rights from now on. We'll stop telling the seagull story every year, and instead we'll relive how you were too scared to eat a shipworm." I turn to Ian. "What about you? Are you also too scared?"

Ian's eyes fasten with mine and I can tell he understands the gravity of the situation. "No. I'll eat a shipworm," he says, with just a speckle of conviction.

I look over at Jack. "And you're in?"

He raises his eyebrows and his arms in resignation. "Sure. Why not? What do I get if I win?"

"Redemption," I say. And just at that moment Monty comes back.

"Nobody's very happy right now," he says, "so we're heading out."

"Not yet," I demand. "Lucy would want you to stay and take part in the shipworm challenge."

Monty frowns with a slight shake of his head. "What?"

"Ian, Jack, and I are all going to eat one but Ted's too scared."

Monty's eyes narrow when he notices that his brother has returned. "All I have to do is eat a shipworm?"

"Yes," I say, "but to win you have to eat it the fastest."

Monty looks around at Jack, Ted, and back at me, a line of tension creasing his forehead. He's silent for a moment, processing all the unspoken pressure that's floating between us. "I'm in," Monty declares, putting his hands on his hips. "I just need to let Lucy know." He strides towards the living room. I walk over to the buffet and grab five small plates for the shipworms.

"This is asinine," Ted says. "And it won't prove anything."

"Of course it will," says my dad. "You said so yourself when you thought it would just be Robin eating one."

I place a plate with a shipworm in front of both Ian and Jack, and in the empty spots where Monty and I will be sitting. Monty comes back, occupies the chair he had abandoned, and talks to Jack. "Lucy's parents are taking the kids back now but she's passed out on the couch."

"Lucy's still passed out from her fingers?" Jack's voice raises an octave.

"No, no… she just fell asleep because Mom drugged her."

Jack lurches towards his mother, and she responds to his shocked expression. "Not on purpose!" she exclaims. "And I didn't know she'd be drinking wine."

"Anyway," says Monty, "when we're done I need you to drive us back."

"Fine," says Jack. "But can we get this competition over with first?"

"Natalie," I say as I take my seat. "You'll be the judge."

"Okay…" she says. "What do I have to do?"

"Just watch, and the first person who swallows down their shipworm and shows you their tongue, wins. If they puke it up they're automatically out."

The spouses and the kids who are old enough to understand all groan in disgust. Monty addresses Ted.

"I can't believe you're not going to compete, when it was your idea to order the shipworms in the first place." He shakes his head. "Lame. Really, really lame."

Ted makes a long, loud exhale. "Fine," he says through clenched teeth. "I'll do it."

"I thought you might change your mind," I smile as I pass down the fifth plate of shipworm.

"Okay," Natalie says, imitating Joe Pine. "Hands on the table and wait for my 'go'." She looks around at all of us, as we sit, poised and ready to win. "Are you all ready?" We nod and murmur yes. "Go!" she yells.

This time I don't hesitate, I just pop the slimy, slurpy noodle-worm into my mouth, and it's so much easier to convince myself that I'm eating overcooked pasta now that the shipworm isn't alive.

"Go Robin! You can do it, Honey!" My dad cheers me on. I barely have to chew, and in moments I get it all down. On my first and last monumental swallow I jump up and stick out my tongue, waving my arms and hooting in triumph.

"Robin wins!" Natalie yells, and my father claps.

"Yes!" I cry.

"Second place!" Jack shouts, sticking out his tongue. "I got second!"

I leap over to where he's sitting and give him a high five. Ian spits out his shipworm and wipes his mouth. "Why are they still going?" he asks, gesturing to Ted and Monty, who are both struggling not to gag while they attempt to swallow.

"Come on, Monty," Jack bellows. "Just pretend it's sushi."

Ted's eyes swell as he looks sideways at Monty. Monty swallows roughly and gasps, sticking out his tongue in the process. "Third place!" Monty yells and Jack cheers.

Ted gulps the last of his shipworm and takes a huge swig of wine. "Fourth place," he says dejectedly, pointing at Ian. "At least I didn't quit."

"I thought we were just going for a winner," says Ian. "Nobody said otherwise."

Eddie rubs Ian's back with a flat palm. "Don't worry about it, Sweetheart." But Ian hangs his head.

"Oh, get over it," I say, sitting back down in my spot. Now that I finally get to eat some real food, I grab my plate of cooling turkey, potatoes, and asparagus casserole. "But before we move on, I need to make one thing clear."

I pause, enjoying that I have the floor. With a swift inhale, I glance past the faces who are staring back at me. "The camping trip when I was eight? I'll concede I had new shoes that gave me blisters, and I'm sorry you all had to take turns carrying me on that hike." I paste on a sardonic smile, one like the frat-boy lawyer would wear. I even attempt his casual, assuming tone. "But the real issue here is that the seagull pooped in my hair, not in any of yours, but in *mine*. And you all judged me for my reaction," I grasp my fork like it's a gavel and lower it against the table with a thud. "Because of that, last year at this time you thought I'd be a disaster on *The Holdout*. While I admit I made mistakes, I think we can all agree that I would, in fact, kick all your asses." I pause and take a moment to meet eyes with both my brothers and my cousins. "So I'll accept your apologies now."

I sit back and wait for my verdict, a unanimous vote in this civil case, and the awarding of damages to the tune of "we're sorry."

"You'd win over me, Robbie."

"I'd probably get voted out right away," says Monty.

"Sorry…" mumbles Ted with a sigh.

§

I turn to Jack. He's eating his turkey with his head down. When he feels the silence he looks up. "What?" he demands. "I killed that ropes course. I'm thinking I might apply and get on the show. I could use a million dollars." He smiles. "Do you think you could pull some strings for me, Robin?"

Later I've gone to the bathroom, and after checking my reflection for any lingering shipworm between my teeth, I stroll back through the living room. Jack and Monty are both there, standing over a sleeping Lucy.

"Do you need help lifting her?" Jack asks.

Monty rolls his eyes "Of course not," he says, clearly offended at the question. He puts on his coat, and then sits on the edge of the couch. "Sweetheart," he says, "can you sit up and put your arm around my shoulder?" He doesn't wait for an answer; he just hoists her up, and wraps her coat around her.

"Who won shipworm challenge…" she murmurs.

"Robin," Monty replies, half of his mouth sneaking up in a grin. Lucy smiles and falls right back asleep.

"Best Christmas ever," he mumbles as he easily lifts Lucy into his arms. Her head nestles into the crook of his shoulder as if it's second nature.

Monty turns his head and notices me. "Congratulations on the shipworm challenge. I'm glad you won."

"Thank you." I kiss him on the cheek and then look down at Lucy. "I hope she feels better. It's good she trusts you so much."

Monty's face wrinkles in surprise. He laughs. "I suppose. Although, right now I could be Donald Trump and she'd still let me carry her to the car."

Jack laughs. "Yeah, but it would be the last time she'd ever let you carry her anywhere."

Monty laughs too, and suddenly they're two brothers sharing some inside joke, completely opposite of how they were hours before.

"Merry Christmas, Robin." Jack hugs me.

I hug him back and whisper in his ear. "Do you need to sleep on my couch again?"

He pulls away and shakes his head. "I'll be fine." He turns to Monty, who is shifting his weight. "I'll get the door for you."

"Thanks," Monty replies. "Take care, Robin. Good seeing you," he says over his shoulder, and then he rotates back to Jack. "So what happened with Jessie?"

"She freaked out on me…" As Jack explains, they walk together out into the night. Only siblings can be mortal enemies one minute and allies the next, with no words of apology passed in between.

I burp, which vacates just enough room in my stomach for dessert. I will go back for some pie but Dad's compliment still rings in my ears. I've tried all my life to be brave, believing that doing so involves putting myself on the line and going it alone.

But that's only half of it.

I find my purse in the back bedroom and dig for my cell phone.

"Hello?" I hear him say. Happy anticipation rises inside me.

"Hi," I answer. "I'm sorry it took me so long to call."

Epilogue

January, 2013

It's amazing how quickly things can happen. The money I won has already been invested in studio space, supplies, and a web page for my clothing business, and I'm keeping myself busy and working hard. But I haven't been too busy to figure some things out.

For instance, I can't go for a relationship that is based on dishonesty, or for one that began as a game. I never even called Grant to let him know I wasn't interested. Sometimes it's better to let lying dogs sleep by the phone, waiting for it to ring.

But I am interested in starting something real. It's a lot scarier, but I've come to a conclusion. It's time to be brave and let go.

New Year's Eve we stay in. I make him dinner and we watch *Twelve Angry Men*. "You're definitely the angry, judgmental one," Nick says. "And I'm the rational one that finally sways people to do the right thing."

"I completely disagree."

He laughs, and to show me he was joking, pulls me in for a kiss. It's warm and lingering, and my pulse races just from the feel of him. I pull away first because there's no need to take things super-fast. We have plenty of time.

Nick looks at his watch. "Only twenty minutes to midnight."

I grab his arm, bring his watch close and look at it with scrutiny. "What's the story behind this watch?"

"What makes you think there's a story? Maybe it's just a watch."

I look into his eyes and take in the whole of his face. How could I have ever missed how striking he is? "I think there's a story."

He glances down at his arm and his finger gingerly traces the rim of the timepiece. "It was a graduation present from my mom. She died before she could give it to me, but my dad says she shopped for it on the last good day she had."

I reach out and clasp his fingers with mine. "Well," I whisper. "I think it's really beautiful."

He brings my hand to his mouth and kisses it. "I think you're really beautiful."

And then my moment happens. I let myself trust him, just a little bit, enough to draw him closer rather than pushing him away.

We kiss some more. He lowers me to the couch and soon we're engaged in some very heavy petting. I don't even notice when his watch strikes twelve, but that's okay. Endings and beginnings merge all the time, so it's not always easy to distinguish when change happens. And it's not always necessary.

Because this time I could feel the change. And this time I knew it was right - absolutely.

To learn more about Laurel Osterkamp and her writing, visit her website:

LaurelOsterkamp.com

PMI Books

Boulder, CO

www.pmibooks.com

9 781933 826400